SLOW
SURRENDER

SLOW SURRENDER

CECILIA TAN

FOREVER

NEW YORK   BOSTON

Copyright © 2013 by Cecilia Tan

Excerpt from *Slow Seduction* copyright © 2013 by Cecilia Tan

Forever
Grand Central Publishing
Hachette Book Group
237 Park Avenue, New York, NY 10017
www.hachettebookgroup.com
www.twitter.com/foreverromance

Printed in the United States of America

RRD-C

First Trade Paperback Edition: August 2013

10 9 8 7 6 5 4 3 2

Forever is an imprint of Grand Central Publishing.
The Forever name and logo are trademarks of Hachette Book Group, Inc.

The publisher is not responsible for websites (or their content) that are not owned by the publisher.

The Hachette Speakers Bureau provides a wide range of authors for speaking events. To find out more, go to www.hachettespeakersbureau.com or call (866) 376-6591.

Library of Congress Cataloging-in-Publication Data
Tan, Cecilia.
    Slow Surrender / Cecilia Tan.—First trade edition.
        pages cm.—(Struck by Lightning ; book 1)
    ISBN 978-1-4555-2927-8 (trade pbk.) —ISBN 978-1-4555-2926-1 (ebook)
1. Self-realization in women—Fiction. 2. Erotic fiction. I. Title.
PS3570.A483S64 2013
813'.54—dc23
                2013004656

To the stars in my life.

You know who you are.

Every girl dreams she'll be the one who catches his eye, who catches his heart.

Do any of them dream of being the one who's caught?

One

Out of the Blue

The night of Lord Lightning's good-bye concert was a crazy night to say the least. I was doing one last waitress shift at the bar my sister managed in Midtown, the concert having taken place at Madison Square Garden, just a few blocks away. The bar was packed with "Lord's Ladies," who were inconsolable and tearing their hair out (or wigs, actually) while smearing their face paint with tears. My roommate Becky was at home crying about the same thing. Me? I couldn't care less what some self-absorbed rock-star asshole was doing as his latest publicity stunt, but it was all over the big-screen TVs: his masked face projected sixty inches wide along with footage of the screaming fans at his supposedly last public performance. The whole city was turned upside down, and I remember so clearly the Lord's Ladies because they were such a royal pain in the arse! Ordering as little as possible, taking up the best tables all night long, and I could already tell they were going to be lousy tippers.

I'd even had one table dine-and-dash on me. I didn't think

the night could get any worse until I got to the hostess station and caught a glimpse of my thesis advisor walking through the front door. The same advisor I'd told I couldn't meet tonight because I was "too sick to leave my apartment, *cough cough*" when my sister Jill had convinced me she was desperate and needed me to work. She had promised a great night for cash tips, which was the only reason I'd agreed to this madness. Even worse, on top of it all was the fact that he'd come in with the man I'd had a job interview with that afternoon, a project manager at a design firm where I hoped to work as soon as I graduated, if not sooner. Theo Renault's approval of my thesis was the main thing standing between me and graduation, and I knew from department talk he wasn't one who would casually accept being lied to.

In other words, I was fucked, and all because I was doing Jill a favor. I forced myself to stop looking at Renault and the guy—Philip Hale was his name—as they fought their way through the crowded room toward the bar. Maybe they would have a quick nightcap and get out of here. I tried to focus on the customer stepping up to the stand now, a tall man in a hat and a bittersweet-chocolate-brown suit that was clearly tailored to perfectly fit his lean frame, like something out of a fashion magazine.

Not the kind of guy who was alone, usually, but I hurried to seat him. If I took him upstairs, maybe Renault wouldn't see me. "Table for one?" I chirped as I thought, *Please don't be waiting for someone.*

"Yes, plea—"

"Great! Follow me!" I practically grabbed him by the arm and led him quickly to the stairs. "Kind of a busy night in here. It's a bit quieter on the second floor. I'll get you away from these crazies." I waved the menu in the general direction of the Lord's Ladies, who were starting a group sing-along of some kind.

"I'd like that," he said, his voice deep. He sounded faintly amused.

Probably because I was acting so flustered. "It's not always like this in here," I assured him, as if it mattered. The second floor, unlike the crowded, chaotic first floor, was devoid of both TVs and singing fans and had only a few customers scattered throughout. A group of four women in one corner had already cashed out but had been lingering for an hour. A couple sat near the top of the stairs.

I led him all the way to a table by the windows, overlooking the street, desperate to kill as much time as possible. I had the funny urge to pull out his chair for him, as if this were a white-tablecloth kind of place, but I hung back until he seated himself. He had a topcoat folded over his arm, and he hung it over the back of his chair, put his hat on the wide sill of the window, then sat. I set the menu down in front of him.

"The kitchen is already closed," I said, going into my automatic "after 10:00 p.m." patter, "but the full list of cocktails is of course available, as are the selections on the dessert menu." I turned the menu over to the list of desserts. "Today's sorbet is passion fruit."

"Passion fruit?" he asked, one eyebrow raised like he was skeptical of it.

"Nah," I joked. "That's the name of my Lord Lightning cover band."

That made him laugh. In the streetlamps that shone through the window, I couldn't tell the color of his eyes, blue, hazel, green? The light from outside was stark and bluish compared to the soft amber lights in the bar, making his cheekbones look impossibly sharp. His hair was dangerously blond, almost white, and cropped close to his head. His age was impossible to gauge; he could've been a young forty or a haunted twenty. He was gorgeous and striking and his voice had a slight British tinge to it as he said, "Oh, just try to work it into every conversation, do you?"

"Yes, exactly." I grinned. Normally, flirting while waitressing was asking for trouble and I avoided it at all costs. I didn't like men thinking just because I was female it was okay to treat me like something on the menu. But I was on a mission to waste as much time as I could. Besides, he was quite attractive and that was an understatement. "Actually, I think the sorbet is lemon with a little orange food color. It all tastes the same."

He chuckled. "So, you don't recommend the sorbet?"

I chewed my lip a moment. "I lied," I said. "I've never actually had it."

"Well, at least one of us should embrace new experiences," he said. "Bring me a dish of the sorbet, and a bourbon. Something better than Maker's Mark." His eyes were on me, very intent, as if he had no intention of actually opening the menu.

I collected it from him.

"Coming right up." I couldn't resist making a fake little curtsy and then hurrying away.

That worked out perfectly, I thought. I punched in the drink order from the upstairs server station, then went down to the kitchen to dish the sorbet myself, completely out of the view of Renault and his friend. I picked up the bourbon from the back station, added it to the round tray with the sorbet, and headed right back upstairs.

"Here you are," I said as I set down the napkin and the drink, then the small metal dish of sorbet and a spoon.

"Thank you," he said, and sounded sincere about it.

I busied myself for a little while, refilling the water glasses for the four-top and checking that the couple didn't want a round of dessert. They didn't, which was just as well, because the sugary sweetness coming from the two of them cooing at each other was enough to hospitalize a diabetic. I guess they were having each other for dessert. It was hard not to feel bitter watching them when I'd never met a guy who could act like that and actually mean it. While I wiped down some of the empty tables, I glanced over at my solo customer. He was sipping the whisky very slowly and looking out the window. Maybe it was that a man drinking alone always looks melancholy, but I got the feeling he was a little sad about something. Wistful, maybe.

I also noticed he wasn't eating the sorbet. I went back to his table. "Was it not to your liking? I can take it away and bring you something else you might like."

He settled back in his chair and gave me a thoughtful look. "Actually, there is something I'd like."

"Name it." I gave him my waitress smile.

"I'd like you to try the sorbet." He picked up the spoon, which was still resting exactly where I'd left it, and cut into the perfect scoop that had clearly been untouched.

"Me?" I asked, as if he could have meant anyone else. "Why? To make sure it's okay?"

"No, no. Because you said you hadn't had it before. I thought, what a shame, she works so hard in a place like this, and she's never tasted the sweetness right in front of her?" He held up the spoon, waving it enticingly.

I glanced behind me to make sure Jill or some other server wasn't watching. Normally one didn't do this sort of thing with customers, but I wanted to see what would happen if I did. "All right."

He held the spoon still, then up toward my chin. I leaned forward, my hands on my apron, and I slowly closed my mouth over it. The spoon was cold and the sorbet tart at first, then sweet as it melted in my mouth. "Mmmm."

His gaze never left my face and he smiled as I straightened up. Attention from guys often felt slimy to me, but from him all I felt was warmth, his eyes like hot spotlights.

I wanted to shine in that light. "Anything else I can get for you?" I asked, one of my standard lines.

He ran his finger along his chin, as if I had proposed a question requiring deep thought.

"Er, you know, I can have the bartender pour you something else, if you don't like this," I blathered.

"Oh, I like this," he said, a half-smile coming onto his face, and I felt he wasn't talking about what was in his glass. His neck was long and graceful, and he had not the slightest bit of slouch in his posture, like a male figure skater. Or a model. He seemed more gorgeous the longer I looked at him, with high cheekbones and a luscious-looking mouth. He tilted his face up at me. "Your name tag says *Ashley*. Is that your name?"

"Yes, of course," I answered. It was a lie, actually. Ashley was the girl I was filling in for tonight, the one who was actually too sick to come in. I'd quit working here a few months ago to concentrate on my thesis; the "Karina" name tag had been lost or repurposed by now. For a second I wondered if Ashley was really sick or if she'd lied just like me, while she covered the ass of someone else, and so on and so on. Sadly, there was no one who could cover for me if Professor Renault caught me.

"Ashley, Ashley, gray as a cat, as you drift to the floor from the end of my cigarette," he said, as if reciting a poem. His voice was cultured and smoky like a deep jazz saxophone, making me feel melty inside. There was something charming about him, even if what he said made no sense.

"Ashley, tell me something," he said, angling his head as if to see me better. "Would you like to try something else new?"

"Something else?" I echoed. "What do you mean?"

"Are you bored? Tired of the rat race? Looking for a little adventure?"

"Well sure, who isn't?" I said.

He nodded at my automatic response. "Indeed. Ashley, I'm bored. I would like to play a game. And I would like someone to play it with me."

"I bet you say that to all the girls," I joked.

His expression darkened, surprising me. "Actually, it takes a very special person to pique my interest."

He thinks I'm special? I thought.

"If you don't want to play, that's fine," he added. "I'll leave and never come back if you say no."

Right about then, my weirdo meter should have been pinging hard. But my inner alarm bells were silent. Maybe because he wasn't giving off a weird vibe and he seemed sincere about leaving me alone if I didn't want to play along. And maybe because it was hard to say no to such an attractive man. I decided to test him out a little, though. "I'll play if you'll answer a question."

He smiled. "Name it," he said, imitating me perfectly.

"Tell me why a wealthy, well-dressed man like yourself is drinking alone."

"You mean, am I here fleeing a harridan wife or escaping my supermodel girlfriend?"

I shook a finger at him. "No answering a question with a question, mister. That's rude."

He flattened a hand against his lapels. "I beg your pardon. You're right. An honest question deserves an honest answer. The truth is I've come to the end of a very long and tiring episode in my business. I'm at loose ends for the first time in a long time, and to celebrate, I wanted to be alone for a while, something I haven't had a chance to do recently." He glanced out the window, then turned his full attention back to me. "In fact, I was just working myself up to a promise to spend more time by myself"—he paused and swirled the bourbon in his glass—"when you came along. There, was that a satisfactory answer?"

I smiled. He seemed confident, sophisticated, and eminently reasonable. He seemed real. "Yes, it was. Okay, so what's the game?"

"The game is very simple. I ask you to do something, and you do it."

"Something like what?"

"Something like this: I have a marble in my jacket pocket. I'd like you to reach into the pocket, take out the marble, and put it in your mouth. I'll also have another bourbon and a glass of water, and when you bring me back the drinks, put the marble into the glass of bourbon. That's how you'll return it to me." His voice deepened and it felt like silk sliding over my skin. "Would you do that, Ashley?"

No one had ever said something like that to me before. It

was like a dare, like a secret, like something private just the two of us were getting away with, exciting and a little bit illicit. "If this is a game," I said, "what do I win if I play?"

His full smile was like a prize itself. "I'm a genie. I'll grant you a wish," he said with a laugh. His voice was as rich as melted chocolate, even when he lightened it playfully.

"Okay." I gave him a goofy little curtsy. "I get it." Playing the game and sharing a secret *was* the prize.

I stepped closer to him, glanced back to make sure Jill or someone wasn't watching me from the stairs or server station across the room, and then bent over to reach into the pocket nearest to me. The jacket was a surprisingly soft fabric that felt almost like suede, a stylish cut, but it still had pockets like a traditional suit.

The pocket was empty. His eyebrows twitched with amusement. Okay, other pocket. Now I had to lean across him.

As I did so, he probably got an eyeful down my white, button-down shirt and I kind of liked that thought. My nipples tightened as I wondered if he liked the view. I slid my hand into the pocket and found it empty also. "Hey—"

Before I could voice my protest, he spoke. "There is *one* more pocket."

Oh. The exterior breast pocket was clearly a fake one, which meant the real pocket was inside the jacket. The expression on his face was bemused. Well, what did I know? I'd never played this game before. Maybe I should have thought of that first. Whatever. I gave him the old eyebrow right back, and slid my hand inside the jacket.

As I did, I caught a whiff of a spicy, masculine scent, not quite strong enough to be cologne. It was as if I could feel his body heat with my nose.

Intoxicated by his scent, I finally felt something square and hard. I pulled it free: a ring box? Now I really wondered why he was drinking alone, if this was an engagement ring or something like that . . .

I glanced at him before I opened the box only to find a marble perched on a bed of velvet. I plucked it free.

The marble felt warm from being kept close to his heart. Just a round, glass marble with a swirl in it.

So, what were the instructions again? Put it in my mouth? I shared a look with him as I held the marble between two fingers. The request was a little bit dirty and a little intimate without being overtly sexual, and I think he knew that. It was a dare.

Did I dare?

I did. I made a show of dropping the marble into the alcohol he had left, swirling the glass around with a clinking sound, and then fishing the marble out and popping it into my mouth.

"Don't swallow," he warned.

I smiled, took up his glass, and went to fill his order.

Thankfully I didn't have to speak to send his drink order to the bar. I typed it on the upstairs order station, and then went down to put the glass in the bus bin.

Then what? I couldn't chance going into the main section of the bar, and I had to keep busy or it'd be obvious I was slacking off.

The ladies' room. I'd take a quick "powder" and then see if the drinks were up.

In the employee restroom, I straightened my hair and my shirt. Normally I wouldn't give a damn about what a customer thought of my appearance. In fact, normally I hoped they didn't even notice me. But he was so impeccable and smooth! I wished I could seem even half that sophisticated, and since I couldn't, usually being invisible was better. I'd gotten some ketchup on the cuff of one sleeve at some point during the night. Sloppy. And this was my last unstained shirt. I made a note to ask Jill if she could cover that, too, at least a thrift store one. I hated being broke. I needed to get the hell out of grad school and start making some money. I had to find something to do with my life other than staring at pre-Raphaelite art and writing pretentious analyses of it. My mother told me endlessly that grad school was a waste of time, except for the fact that I might meet a well-educated guy to marry. I hadn't even gotten that part right.

A knock on the door jolted me. I hoped it wasn't anyone I would have to say much to. I tucked the marble into my cheek. "One sec!" I ran the water and washed my hands.

When I came out, Jill was standing there, her beefy arms crossed. "You okay in there? I've been waiting."

Well, nothing like the truth at a time like that, right? "I'm hiding because the advisor I blew off tonight to cover your ass is out there right now!" The marble clicked against my teeth as I tried to make myself understandable. Hopefully she would think it was a cough drop or an ice cube.

"What advisor? You didn't tell me you blew someone off!"

"Would it have mattered? 'Karina'"—it came out "Kawina" with the marble in the way—"'I'm desperate. You're the only one who can do this. I need you,'" I hissed, imitating the way she had wheedled me on the phone.

"Of course it would have mattered."

I shook my head. "Last time I told you I had plans and didn't drop everything to work for you, you got Mom all pissed off at me and made my life a living hell for months."

"You had 'plans' with stupid Brad, who was no good for you anyway! I really did need you, and that night blew chunks without you." Jill had just turned thirty and was a good deal heavier than me. When she smacked the door frame next to my head, I swear the door felt it.

"Well, this is it, the last time. Now excuse me, my order's up." I pushed past her. I loved Jill, but she thought because she was the oldest that my brother Troy and I were her lord- and lady-in-waiting or something. Troy was only a year younger than me, but he might as well have lived on another planet for all I saw of him or understood of him. And that was a cheap shot bringing up Brad. He was a failure in every sense of the word. I had thought dating an older, more distinguished guy was a good idea for someone about to leave grad school. He was thirty-three, seven years older than me, and I'd made the mistake of thinking that meant he was a functioning adult. Instead, he'd bounced between acting like he was fifty-three and in need of a geriatric nurse and acting like he was *three* and in need of a time-out. Worst of all, he was already trying to get a prescription for Viagra.

I meant it when I said failure in every way.

Thankfully, the order was up. I took the glass of water and the bourbon up the stairs, thinking, *So far, so good.*

The four-top of women had left, and the couple was holding hands and had their faces close together. I could see the tatters of wrapping paper on the table from the gifts they'd exchanged. I'm sure they were perfectly nice people, but all I wanted was to tell them to get a room.

As I approached my mystery man's table, I realized I had no idea how I was going to get the marble out of my mouth.

It was too late to go in the back and drop it into the glass there. He'd already seen me, and his gaze seemed to be drawing me toward him. His eyes never left mine as I crossed the floor, feeling like each step was getting heavier and heavier.

At last I stopped in front of his table, drew in a deep breath, and set down the glass of water. I then held up the shot glass of bourbon as if I were smelling it, brought the marble out until I held it with just my lips in an O shape, and let it go, almost like I was blowing him a kiss. The marble fell with a *plop* and I set the bourbon on the table, resisting the urge to wipe my lips. I settled for licking them.

He ignored the glass on the table, his eyes never leaving my face, and I saw his gaze sharpen at the momentary appearance of my tongue. I wondered if he was as turned on as I was. I had never flirted with a customer. Not like this.

He lifted his drink and smelled the bourbon, waving the glass under his nose and then closing his eyes for a moment as if savoring the scent. I nearly sighed when he did, as if I'd been released from a magic spell. A moment later he stared at me again as he took his first sip.

He nodded, as if satisfied, and set the glass down. "How did you choose which bourbon to give me this time? This isn't the same one."

"Well, you seem in the mood to try new things tonight," I explained. "Plus I figured you for the type that wouldn't go down in quality, so I went up."

He nodded again, approvingly, as if I'd answered a particularly tricky test question.

"Do I get my wish now?" I asked jokingly.

His face remained stern as he laid his hand on the tabletop, fingers curled as if he were holding a live moth. "Think very hard about what you want, then close your eyes."

I did as he asked, without hesitating. Well, I closed my eyes, anyway. But what did I want? What should I wish for? I supposed this was like making a birthday wish before blowing out the candles. Wishing for happiness seemed way too general. Wishing for money felt wrong. Wishing to graduate . . . *I shouldn't have to wish for that, damn it.* I deserved to finish and move on with my life. Wishing for that job I'd interviewed for? That was like wishing for money. And I wasn't even sure I wanted to work for Philip Hale. Something about him creeped me out a little.

"Make your wish," he whispered, and yet I heard him perfectly clearly. "Then take the wish out of my hand."

I want to know what love is, I thought, and opened my eyes. He was grinning as he opened his hand and there was nothing there, but I played along by snatching up a bit of air and pretending to shove it into the breast pocket on my button-down shirt.

He startled me then by standing up, very close to me. I didn't back away. Instead, I looked up at him wondering if he was feeling the effects of the alcohol. He was tall and he looked down to meet my eyes, his now shadowed, hawkish and intense.

"Thank you for playing this game with me," he said, voice low. I heard glass clink as he held up the marble, glistening with booze. He licked it clean, his tongue long and sinuous like a cat's, and I imagined what it would feel like licking me instead of the piece of glass. "You're very rare, Ashley. I would like to play another round with you sometime."

"I, um, okay," I said, hardly able to speak. I felt more like

I was the one who had downed a shot, fueled with liquid courage.

He handed me a card with his other hand. "Call the number on that card if you're interested."

"Could we, um, play another round right now?" I heard myself ask. He was mesmerizing. He was different. I'd never met a man who made me feel like this: turned on and intrigued and challenged, and yet I felt safe, like he was someone I could trust.

He chuckled very low in his throat. "Desire is good," he said. "Being pushy is not."

"Oh. I'm sorry."

He closed his eyes a moment, as if he were thinking it over, and that helped. We were still standing far too close for far too long in a public place. I wanted to lick the shine of bourbon from the edge of his lip. He'd used the word *desire*, which made it clear what we were talking about, didn't it?

What he said next surely did. "Very well. One more round. Take the marble, and put it into your panties. You'll keep it there the rest of your shift. When you get off, call the number on the card to get your next instructions."

My heart was beating in triple time. "Okay," I said, sounding a bit breathless.

He handed me the marble and then raised his eyebrow.

"Right now?" I squeaked.

He nodded. The couple had stood to leave and were paying us no mind.

Under the front knot of my apron, I reached inside the waistband of my jeans, sucking in my stomach to make room for my hand. From there I dug my fingertips under the elastic of my panties and let the marble drop. I held in a gasp as it slid straight down the seam of my body, to where it found a pool of dampness I hadn't realized had gathered there.

I hadn't been this turned on in months. Possibly I hadn't been this turned on *ever.*

He leaned in to whisper, "Good girl," and I felt like I had won another prize. The feeling only deepened when he ran one finger along my jaw, such a light touch I barely felt it. "If you don't call, I'll know you decided you didn't want to play after all. I won't be— No, that's a lie. I *will* be disappointed if you don't. However, I'll respect your wishes."

"I'll earn another wish from you," I said in return. In the back of my head I was already thinking that if I wanted to back out, it would be easy. My name wasn't even Ashley, and this wasn't my actual job. But in the front of my mind all I could think of was how much I wanted to keep playing . . . with him.

He grinned. "Excellent." He nodded, then stepped back to put his topcoat on and walked out without looking back at me.

I stood there for a few more breathless seconds, until he was out of sight. Then I looked down and saw that the two twenty-dollar bills I thought he'd left on the table to cover his tab were actually fifties.

I shoved them into my apron pocket and collected the glasses from all the tables before heading down the stairs, carrying the tray over my shoulder. With each step I took, the marble rubbed back and forth in my panties, inflaming me. I wondered if anyone would be able to tell how turned on I was and was thankful for the amber and red lights in the place.

This was by far the kinkiest thing I had ever done. If Jill

knew I had flirted with a customer like that, or with *anyone* for that matter, she'd freak. So it was imperative that I keep our secret. I suddenly realized I didn't even know his name. I looked at the card. All it had on it was a phone number. I slipped it into the back pocket of my jeans, wondering what his hand would feel like there.

I was so wrapped up in thinking about him that I almost dropped the glasses I was holding when someone grabbed me by the arm.

"Karina Casper! You told me you were too sick to get out of bed! What do you have to say for yourself?"

It was Professor Renault. And I was plain caught.

Two

In the Back of a Dream Car

Professor Renault would have launched into a lecture right there, I'm sure, except that the throngs of Lord's Ladies picked that moment to break into song. The HD TVs were all showing a video from the concert earlier in which the singer flew over the audience while riding a giant white swan. I could see Renault's mouth moving but couldn't hear a word he said. I pointed to my ear and shook my head. He made a frustrated noise. Hale stood behind him looking boozy and amused.

Renault took my arm again, this time to pull me close enough to say directly into my ear, "You will be at my office first thing in the morning. Bah, no, I have another appointment. Come to my house at eight."

"In the morning?" I protested. "Professor..."

"You are the one who lied and inconvenienced me, so now you must make it up to me. Eight o'clock." He let me go again with a sneer on his face so spiteful he might as well have said, "Or else."

He rattled off his address before he turned to leave, and

Hale kind of leered at me and gave a wave of his pudgy fingers, then followed Renault through the crowd of outlandishly dressed fan girls (and a few boys). Maybe Hale was too drunk to recognize me, though he'd probably heard my name. Whatever. I'd had enough. I didn't care that there were still two hours to go until closing time.

I went directly to the back room, took off my apron, and flung it into the laundry. Then I remembered the cash in the pocket and had to pull it back out of the bin. I went to clock out and then remembered I wasn't actually a clocked-in employee. Right. That was how I got into this mess in the first place.

I didn't see Jill anywhere to tell her good-bye, which was just as well since I was so angry I might have said something I would regret. I grabbed my coat and stormed out the back, half thinking I should stand in the alley until I cooled off and then go back in and finish the shift after all. But there were people out back, a busboy having a smoke and getting an eyeful of two LL fans whose genders I couldn't even determine making out against the wall. They were dressed identically, with purple wigs, electric-blue jackets, and thigh-high red boots. At any other time I would have found it comical. Right now I was just pissed.

I hugged my jacket around me and hurried out of the alley. The Seventh Avenue sidewalk was crowded with concertgoers and roving packs of glam rockers, even though the concert was long over. Normally I'd go over to 34th to walk on the busier—and therefore safer—street, but right then I was too mad to care. I turned and stalked for half a block on 32nd Street, fuming about my advisor, about my ketchup-stained shirt, about everything, but then something very insistent caught my attention. The slippery, round nub of glass in my panties.

Remembering it suddenly brought back the lust and attraction in a rush and my cheeks heated up, even in the chilly March wind. I sagged against a building, but that caused the sensation of the marble to stop. I started walking again, imagining it was his finger moving back and forth. Teasing.

I felt in my coat pocket for my phone. Should I call now? Or wait until I got home? He wasn't expecting me to call so soon, was he? He probably thought I didn't get off until two in the morning. I glanced at the time on the cell's screen. It was barely midnight.

I was almost to Sixth Avenue, almost to Herald Square where I normally caught my train, but now I wasn't sure. Maybe I should go home and forget all about him. I mean, seriously, what if he turned out to be a psycho?

Who was I kidding? What we'd done at the bar was far from normal and yet that was what was so interesting about him. I couldn't help but think about what else he had up his sleeve ... or better yet, in his pockets.

I sucked in a deep breath and dialed the number on the card. I heard a ring, then what sounded like a connection. "Hello?" I said when I didn't hear anything else. "Ah, piece of crap phone, did you drop the call? If anyone's there, I'll try you again. I need a new phone."

I hung up and tried again.

This time a male voice, deep even through the phone, answered. "Hello?"

"Hi, it's me. K—um, Ashley. Is this ...? Ha-ha, I don't even know what to call you. I mean, that is, I'm calling for my next instructions." Why was I always such a dork on the phone? I felt pretty good for having put together a nice full sentence at the end, though.

I heard his amused chuckle. "Your shift is over?"

"Very over," I said with some vehemence. "I quit."

"I see. Well, where are you now? Sounds like you're out-doors."

"I am. Thirty-second Street, just west of Sixth."

"The north side of the street?"

"Yeah, the mall side."

"Say *yes* instead."

"Yes?"

"Instead of *yeah*. Say *yes*."

"Okay. Yes." I held on to the *s* a little too long. *Yes* had a kind of sexy hiss to it.

"Lean against the wall, like you're waiting for a bus," he said. "I'll be there in a moment. Stay on the phone."

"Yes, I will." I did as he asked, leaning one shoulder against the wall and cradling the phone to my ear. In a moment? I guess he hadn't gone far after leaving the bar. Had he been expecting my call? I looked around the sidewalk, expecting to see him walk around the corner at any moment.

Instead, a long black limousine pulled up in front of me.

"Stay against the wall," he said, but the window rolled down a crack, just enough for me to see his eyes. That was all I needed to see to know it was him.

"Reach into your jeans and pull up your panties until I can see the edge."

"Okay."

He clucked his tongue. "Say *yes*."

"Right. Yesss." I did as he asked, tugging on the waistband,

which had the effect of bunching my panties between my
lower lips, in addition to pulling the marble against the center
of my pleasure. I gasped out another "Yes!"

"Very good," came his voice. "Keep tugging like that."

"Yes, I will." I wondered with some disbelief whether a total stranger was about to make me come right there on a New
York City street.

"Not very lacy, are they?"

"Excuse me?"

"Your panties."

"Oh, um, no." My cheeks flushed. I was wearing plain
white cotton, the kind I bought in a pack of ten. "I'm not
much of a girly-girl, really." My breath caught.

His voice was a whisper. "Don't come."

"But I'm so close."

"What did I say about being pushy?"

Oh. *Oh.* "Isn't desire good?" I asked.

"Yes. Very good."

"What do I have to do to come?"

"Be patient," he said, with another chuckle.

I squeezed my legs together. "Damn it, how did I know
you were going to say something like that?"

His chuckle turned into a laugh loud enough that I heard
it through the cracked window. "Because your instincts are
good, that's why. How about this? What would you do to earn
an orgasm? And don't say *anything.* I can't stand clichés."

That made me laugh. "All right. Besides, I wouldn't *do*
'anything.' I'm not that kind of girl."

"No, indeed you aren't. I can tell you're a good girl, and
that's one reason why I like you," he said softly, and it made
me feel warm and tingly inside. "Now, answer the question."

I looked at him, those eagle eyes staring out from the slit in the window. "It's hard to say what I'd do when I don't know the rules of the game," I said.

"Oh, but learning the rules is part of the game," he answered. "Indeed, your answer will help make the rules."

"Oh." I racked my brains, but it was hard to think when I was so turned on. "Well, I should do something that you'll like so that you'll let me come. But I don't know you well enough to guess."

He laughed again. "Learning what will please me is nearly the same thing as learning the rules."

"I see. Well, I think two things please you," I said, tugging on my panties again. "One is watching me obey, and the other is watching me squirm."

"Both are correct."

"If you don't tell me what to do, I can't obey, and, well, I sure as hell am squirming now."

"That you are, and it is lovely."

I felt the flush creep up my face again. "Thank you." No one had ever called me lovely before. And meant it.

"Do one more thing for me, and then you may come only if you can do so without reaching into your jeans."

"One more thing?"

"Yes. Walk around the block."

"Which direction?"

"So that the car may follow you, of course. Go up to Sixth and turn left."

Of course. "Okay. I mean *yes*."

"Very good."

I started to walk. I was wearing a stained shirt, black jeans, and my clunky black work shoes, but I felt like I was in stilettos and a miniskirt. I was completely slippery down below, and I could feel his eyes on me as I walked.

After midnight there weren't a lot of people on Sixth Avenue, but in New York the streets are never completely empty. There were small crowds waiting for the bus, loitering, doing whatever the hell people do...None of them paying any attention to me, but the thought that they might look up, might wonder why my face was so red, why my steps were so slow...

I turned the next corner heading back toward the Garden and could hear the engine hum as the car followed around the turn.

Suddenly his voice was sharp. "No, don't." The car and I both stopped where we were. "Too many people in the street at the other end." I heard him curse away from the phone and say something I couldn't make out, possibly in some other language. He must have been talking to the limo driver.

"It's the crowd from the Lightning concert," I said while I waited for him to tell me what to do. "New York is infested with roving gangs in platform glitter boots."

He chuckled nervously. "Indeed. Well, judging from the look of things in this direction, we won't be getting through there."

"What should I do?"

There was silence. I guess he was thinking about it.

"Get in," he finally said, and I heard the door unlock on the limo at the same moment his eyes disappeared from the window.

I didn't even hesitate. I didn't think about how stupid it could be to get into a stranger's car. I opened the door and slid onto the seat. I could still feel his warmth.

He had moved to the other side of the car. The compartment was spacious and he seemed too far away.

"Give your address to the driver," he said.

The driver was a young man in an actual chauffeur's uniform and hat. Brown curls escaped from the hat. He said nothing, waiting for me to speak. I rattled off my building's address, and then the window between the front and back seats closed, the black plate glass sliding slowly across like an eclipse.

I turned toward my companion. He brushed his hand over his hair, as if he was used to having it much longer and was surprised to find it cut short. He exhaled a shaky breath as the driver made an illegal U-turn, then pulled out of the street the wrong way.

"I apologize for my error in judgment," he said, a bit of a quaver in his voice. "I would've liked to watch you walk the entire block very much."

"Yes, well," I said, because I felt I had to say something, "that's New York. Never know when you're going to hit traffic."

My lame joke seemed to make him relax. "Now, about that orgasm," he said, as casually as if we were discussing the weather. "You must come before we reach your home."

I swallowed, almost said "okay," then remembered, and said, "Yes. Same rules as before?"

"Yes," he answered, a catlike smile settling on his face.

Okay, so no reaching into my jeans, but I could still pull on my soaked panties that held the marble. The sensation was nothing like what I was used to and I wondered how long could it take.

I slid down in the seat a little and spread my legs, unbuttoning the bottom few buttons of my untucked shirt and getting a grip on the edge of the waistband of my panties.

I pulled slowly this time, rocking my hips as I did it so that the marble went up and down over my clit. I shivered. It wasn't hard to imagine his finger, or something else, touching me there, given the smoldering way he was looking at me.

I couldn't look away. Even in the dim interior of the limo, his eyes were intense. He sat perfectly still, his spine straight and his head held high.

I doubt I had ever been so aroused in my entire life. My skin tingled all over even though I was clothed, causing me to speed up my movements.

The limo sped down Broadway, I think, and for once I wished for traffic. Although my climax was close, my arousal seemed to have leveled off. I tugged harder on my underwear, then reached down and rubbed myself on the outside of my jeans, but there was no way that was going to work.

Then the marble slipped out of place and fell somewhere around my tailbone. I cried out in dismay.

Wait, maybe that was a good thing. The roughness of my wet panties seemed to help, but again I went up and up and then stuck on the edge of coming, but not going over the edge. I made a helpless noise, whimpering, then moaning with need.

His tongue darted out to moisten his lips briefly, but he said nothing, watching my plight.

"What . . . what happens if I don't 'get there' before we get there?" I asked.

He shook his head slowly. "You can do it," he murmured.

"I'm not sure I can! I . . . ungh." I tried again, rubbing from outside as well as tugging on my panties.

"You can," he said firmly. "I'll be very disappointed if you don't."

"So will I!" I wailed.

I looked frantically out the window and saw we had only a few blocks to go. *Damn it!*

"Please," I begged. "Please..." But I didn't want to actually beg for a change of the rules.

"You can do it," he said again, leaning forward now and clasping his hands. "You can. Relax."

There was no way to relax, riding in this car, with this man, not allowed to touch myself with my fingers and with maybe only a minute or two left before I ran out of time. I was crying out now from the intensity of the stimulation, but I still wasn't coming.

And he knew it. "Almost there. Do it for me, Karina."

I bucked my hips frantically.

He moved next to me, and I caught that scent of him, so spicy and sweet at the same time. He didn't touch me, but he leaned closer so that I could feel the warmth of his breath in my ear.

He whispered one command. "Come."

And I did. I screamed hard and loud as I finally went over the edge. I was falling, soaring, speeding, all at once, my body spasming as I came. One knee knocked against the door and I writhed at the waves of release washing through me.

Normal awareness returned bit by bit. His masculine scent first. Then hearing, the roughness of my panting, and the silence that seemed odd after all the noise I'd been making.

Then I realized I was lying on my side with my face in his lap. What was under my cheek? That was not a baseball bat, though it felt like one. He was intensely hard just from watching me, listening to me?

I sat up abruptly and felt dizzy, blinking. He was looking at me as intently as before but made no move. I wondered if he was going to ask me to suck him off now. That was what guys in cars wanted, wasn't it? This was the moment when he'd become like every other horny guy who met a waitress in a bar and ask me to give him head.

Except he didn't. "Are you all right?" he asked, his words very careful, very precise.

I nodded. "Think so."

"Good. Is this your building?"

I looked through the tinted window. "Yes."

His tone was oddly cordial, warm. "If you think you can stand, you may go. I'll wait here until you are safely inside."

I was surprised and I'm sure it showed on my face.

He smiled a benevolent smile. "You did well. I'm pleased."

I nodded. I would have asked, "Are you sure you don't want something?" except the way he said he was pleased, it felt like I would be contradicting him. I got the feeling he wouldn't like being contradicted. I didn't want him to pull away emotionally yet, so I said, "Does that mean I get another wish?"

His smile turned into a grin. "Yes. Yes, it does."

Don't think that in the throes of passion I didn't notice that he'd used my name, my real name. He must have some special kind of caller ID, I thought. "I wish I knew what to call you," I said.

That made him laugh. "You are a delight," he said, but did not introduce himself.

"Well, don't you think that's fair?" I asked. "This is a game, right? And games should be fair. You know my name"—*and where I live*—"but I don't know yours."

His smile was indulgent, but his answer wasn't. "You didn't wish for my name. You wished you knew what to call me."

"Um..." I supposed that was true.

"You'll know what to call me when it comes to you," he said. "*If* we play again."

"If I call you, will we?"

"Yes." He paused a moment, looking away, then back at me. "When do you think you'd be most likely to call?"

"Honestly? The way I'm feeling right now, I don't know if I'll be able to resist calling you the minute I get upstairs."

He laughed, delighted. "Thank you so much for brightening up an otherwise maudlin evening for me, Karina. How about this? Call me on Friday, at seven p.m. sharp. If you're late, I won't answer."

"I won't be late," I promised.

Had we made a date? I wasn't sure, like I wasn't sure if we'd had sex or not. I mean, he hadn't even touched me. I hadn't even touched myself...well, not skin-to-skin contact. I had no idea what to call what had happened.

I opened the door of the car, but with one foot on the curb I paused and asked, "What about the marble?" The marble he'd kept in a ring box in his jacket pocket.

He thought a moment before saying, "It is as special as you are. Keep it as a token of my affection."

So I did.

Three

Where Things Are Hollow

In the light of morning, my mystery man might as well have been a prince of Elfland in a pumpkin carriage. That was how unreal it seemed. Stuff like that didn't happen to people. Or at least it didn't happen to me. I know they say the city is full of stories and strange things, but it hadn't been a fairy-tale city in my experience. It was just a place to live, a place to work, a place to study along with eight million other people, including one very pissed off thesis advisor.

I rolled out of bed at 7:30 a.m. I brushed out my hair, but I'd gone to sleep with it wet, collapsing into bed practically the minute I was out of the shower. So it was hopeless-looking unless I was going to wash it again. But there was no time for that if I was going to get to Renault's by eight. I stuck a baseball cap on top of it, threw on some clothes, grabbed a granola bar, and hurried out.

I ate while I walked. The streets were crowded at this time of day with tons of people trying to get to work. At least it wasn't raining. The walk across town took about twenty minutes. There was no convenient way to travel by public transportation, so I hoofed it.

I rang his doorbell at five after eight.

Professor Renault yanked the door to his brownstone wide open. I guess he was still pissed off. He was a skinny man, with a pinched-looking face even at the best of times. "Take your shoes off," he barked. "Come into my office."

He stalked to the back of the house while I untied my sneakers and put them onto the rack of other shoes by the door.

I found him sitting at his desk in his cluttered home office, his back to the window that overlooked a small patio. His hands were folded on the desk blotter and he had a very stern look on his face.

There was no chair for me, so I stood there on his oriental-style rug in my socks, wondering which one of us was going to speak first.

I figured it should be me. "Look, I'm sorry about last night. My sister is the manager of that bar, and she begged me to work for her. I didn't think it would be a big deal to reschedule the meeting with you."

He moved his mouth like he was sucking on something sour. "Your petty family problems are not my concern."

"I know, which is why I didn't bother to tell you about it last night."

"Instead you lied, creating an elaborate fabrication. This is unacceptable behavior for a grown woman." He looked me up and down, as if jeans, a sweatshirt, and baseball cap were also not acceptable in his eyes.

I couldn't really argue with him, though. I had lied, and had gotten caught. What I didn't know was what to do about it.

Then he opened a drawer in his desk and pulled out a

folder. He laid it on the desk and opened it, and I could see the title of my thesis on the first page in large letters. It was the printout of the latest draft I'd given him to read. The thing we were supposed to talk about last night. I relaxed a little, thinking the lecture and scolding portion of the meeting was over and that now we'd talk about the actual work. When it came down to it, I didn't give a damn what Professor Theobald Renault thought about me as a woman. His job was to judge me as a scholar.

He picked up the pages by the corner, as if he didn't want to handle them any more than necessary. He moved it to the side, until he was holding it over a round wastebasket.

"What are you doing?"

He let the pages drop into the trash. "You are not fit to graduate."

"Are you kidding me? Nobody knows more about pre-Raphaelite art in the city than me!"

"Is that so? And what were you planning to do with your degree anyway, Karina? Why are you here? Don't tell me the pre-Raphaelites are your burning passion in life."

I shifted from foot to foot on the carpet. "I like the pre-Raphaelites," I said, but it sounded weak. Very weak. The truth was I had only gone to graduate school because I hadn't figured out what to do with myself otherwise. I'd qualified for the loans, so I figured why not? It would give me time to figure things out, I'd thought. But I'd pursued my studies so single-mindedly, even my hobbies had been neglected. I didn't know what was next for me after graduation, but that made it all the more important, in my mind, to get the degree and get going. My previous advisor hadn't really cared one way or the other what I did, but his failing health had forced him to retire suddenly. That was how I ended up with hard-nosed Renault. "Did you even read it?"

He didn't answer. He exhaled slowly through his nose. "You should've dressed better. You're supposed to be trying to impress me. You're supposed to be making me think you're not a total fuck-up."

"This is about my clothes? If you wanted me to look like I didn't just roll out of bed, don't make meetings at eight o'clock in the morning!"

"You dress like a lesbian. Do you want people to think you're a lesbian?"

"What?" I wasn't a lesbian, but I failed to see how that could be relevant. "Are lesbians not allowed to graduate?"

"Every advisor has his own standards that must be met," he continued. "Mine are a bit more stringent than your previous advisor's."

"What is this really about, Professor?"

"I take my job as a mentor to you women students very seriously. It says right in the university handbook that judging a student's readiness to participate and compete in the world outside the university is my job and that I shouldn't allow any student to pass who is not ready." He looked around the office, for what, I didn't know. His face became increasingly red, as if I was embarrassing him. "You have not shown the proper accommodation to the situation."

"Proper accommodation? Would my apology have been stronger if I'd gotten my hair done and dressed up?"

"Yes, very much so," he said, clearing his throat. "A floral skirt would have been best and would have signaled your receptivity. You have utterly failed to mitigate the situation. You are a disappointment."

"So...I was supposed to dress up in a completely *fake* manner to prove that my apology was *sincere*? That makes no sense."

"Certain things are going to be..." He cleared his throat. "Certain things are pleasing, and if you showed proper deference and receptivity, we could put your egregious lapse behind us."

"Speak plain English, Professor. I have no idea what you're talking about."

"Which only proves my point." He sighed and shook his head sadly. "Do I have to spell it out for you?"

"Yes, damn it, I apparently lost track of this conversation a long time ago. Do you want me to rewrite the thesis or what?"

He shook his head again. "No rewriting will be necessary, if you will simply...bow to the needs of the situation."

Maybe it was the way he said "needs" that suddenly clued me in. Receptivity. A floral skirt would be "pleasing." He had wanted me to make myself pretty for him. His face was red and he was shifting uncomfortably in his chair. My eyes were probably as wide and round as my mouth when I said, "Oh."

He sighed in relief as if thinking, *The idiot finally understands!* and then unbuckled his belt.

I froze where I was. He stood to let his trousers drop, but thankfully the tails of his shirt hid whatever he had under there. The sound of the loose change in his pocket jingling when it hit the floor shook me out of my paralysis.

"You're crazy," I said.

"Come now, don't be difficult," he insisted as he sat back down in the chair and waved his hand at his lap like a waiter showcasing a meal. "This is the way the world works, Miss Casper. Using your mouth will incur no risk of pregnancy and it will be but fifteen minutes of your time at the most. Is it worth it to throw away years of work by refusing to do this one thing?"

"You're seriously saying if I suck your dick you'll pass me, and if I don't you'll fail me? Did you even read my dissertation?"

He waved his hand as if dispelling a bad smell. "It doesn't matter." Then he gestured to his lap again. "Oral sex is not only much safer for you, it is also more satisfying for a man my age. There is a pillow on the bookshelf for your knees."

"You're out of your mind," I said, looking in horror at the embroidered pillow jammed into the bookshelf right next to him. "Completely and utterly out of your mind." With that I turned and practically ran to the front door. I grabbed my shoes and bolted out, right onto the sidewalk, and didn't stop until I had rounded the corner in front of the Korean grocer.

There I paused to catch my breath and put my shoes on. I dared a look around the corner of the building, wondering if he'd chase me with his dick hanging out. There was no sign of him.

I leaned back against the building, my heart pounding. If I'd thought last night was unbelievable, this was in a whole different class. The nerve! I wondered how many female students had polished his knob over the years. And how many of them hated themselves for it later. I shuddered. Disgusting. He even had a pillow there like it was a regular thing!

I should report him, I thought. Shouldn't I? Or would he claim I came on to him? *You're being naive if you think this kind of thing doesn't go on all the fricking time,* I told myself. He'd been at the university a long time. He probably had friends in high places. For all I knew, he went to orgies with the dean. I didn't know what to think. Hah. Wasn't that the lesson he thought he was teaching me, to make me ready for the job market? That this was the way it was? Women have to put out sexual favors to powerful men if they want to get anywhere?

A sudden thought struck me. Had he seen me do something at the bar last night, flirting or whatever, that made him think I was a slut? Why did he show this side of himself now? I tried to think. I hadn't done anything. Well, except screaming at the top of my lungs as I came inside a limousine, but I was sure no one knew about that. Maybe he'd seen me drop the marble into the glass?

I needed to talk to someone about it. Jill? No. I'd only get a lecture about how I must've brought it on myself somehow. Or she'd say it was his way of saying the thesis was no good. Mom? No way. She'd lecture me on how I shouldn't have moved to the city in the first place because it was full of perverts.

If you only knew, Mom. I forced myself to go into the grocer's and buy a bottle of water. The clerk gave me a strange look. My face was probably all blotchy, even though I hadn't actually cried. Some women look elegant and tragic when a tear comes to their eye. I always looked like I had a bad case of the flu.

I stood outside and concentrated on drinking the bottle of water. My hands were shaking a little. Who could I tell?

I held my phone in the palm of my hand. Could I call *him*? I was supposed to wait until Friday, but did that mean I couldn't call before that time? Those were the rules of the game, but...

This wasn't a game.

I went ahead and dialed the number, which was still in my recent call list.

It rang, and my heart rate, which was still high from the incident with Renault, doubled.

It rang again, and I clutched the phone close to my ear.

Then it rang a third time and a generic voice mail message played.

I swallowed, wondering if I should hang up. No, if he saw there was a missed call from me, he'd think...he'd think I was stalking him. I realized he was probably asleep. It wasn't even 8:30 yet, and I knew where he'd been last night. Stupid.

The beep sounded. "Hi, sorry to bother you, but it's Karina. I normally wouldn't call, but something sort of happened, and I kind of feel like I need to talk to someone about it. And you seemed like you might be one of the only people, well, okay, the only person I know who I think I could tell. That sounds weird I know, but it's...a very private thing and...and...oh God is there a way to erase messages on this thing? I must sound like such a nut. I'm sorry, never mind, I'll handle it. Forget I called. I'm okay. I'll talk to you Friday." I hit the pound key, hoping it would take me back to the menu so I could erase it, but no such luck.

"Message sent," the voice said.

I let out a sigh. I'd probably torpedoed the whole whatever it was with whatever his name was, too. Great way to start the day.

I went home and went back to bed.

* * *

I must have been really tired, because I fell asleep even though my mind was still turning in circles. I woke with the phone ringing under my pillow a while later.

I answered it sleepily, without looking at who it was.

It was *Him*. "Karina. Are you all right?"

"Um." I sat up straight in bed. "Sorry." It took me a while to wake up enough to use full sentences. "I mean, sorry for calling so early this morning and for leaving you such a crazy message. Everything's fine now."

"Is it? Or are you just saying that?"

I blinked. Why did I say that? Because I didn't want him to think I was some kind of basket case. "I'm not actually sure. I'm not in danger or anything like that."

"If you're sure..."

"Look, I don't want you to think it's like I have a...a..." I tried to imagine what kind of mysterious trouble someone could get into. All I could think of was dumb stuff from movies, but okay. "...loan shark after me, or the Mafia or something. It's nothing like that." I especially didn't want him to think I was after his money. I had no idea what he did, but your average, middle-class corporate drone didn't tool around Manhattan in a private limo.

"All right," he said. "If you need my help, you should ask for it."

I almost said "Really?" in a skeptical way. We'd only shared a kinky ride in his limo. I didn't see how that made him a knight in shining armor or why he'd feel obligated to be one. But it was nice to have his support, so I didn't argue.

"I think I'm okay now," I said. "But thank you. I appreciate it." I still didn't know what I was going to do about Renault.

Sure, there were cases in the news of sex abuse victims winning against their abusers. There were also plenty of cases of them being vilified, their lives ruined. If I wasn't the first woman Renault had done this to, and I clearly wasn't, then he had some way to silence his victims. I didn't want to find out what it was. Maybe I could just go to the dean and request a new advisor for "personality conflict" or something and we would both let it drop.

"Karina, are you still there? Are you sure you're all right?"

"Yeah, I mean, *yes*, I'm all right." I blew out a breath. "I still don't know what to call you."

"What do you want to call me?" came his rejoinder.

"I mean, even in my head, I'm just calling you Him, with a capital *H*."

He laughed. "I rather like that. No other man but me, if I'm the only 'him' you think about."

"Yes, but it doesn't work on the phone," I insisted as I lay back down. "Hello, is this Him? Oh, wait. That kind of does work." I started to laugh myself. "You know what I mean, though! Like you can say my name to get my attention, but I can't exactly say 'Hey, you,' can I?"

"You can't?" he teased.

"No, it's rude and uncouth, and you don't like rude and uncouth things."

"I don't?"

"Clearly not. So I need something to call you."

There was a beat of silence, then, "What about *sir*?"

"Because you're my knight in shining armor? Sir Limos-a-Lot?"

His chuckle was dark and rich. "I was thinking of it in a less innocent context."

"There's nothing innocent about that limousine," I said. "But really? Sir, like Daddy or something?"

He sounded a little tentative. "Would you prefer *Daddy*?"

"Hell no. Oh gosh, that would just... *yuck*." I couldn't even make a coherent sentence. I wasn't sure why I found the idea so off-putting. My father had left us when I was six. Maybe I never had time to be a "daddy's girl." "Why can't I call you what other people call you?"

"Because you are nothing like other people," he said seriously. "Now, really. I want a special name, one that's only for you to use."

"Hmm." I tried to think of something. "This is like trying to name a cat."

"I reserve the right to veto any name like *Mittens*." He sounded a bit worried.

"You're like a British fashion model, so you need a name like Bastian or Antonio," I said, "except you're not really British, are you?"

"I spent some time in school there," he said. "My mother was from there, but I was born here. You know, neither *Bastian* nor *Antonio* is particularly British."

"Oh, hush. I'm just trying them on for size. I suppose I meant European anyway. Lars? Marco? Gideon? None of them seem like you. Maybe something British after all."

"The most British names of all are those of kings," he suggested helpfully.

"Aha, is it a guessing game, then? Arthur? No way, that is way too old for you."

"Is it? How old do you think I am, Karina?"

I closed my eyes. I'd thought his age was hard to gauge in the bar. He seemed so self-possessed and refined, which made him seem older than he was, I thought. So if the oldest he physically could be was forty, then he was probably more like: "Thirty-four."

He whistled. "That is amazing."

"I'm right, aren't I? Yes!" I pumped a fist in triumph. "In that case, Henry sounds too old, too."

"You could try James."

"You mean like the Bible? The King James Bible?"

"Well, the Bible isn't exactly what I hope you'll be thinking about when you're thinking of me."

"Okay, James what?"

"Excuse me?"

"You need a last name, too."

"Do I?"

"If you don't, you're even more like a cat. Or like Cher or Prince," I teased. "Here, I'll give you a last name, too. Rich. James Rich. Then you can be Mr. Rich when I want to be formal about it." I blushed and hid my face under a pillow. I don't know where I got the nerve to be so forward with him, but it was easy somehow. It didn't even feel like flirting, really, but more like I was letting my real self out.

He chuckled. "So it's more of a title than a name?"

"Yes, Mr. Rich," I said, trying on a sort of sexy secretary voice.

"Oh, I *do* like the sound of that. Are you ready to run an errand for me, Karina?"

"Most certainly, Mr. Rich."

"Good. I want you to buy a pencil skirt, stockings, and pumps. Ones that fit you, I mean."

"Yes, Mr. Rich." I wondered if I should get a dictation pad

as a prop, too. "Should I be wearing them when I call you on Friday?"

"Yes."

"And the marble?"

A thrill ran through me like he'd plucked a string deep in my middle when he said, "There are more where that one came from." His voice was low with promise before he disconnected the call.

Four

Innocence in Your Arms

I was tempted to reach my hand into my panties right at that moment, but the door to Becky's bedroom was open a few inches and I couldn't tell if she was in there or not. The day had been mortifying enough without having her walk in on me touching myself in the living room. I don't think I'd ever be able to face her again if that happened.

When I'd first rented the apartment, I'd been working three jobs, the one at Jill's bar and two on campus, so I'd been able to afford the place by myself. Last summer one of the campus jobs got eliminated and to make up for it, I got a roommate. The problem was the place was a one bedroom, which meant I gave Becky the bedroom to convince her to move in while I moved onto the futon couch in the living room. The room was perfectly fine as a bedroom except that it had no door.

Come to think of it, I wasn't even sure Becky had been there last night when I'd gotten home. I went and peeked through the open door. Her cat Milo (which was short for Mr. Millennium Meow) looked up sleepily from the bed and then put his head back down on his folded paws. He appeared to be sleeping on top of a pair of ripped up fishnets. There was no sign of her.

Well, good. Just because her favorite rock star was retiring was no reason to lie around wallowing in depression, was it? Lord Lightning's masked face adorned every inch of the bedroom walls. Becky was Asian American—I was too embarrassed to ask whether she was Korean or Chinese—and I got the impression she had uptight parents and a repressed childhood. She told me when she moved in that wearing punk-glam clothes was a way of rebelling, but she was too timid to actually go out to shows or clubs. She spent a lot of time on the Internet. It was really good to see she was out of the house.

I did want her advice on clothes, though. I went into our tiny galley of a kitchen to find something to eat while I speed-dialed her.

She picked up after a few rings. "Hello?"

I could hear music in the background and people's voices. It sounded like she was at a party. Becky, at a party? At eleven in the morning on a Thursday? "Hey, Becks, I need some advice on the best thrift store."

"Depends on what you're looking for."

"A pencil skirt, stockings, and pumps," I said.

"Holy crap, you? What for?" Becky's disbelief was understandable. She'd probably seen me out of sweatpants or jeans all of once in the five months since she'd moved in.

Damn but she could be nosy. Fortunately it was a lot easier to lie to her over the phone than in person. "Oh, for a drama school play I'm helping out with. Secondhand and inexpensive is best."

"If it's just for the one time, dig around in my closet and see if you can find something first," she said. "I think there are a couple of skirts in there, and stockings are in the top-right drawer of my dress—" She was cut off by a gale of laughter and I heard her saying, "You guyyyss!" off to the side before coming back. "What was I saying?"

"Stockings. Top-right drawer. By the way, I think Milo ate a pair of your fishnets."

"Oh, that's okay. They were getting too ripped to wear. Actually, most of the stockings are pre-ripped. Is that okay?"

"Um, maybe."

"Yeah, sorry, I know, I'm soooo retro-punk. What size do you wear? In shoes, I mean."

"Eight."

"Dig around in the bottom of the closet for shoes, too, then. I never wear any of them and there are a ton. Crap, I hope Milo hasn't been peeing in there or anything."

"Me too. Thanks, Becky. That's really nice of you."

"No problem, Rina. Hey, would you feed Milo for me? I'm not sure when I'll be home."

"Where are you, anyway?"

She hesitated a bit. "Just out with some girlfriends I met last night. I'll tell you about it when I get home. Eventually."

"Looking forward to it!" Sounded like she was having quite the adventure. Well, good for her. I gave up looking for a real breakfast and decided to look for the clothes instead.

First I poured some kibble into Milo's half-full bowl on the side table by her bed. The cat deigned to open one eye and then closed it again.

I decided to start with the dresser. It was an old wooden thing she'd gotten at Goodwill, so bulky we had to get help from two neighbors and the building's super to get it in here. The top-right drawer almost wouldn't come open it was crammed so full, but I finally pulled it loose, and several balled-up pairs of stockings sprang free.

I ended up dumping the whole drawer out on the bed, which made Milo's whiskers twitch, but he didn't bother opening his eyes. I wasn't worth spending the attention on, apparently.

It looked to me like Becky had never thrown away a pair of stockings. It seemed every pair of L'eggs, drugstore-brand knee-highs, or Victoria's Secrets she'd ever bought had been packed into that drawer. Who needs four or five dozen? Black ones, patterned ones, nude ones, opaque ones . . . some seemed new, while others had runs in them. I guess if you wore them under torn jeans runs were okay. I had never been much of a fashion plate myself.

I sorted them out as I looked through the pile. Among them were some that were separate, more like thigh-high socks than stockings. I suddenly had a thought.

I speed-dialed Becky again. "Is there a difference between stockings and pantyhose? I mean, aren't they all considered stockings? Or are stockings only the ones without the panty built in?"

"Why don't you ask the director?"

"I couldn't get him," I lied.

"Well, is this a period piece? A retro thing?"

"Maybe? I think I'm playing the part of sexy secretary."

"Then you better go with real stockings and not panty-hose," she said.

"Uh, sure."

"There should be garter belts in there somewhere, too."

"Okay, thanks."

Indeed, digging through the mass a bit more, I found a black elastic thing that had to be a garter belt and some individual stockings that had a faint pattern to them with a thick, black seam up the back. Bonus, these didn't have any holes.

Next I tried the bedroom closet. There was so much crammed in there, the door wouldn't shut. The rod was completely full of hangers and then more hangers hung crosswise on those. Thankfully, there was a skirt that looked like it might do. I almost missed it, because it was hidden inside a jacket on the same hanger.

I went back to the kitchen to get the flashlight to spelunk the bottom of the closet. What I found was a graveyard of old shoes, all flung together. A lot of them looked like they must have been bought to go with bridesmaid dresses or something. I eventually pulled out one slim, black pump that looked like it might work, but to find the match I had to excavate forty or fifty other shoes until I came to it.

I spent more time putting everything back than I did digging it out.

* * *

I didn't try the whole outfit on until Friday. I figured since I had to call him at seven, I'd start getting dressed around six-thirty. What I hadn't counted on was getting into a discussion with Becky.

I had the skirt, stockings, and garter belt sitting in a little pile on the corner of the futon. It only occurred to me as I looked at the pile that it didn't include a top. Maybe he wanted me topless . . . ? He probably thought I had a bedroom to myself like a normal person. He hadn't said whether this was just phone sex or if we were going out. He wanted me to wear shoes—that probably meant going out, didn't it? Oh, how could he have specified some things and not others? He had said figuring out the rules of the game was part of the game itself, though.

I could hear Becky's voice in the hall as she came toward our door from the elevator, singing one of her favorite songs. I picked up the clothes, went into the bathroom, and stripped down to a T-shirt and my white cotton underwear and started putting the stockings on. This turned out to be more complicated than I expected.

"Becks?" I called into the hall, holding the bathroom door open a crack.

"I'm home!" she yelled back from where she was still getting her coat off. "Rina, the most amazing thing happened!" She came running up to the door and held up a white square of cloth, slightly smeared and stained-looking. "Look at this!"

"A handkerchief?"

"It's *his*!" She rubbed it on her cheek. When she said *his* like that, I knew she meant her rock-star idol. She had her mystery man and I had mine.

"How do you know it's his?"

"At the Madison Square Garden show, you know how he always wears a mask, right? He kept wiping his forehead and then throwing the handkerchiefs into the crowd!"

"But you weren't at that show."

"No, no, I wasn't. But one of the other girls was, and she got two, and she put one into a raffle for charity that the Lord's Ladies were running, and I won it! I won it! I never win anything!" She positively bounced.

"That is awesome!" Her glee was infectious and I found myself grinning. "But, hey, can you help me with this?"

"Of course. What do you need, Rina?"

"Um . . ." I opened the door all the way so she could see the disaster I was making. Among other things, one of the stockings was twisting around my leg like a barber-pole stripe.

"Here. Sit." She dropped the lid down on the toilet and I sat. She took the stocking off and bunched it as she went, then handed it back to me. "Just let a little of it out at a time as you go up your leg."

"Aha! I knew there had to be a trick to it."

"You've really never put on stockings before?"

"Well, only a few times. I always just kind of tugged at them until I got them on all the way, like you do with dance tights." I started pulling it up my leg and she put a hand on mine to slow me down a little.

"I didn't know you danced," she said.

"I used to, just for fun, when I was in high school and a little in college. I wasn't very good at it, though." I shifted as I got the stocking most of the way up my thigh. "And dancing was something feminine, so my mother approved." That was before I'd figured out that I'd never be feminine enough to please my mother.

"You've got the garter belt on backwards," Becky pointed out.

"How can you tell?"

"There's a little bow that goes in front."

I shimmied the belt around while she bunched up the other stocking.

"I had ballet and violin lessons," Becky said, "but so did

every girl I knew. I started both when I was five and quit ballet when I was ten."

"Why?"

"So I could spend more time on the violin. Ugh," she said.
"That was my mother's idea, too." She fastened the stockings
to the dangling bits of the belt and then made a face.

"Rina, those panties totally don't go."

"Well, I wasn't gonna borrow *those* from you," I said. Then
I blushed furiously as I realized panties hadn't been on his list
of things to wear. Maybe he intended for me to go without. I
felt a deep thrill between my legs thinking about it.

Becky was still sitting on the bathroom floor. She looked
up at me seriously. "What's this all about, Karina?"

"What do you mean?"

"You getting dolled up like this."

I tried for indignant. "I'm not allowed to get dressed up?"

"You told me it was for a play," she said. "So why are you
getting dressed here and not at the theater?"

Oh, I was so busted.

"Look, I know you're having money troubles," she went
on.

"What does getting dressed up have to do with...? Oh."
I was already blushing like crazy between thinking dirty
thoughts about James and being caught lying to her, so I
doubted it could get worse. She was implying that I would
only be getting dressed like this for one reason. "You think
I'm hooking. Is that it?"

"Can you seriously tell me you're not?"

"Jeez, Becky, I'm just trying to—"

"Karina. I know we haven't known each other that long,
but when a woman who doesn't even own a skirt suddenly

wants to put on a whore-y outfit, you gotta wonder." She was giving me a look over the top of her glasses a lot like a disapproving librarian. "Right? I know there were those girls in Palladium Hall caught last year. I read that Manhattan call girl book. What's the real explanation, if that's not it?"

I sighed. "I met a guy, that's all." Her expression didn't change. "Just for fun." Argh, even worse. "It was his idea." Oh, fuck. Could Becky be right? I admit I thought he was probably filthy rich, and he'd told me to ask him for help if I needed it. Just what kind of "help" did he mean? Was he going to pay me to be his whore?

Becky nodded. "I don't know what's worse—if he hasn't offered to pay you and thinks he's going to get away with it, or if he's going to stuff a couple hundred in your bra when you're done."

"I really don't think that's what it's going to be like," I said. But what if she was right? What if I was being as oblivious to the way things were with James as I was with Renault? I had no idea what I was getting myself into.

Wasn't that the point, though? I didn't know what to expect, and that was part of the fun. I was tremendously attracted to him; my whole body felt alive for him in a way it hadn't for Brad or anyone else. So far, I hadn't felt scared or weirded out by him at all. He felt more like a prince than a pimp. I had to go with my feelings.

"He's really very nice," I said, which came out sounding lame and a bit like a lie since I had no idea if he was nice or not. "It's okay, Becks. We're just having a little fun. Experimenting." Jeez, now I made it sound like we were doing drugs.

She sighed and got up. "Well, when will you be home?"

"I'm not sure. I don't even know where we're going. I'm supposed to call him at seven."

"Okay, say he takes you out or to his place or whatever. Tell him you have to call me at eleven p.m. sharp or I'm calling the police."

"What? I can't tell him that!"

"Lie and say I'm your mother. Come on, Rina, you're good at little white lies. He'll fall for it. It'll keep him on his toes knowing you've got someone waiting up for you."

"You're not actually going to wait up for me, though, are you?"

"Well, I'm going out, but I'll have my phone."

I could see how it made sense to have a check-in with a friend if there was even the slightest chance things could get sketchy. But I didn't want to go overboard. "What if I forget to call you? I don't want you to put out an APB if I'm having a nice time."

She sighed again and leaned against the bathroom door frame. "Set an alarm on your phone. I'm serious about this, Karina. Call or text me to say you're okay. If you're not okay, don't call. Or if he's listening and you're pretending it's okay but really it's not—" She snapped her fingers, her eyes brightening. "I know! Let's have a code word!"

"Becks, I really don't think we need to get all James Bond about this."

I think her enthusiasm was only heightened by the mention of James Bond, though. "No, really," she insisted. "If everything's fine, use the word *sunrise* somehow, and if it's not, use *sunset*."

"Uhhh . . ."

"You know. Like if everything's all right, you could say 'I

might not be home until sunrise' or 'Don't forget to sign us up for that sunrise yoga class.'"

"I thought you were supposed to be my mother."

"You wouldn't take a yoga class with your mother?"

"I wouldn't tell her I'm going to be out all night with a strange...guy." I'd nearly said *strange man* which was surely what my mother would've considered him, but changed at the last moment to *guy*. Although guy didn't really fit him. Brad was a "regular guy." James, though? He was basically the same age as Brad but was nothing like him, or the couple of other men I'd known. I really was leaping into unknown territory, wasn't I? Maybe that was the point. I didn't know anything about his life, and he didn't know anything about mine. Maybe tonight we were going to sit and talk and find out all those things, though I seriously doubted it. He had asked me to dress a certain way, a way that Becky thought was whorish and that even I had called "sexy secretary." Even if whorish hadn't been his intent, though, I thought he probably picked the outfit because it turned him on.

I *hoped* it turned him on.

Becky cleared her throat. "So are you going to do it, or not?"

"Sorry, daydreaming." I shook my head and stood up. "Do what?"

"Call or text me," she said, exasperated.

"Oh, right. Yes. Okay." I picked up my phone and set the alarm for 10:55 p.m. Then I realized the time on the phone was showing 7:01. "Shit!" I fumbled with the recent call list, trying to pull up his number.

It rang. Becky rolled her eyes at me and went back to her room. My heart was rapid with panic as it rang and rang.

Then, thank God, he picked up. "Karina?"

"Yes, it's me!" *Calm down,* I told myself. *Try to make it sound like you thought you were right on time, not late.* I put on my "sexy secretary" voice. "Um, hello, Mr. Rich."

"Hello," he said, his voice warm and almost dripping through the phone. I think he was amused that I sounded flustered. "I'm in the car outside. Come downstairs."

"Right now?"

"You have sixty seconds," he said with a chuckle, but I didn't think the laugh meant he was kidding. He hung up.

Quick, girl! I stripped off the white cotton briefs, pulled on the skirt, and jammed my feet into the pumps. There was no time to figure out what shirt to put on. I was wearing a black Siouxsie and the Banshees T-shirt, a long one that was soft and comfortable. Maybe it would just look punk with the skirt and all. Maybe it didn't matter because we were only going to play in the car or because he was finally going to collect that blow job I expected to give. Or maybe it was his fault for not specifying. These thoughts were all crowding my head as I rode the rickety little elevator down to the first floor and hurried past the mailboxes in the vestibule.

The same black car as before was sitting at the fire hydrant, and the same young man who had driven before was standing beside it in a well-cut suit, no hat this time. He opened the passenger door as I approached, then shut it after I climbed in.

My date was in the backseat, of course, taking in my appearance with a cool sweep of his eyes. He had one arm along the back of the seat, but he didn't look relaxed.

"Did I make it?" I couldn't help but ask. "In sixty seconds?"

"And if you didn't?" he asked, a slight smirk coming onto his face.

"Um, I wouldn't get my wish?"

He laughed and knocked twice on the glass that separated us from the driver. The car began to move. "If there is a chance to win, there must be a chance to lose, too," he said. "There should be a penalty for failure."

Something about the way he said the word *penalty* made me feel melty between my legs. He put an emphasis on the word that made it sound dirty and delicious. He had a very careful way of speaking, each word coming out at a deliberate pace, and again I heard just a hint of a British accent.

"What sort of penalty?"

"Well, ideally it would be something you don't particularly like but something I do." He reached up and tugged on one ear as he mulled it over. "We'll have to discover those things as we go along. What is considered a penalty for one person might be a reward for another." He gestured toward my legs. "Spread them a bit apart, if you please."

I separated my knees until the hem of the skirt was taut.

"Tell me what you like, Karina."

"What I like?"

He gestured for me to continue, giving no clues as to how to answer the question.

"I like pre-Raphaelite art."

"Indeed? I would love to discuss it later."

"And . . . and Thai food, and real ice cream." Ugh, that made me sound like I was five, but it was difficult to think with him so close. I wanted to crawl into his lap and bury my nose in his collar, among other things.

He nodded as if my answers were acceptable and encouraged me to keep going.

"And..." I tried to think of how to say what I liked in sex. This was my chance to express that, and I knew it. But I didn't really have a good answer. What I did know was that what little sex I'd had, when it wasn't outright painful or uncomfortable, had been mostly disappointing. Brad had been the ultimate example of that, which gave me one saucy thing to say. "I like guys who can get it up and keep it up," I said.

That startled another laugh out of him and he pressed his fingertips to his lips as if he were holding back more. He cleared his throat and said, "I see."

"Are you going to tell me what you like, too?" I asked.

"Oh, but you already know," he said. "I like telling you what to do, and I like it even more when you obey. I like it when you succeed and I like rewarding you. However, when you fail, I also like enacting penalties. So, you see, it's a win-win game for me, so long as you continue to play."

"Huh, okay." I suddenly remembered he preferred me to say *yes* instead of *yeah* or *okay*. "Yes, I think I understand that," I amended.

"Good." His tongue darted out to moisten his lips before he continued. "Then I want you to reach under your shirt and pinch one of your nipples as hard as you can."

"Oka—damn, I mean yes." Why couldn't I remember that?

"Two pinches, then," he said, penalizing me already.

"One on each side?"

"If you like."

I reached under my shirt and held each nipple loosely between my thumb and foreknuckle. I took a breath, then squeezed. "Ouch!" I hadn't even squeezed particularly hard, but they were sensitive. In the moment after the pinch, though, I felt a lovely warm flush spread over my skin. Did he know that was what it felt like?

"Good," he said. "You know, I don't even know what your breasts look like."

That was true. I hadn't undressed for him. He hadn't touched me. And I hadn't seen what he looked like under his clothes either. This is half the mistake I'd made with previous guys. I'd always been told it was better to wait, but all that meant was I wasted a bunch of time getting to know someone who turned out to be a dud in bed. Somehow, I had the feeling this was different. "Would you like to see them?" I asked, my hands already on the hem of my shirt.

"Yes, please, my sweet. I would like to see your nipples now that you've pinched them."

I lifted my shirt just enough to expose my dark nipples and I saw him swallow. He hid it well, but there was that slight shift, a tiny movement that exposed how tightly wound with desire he was. My own need seemed to rise in response. I wasn't used to that feeling. It was heady and delicious.

He nodded and gestured at me to cover myself again. "Thank you. Now, you were eight seconds late. I think you should pinch and hold them for eight seconds as your penalty."

I sucked in a breath. "I'm...I'm not sure I can." That sounded like a long time to be in pain.

"Does that mean you want me to do it instead? I assure you I won't go easy."

"No, I...What if I can't stand it and I let go? Does the timer start over or can I do it in pieces?"

He pondered a moment. "The timer starting over seems a fitting penalty for failure, doesn't it?"

"I suppose." I swallowed. "In that case, maybe you should do it."

"You want me to pinch your nipples?" He arched an eyebrow, reminding me of Becky.

"I want...to feel your hands on me," I said.

His smile was warm and genuine. "I approve of honesty. Come here, then."

I slid closer to him on the seat, thrusting my breasts toward him.

He slid his hands under the shirt and grazed his thumbs over my nipples. They hardened eagerly under the caress, and my breathing went ragged.

"You like being touched like this," he whispered, now that I was close to him.

"Y-yes," I said. None of the guys I had been with had known what to do with my breasts. They'd either squeezed them too hard or their caresses had been more annoying than pleasurable.

"This is your reward for being honest with me about your desires," he said, teasing me with his thumbs, gentle sweeps up the curve of my breasts and then again lightly over the nipple. I shivered, my arousal surging. That was the way I touched myself when I fantasized, only it felt even better when he did it. His mouth was close to mine and I imagined kissing his lips, which looked lush this close up. In the shadowy light of the car, his eyes were almost gray. I could see a dark dot on his ear like he'd had it pierced but wasn't wearing an earring. "And now the penalty."

He squeezed then and I cried out, my voice sounding

loud in the closed space of the car. When my cry trailed off, I realized he was whispering numbers into my ear. "Four...five..." He seemed to be squeezing harder as the numbers went higher, and I realized I was clinging to his shoulders. "Eight," he breathed, and let go, and I held on to him tighter.

He held me also, for a few moments, now that his hands weren't torturing me. His arms felt muscular, surrounding me with strength and that delicious scent. Then he sat back and I composed myself, putting a few inches between us, trying to gather my wits again. The flush I'd felt the last time was stronger, covering my entire body and centering between my legs.

"Too much?" he asked.

I shook my head, but my hand was shaking as I reached up to wipe the sudden tears that had sprung from my eyes. Whew. "Let's just say that's good incentive for me not to fail," I said. I loved how I felt now, but the pain itself, well, it had hurt. Then again, I was surprised by how good I felt now. When Brad had been clumsy in bed and hurt me—like the time he thought it would be sexy to bite my neck like a vampire and had bit too hard—I felt shitty afterward. I suppose there were different kinds of pain. I took a deep breath. "What next?"

He drew a handkerchief from his breast pocket and dabbed his forehead. Nice to see I wasn't the only one affected. When he had composed himself, he said, "Tell me what you have on under the skirt."

My heart rate was already fast, but it sped up even more with excitement. "Well, you didn't say to wear any panties. So...so I thought I shouldn't."

"Is it really that you're such a good girl that you thought you shouldn't?" He chuckled. "Or that you're a dirty girl who hopes I'll do wicked things to her?"

"Can't I be both?"

His grin was one of delighted surprise and he put a warm hand on my shin. "Indeed, my sweet. Life's full of people who want to split everything into either/or, when in reality so often *and* would serve them better. Perhaps that should be our motto. 'Forget *or*—embrace *and*?' I like both, so let's have both."

His hand smoothed up and down the stocking, a sensual touch that felt so different from a caress on bare skin. "You appear to have followed most of my instructions to the letter. Should you get a reward for that?"

"Shouldn't I?"

"Except that you did wear a shirt, and I don't recall telling you to do that."

Damn. He had a point. "Well, I had to wear something or get arrested."

"It's legal for women, as well as men, to go topless in New York," he said wryly.

"Oh. Really?" Who knew? "Did you actually want me to run half-naked to the car?"

His hand drifted up to my stockinged knee. "I want to see what you're not wearing."

I froze, not because I didn't want to show him but because I didn't know how to do it without looking like a dork.

"Put your feet in my lap," he said helpfully.

I kicked off the pumps and settled my feet in his lap, my upper body leaning back against the car door. I could feel the *seriousness* of his erection through the soles of my feet.

"Now spread your knees."

My cheeks went hot as I did it, and I had to look away. I hadn't ever simply showed myself that way before. My wide-open crotch was staring him in the face.

"May I point out that you are dripping wet with desire?" he said.

"Thank you?" I blushed harder. "That was a compliment, right?"

"Yes, it was, my sweet." He settled his warm palms against the insides of my knees. "It reassures me you like this game. As for whether I wanted you to run half-naked to the car, the sight would have pleased me, surely, but your choice to wear a shirt is more prudent and it gives us more options for where to go this evening. After all, restaurants may refuse service to those without shirts.

"This is part of the game. My requests won't always be clear. You have the choice to ask for clarification or to interpret what I've said to the best of your abilities. Your interpretations are part of the pleasure. When you interpret things in a way that pleases me, you are rewarded. Choose a way that displeases me, and you'll be punished, which I'll enjoy in any case. Asking for clarification is not an admission of defeat, but be warned, even the clearest answer may be open to interpretation."

"Okay." Damn. "I mean, yes." His thumb rubbed back and forth at the edge of my knee, and I shuddered as if he were rubbing something else.

"Do you want to close your legs?" he asked then. "Are you uncomfortable?"

"Yes, I'm uncomfortable, but that doesn't mean I want you to stop." I forced myself to look at his face.

He met my gaze, seemingly more interested in my expression than in my exposed private parts. "Tell me your fantasies."

"Ha-ha, get my PhD, a fabulous job, and a penthouse apartment," I joked.

"Are these merely fantasies," he answered with a smile, "or are some attainable?"

"Well, the PhD would be in art history, and I'm close to finished. Unfortunately, I don't know too many art history types with penthouses. And, well, who even knows if I'll be getting the degree now." Just thinking about it was a downer. "Can we talk about that later?"

"Of course. Would you like to answer the original question more seriously?"

"Which question?"

"I would like you to tell me one of your fantasies. Sexual fantasies, if I need to be specific." He switched to his other hand and kept caressing me. I wanted him to touch me somewhere more intimate than my knee. After the way he'd touched my breasts, I had a feeling he wouldn't be too rough or too impatient.

"Oh jeez. I don't know." I racked my brain, trying to at least make something up that would be sexy and sound interesting. "I used to fantasize all the time when I was a teenager. I didn't know anything about what sex would be like, so my fantasies were always vague. Then after I started having sex, I don't know. There really isn't much to tell." I blushed. "I've fantasized more about you in the past three days than I have about anyone else in the past three years."

There it was again: the "Oh, really?" eyebrow.

"Seriously. But I keep stopping myself."

The eyebrow went higher. "Why?"

"Because I get the feeling the real thing is going to be better than any fantasy I could come up with."

"Refreshing," he said with a nod. "But the fantasy doesn't have to be physical. I'll let you close your legs when you tell me one fantasy of yours."

I watched his gaze drift down my legs to my wide-open lips, and my clit throbbed as if his fingers were brushing it. Then he looked back at my face and I had to come up with something to say.

"I guess when I was a girl, I had romantic fantasies, at least, if not sexual ones."

"Go on."

"Although, who knows, maybe that's the whole point of fairy tales. They're actually about sex. We just don't know that we're hardwiring our little girls to mistrust older women and to crave getting pricked—"

"Karina, you may indulge in a feminist critique of your fantasy later. Tell the fantasy first."

"Prince Charming," I said, almost a whisper. "Cinderella, the night at the ball, him kissing her foot."

"I don't recall Prince Charming kissing Cinderella's foot."

"Er, well, maybe that was only in my fantasy version, then."

He smiled. "Perfect. As you're not sure whether closing your legs is a privilege or a punishment, I have one more request."

"Yes?"

He opened a small compartment in the back of the front seat and pulled out an ornate box. He flipped open the lid, and I could see a pair of marbles, these larger than the previous one and with more swirls and colors inside them.

"Have you heard of Ben Wa balls?" he asked mildly, tilting the box at an angle so that the light glinted off the glass.

"I've heard of them, but I wasn't sure they were a real thing."

"Quite real. Supposedly brought to Europe from China in the sixteenth century. They can be made of solid jade or metal with chimes inside, or glass, like these." He held the box toward me. "Traditionally they are for one thing."

"Female stimulation?" I guessed.

"Insertion," he said, his voice roughened by desire.

"Oh." I swallowed. I took the box. "Is it one per...opening?"

"I wouldn't recommend anal insertion right now," he said, as if he were trying to sound quite reasonable. "You're less lubricated there, and things can get lost that way."

Oh. I hadn't even thought of that. Really there was only one thought in my mind, anyway. I reached between my legs, not daring to hesitate, spreading my lips with one hand to keep them out of the way. The marble slid easily inside of me, much more easily than I'd imagined it would, given the size. It was extremely hard and smooth. My body seemed to suck it in deeper. After a moment, I no longer felt it, except when I slid a finger inside me and touched it with my fingertip. It seemed quite snug where it was, and I tightened my muscles around it. "Should I do them both?"

"I think one is plenty for a beginner," he said. "You did very well."

I beamed under his praise and wriggled a bit, then gasped as the movement of my body renewed the sensation of something inside me. Those sixteenth-century Chinese were onto something.

"Your scent intoxicates me," he whispered. He took me gently by the wrist and pressed my still-slick fingertips to his nose. He took a deep breath, then rubbed them on his upper lip, back and forth a few times before sucking them into his mouth. His tongue cleaned each fingertip and made my clit throb harder.

Then he let me go and indicated I should sit up and arrange myself and my clothes. "We're nearly there."

"Nearly where?"

"Somewhere to eat." He inhaled through his nose and licked his lips. "But no matter what I'm eating, I'll be tasting you instead."

Five

Valentine Evenings

The car came to a stop. The driver got out and a few moments later opened the door on my side. He didn't hold out a hand to help me up but instead bowed with a flourish. I emerged from the car to find us at the valet parking stand of a high-rise building. Several white-jacketed valets flanked the glass door, and one of them opened it for me.

None of the men seemed at all dismayed that I was dressed like an extra in a music video or that I wobbled slightly on my unfamiliar shoes and shaking legs. The Ben Wa ball shifted inside me as I walked, while the sensation of it sinking in, pushing apart my walls as it penetrated, was fresh in my mind.

He caught up to me with a loose arm behind my back, steering me not to the elevator but to the host stand outside the entrance to the restaurant, off to one side of the large, marble vestibule.

Once there, I could see the restaurant was built into an atrium, with a high glass ceiling and a water feature that turned one wall into a giant Zen fountain. We were quickly ushered to a table tucked away in a nook from which we could see the other diners, but most of the patrons could not see us.

Which was just as well. He was dressed in a stylish suit, even more posh than the one he'd worn last time, the hint of a gold watch peeking from under one sleeve. I felt like something the cat had dragged in.

He ordered drinks for us both and some kind of multi-course meal, and the server was gone almost before I got a good look at her. He pushed the candle to one side, leaving the center of the table clear.

"Would you like to learn to read minds?" he asked.

"What?" I shook my head slightly, thinking I'd misunderstood him.

"It's clear you're wondering what everyone here thinks of you. Of us," he said.

"It is?"

"Yes. You should see your face."

"So, you're actually reading my face, not my mind."

"Correct." He grinned. "But reading faces is a large part of it. Call it 'reading people' if you want, but it's what's going on inside them that you're reading. Now, lean forward a little and look to your right and tell me what the couple sitting over there thinks of us."

I leaned forward a little and could see who he meant, around the corner of the nook. They were young-looking, probably around my age, checking their phones obsessively and leaning together and whispering from time to time. "They're acting kind of suspicious, but they seem happy, too."

"Indeed. I would say they have decided only someone

ridiculously famous would dare walk in here dressed like
you. They are no doubt trying to figure out who you are so
they can tell their friends they ate in the same restaurant as
you."

"I once ate in the same restaurant as Sarah Jessica Parker."

"Did you try to snap a cell phone picture of her and text it
to all your friends?" he asked.

"No. I thought that would be rude. I told my mother about
it, though, and she refused to believe it and was mad at me
that I didn't."

"You are a good girl," he said with an approving nod.
"Now, how about the older couple off to my left?"

I had a good view of them. The woman took her cell
phone out and began to make a call. A server swooped down
and ushered her out of the dining room. A few minutes later,
the woman came back and handed the phone to the man,
who got up and took the call, then returned. A short argument ensued, but the woman looked happy and almost smug.

"Tourists, I think. Beyond that, I got nothing." I broke off
as tiny plates of salmon mousse were put down in front of
us. The server explained it was just an "amuse," which I took
to mean the appetizer for the appetizer.

It was a single bite of creamy, salty, fatty goodness. For a
moment I was lost in the flavor.

When my attention returned, he gave his theory about the
couple. "I believe they think you're my daughter. I must be
some rich fellow who can bring his bratty teenager to restaurants if I like. They've barely given me a glance, so they
haven't noticed I'm not old enough to have a teenager. Or
perhaps they think I've had excellent plastic surgery."

"I don't look sixteen."

"I beg to differ," he said. "You're far more fresh-faced than many women in their twenties. You haven't caked on the makeup or mascara."

"True. And a lot of older people think everyone who looks the slightest bit young is a teenager. I'm twenty-six, but on campus older people often mistake me for a freshman or sophomore."

"The phone call, that was the woman calling their daughter back home and then having to let Papa talk to her as well." He took a sip of his cocktail, which I hadn't even noticed had come. I'd been so distracted by the salmon mousse and the conversation. By my side was a tumbler of pricey sparkling water, with the bottle set to chill in a container of ice. "The fact that I am drinking alcohol and you aren't reinforces that image in their minds, too."

"Amazing," I said. "You figured all that out by looking at them?"

"I connect the dots. It takes just two points to make a line, so I only need to know two things to get a direction. Three makes a picture. Some of the dots they reveal and some of them I provide, like what we're wearing or drinking."

He gave half a shrug. "I make educated guesses. The thing is, they are so busy making their assumptions that none of them will guess the truth."

"The truth?"

"That I am, as we speak, already fucking you right in front of them."

He meant the Ben Wa ball. My breath caught and I felt warmth rush through me at the thought of it and from his words. I couldn't feel the glass globe now that I wasn't moving, but I knew it was there.

"There is a man against the wall, by himself. He thinks we might be having a date. But even he doesn't dare to imagine that we're having sex at the moment, through words and shared knowledge, even though I'm not touching you."

I had to stifle a moan.

"Squeeze your muscles down below," he murmured quietly. "Do you feel it?"

I nodded, trying not to look like I wanted to collapse onto the banquette and have him ravish me that second.

As it was, he ravished me with his words. "No food they serve me tonight can compare to the lusciousness that you hide under your skirt. Have you had a man suck on your clitoris before?"

"What? No. Lick, yes, suck, no. They tend to suck higher up." I adjusted my breasts, which weren't even held in by a bra.

"Tell me about them." He didn't take his eyes off me as the old plates were replaced with new ones and new silverware set down.

"My old boyfriends?"

"Yes."

"If you want to have a sexy conversation, they're not good topics," I said.

"Truly?"

"Truly. They tended to suck. By which I mean they were sucky, not that they were into oral. Maybe if they had been, they would've been better lovers. And there haven't been that many of them. Every time a guy turned out to be horrible in bed, it discouraged me from bothering to meet another one."

"That seems a terrible waste," he said.

"I guess. Maybe I just wasn't what they were looking for."

"And what do you guess that would've been?"

"I don't know. Someone blonder? Someone with bigger boobs? Maybe that would have inspired them."

"Well." He paused again while more new plates were delivered, this time with a ginger-and-lime-flavored broth poured over a hunk of white fish.

We ate for a few moments in silence.

"Any man who needs blond hair or a bigger chest to be 'inspired' enough to perform well isn't a man worth going to bed with," he said suddenly.

I stopped eating in surprise.

"Every part of your body," he said, holding one tender flake of fish on his fork, "is a gateway." He seemed to consider his words. "I am trying not to sound overly mystical about it. But any part of you could be the key that unlocks the floodgate of pleasure bottled inside. There are the obvious parts, and there are the not so obvious."

He set down his fork and put his hand palm up on the tablecloth, a clear invitation to put my hand in his. I placed it on top of his without further prompting. His middle finger drew a slow circle on my palm. Then he slid his hand back a little, interlacing our fingers. Two of them spread mine ever so slightly while his middle finger probed the soft flesh where my finger and palm met. It felt like he had spread my legs and was teasing my crotch, with his nose, with his tongue, with his cock? It could have been all of the above.

I had a feeling I was going to leave a wet spot on the seat. I pressed my legs together and licked my lips.

Then he let my hand go, and I wondered if he was throbbing the way I was. He finished what was on his plate, and

I did the same, though my appetite now was for something else entirely.

I took a glance at the other diners. None of them were paying any attention to us now.

"You know, there are advantages to the obvious things, too." I felt bold saying it, even though "obvious things" was a euphemism for sexual parts, the one he had used a short while ago. That was the point, that we had a language that we shared only between us, that made me feel even closer to him than before. Closer to him than I'd felt to anyone, even though I didn't know who he was. Not knowing, not needing to introduce him to my friends or family, not worrying about what he might say to people about me was liberating. I could be bolder than I could when I was trying to be what people expected. He expected bold. He expected sexual.

"Are there?"

"Well, I assume so," I said, trying to think of how to say what I wanted to without coming right out and saying, *Touch me, touch me, touch me.*

Maybe the expression on my face and the hungry cant of my body said all I needed to. I felt something against my knee. At first I thought it was his hand, but I could see both his hands. It was the sole of his foot, insinuating itself between my knees. I spread them apart, and his foot slid along my inner thigh from where the stocking covered to where it didn't. Eventually it came to rest against my bare mons. I hadn't noticed him slipping off his shoe and sock under the table, but his foot felt completely bare.

He vibrated his foot and I had to swallow a moan. "Thank you," I whispered.

After the salad course, I wriggled a bit more, spreading

myself open on the edge of his foot. One of his eyebrows twitched as if he was surprised I would be so forward. I hoped my squirming wasn't too obvious to the other diners. I pretended to look around at the decor while I ground my clit up against his skin.

"If you can come, you should, only if you can do so silently, without tipping off the other guests to what we're doing," he said with a pleasant smile.

A busboy came and refilled our water glasses. I waited until he had gone before answering. "I don't think I can come that easily," I said. "But I'm enjoying it."

"Good."

I don't even remember the main course. I remember him pumping his foot gently up and down. The puddle on my seat was going to be huge.

And he was surely going to leave a huge tip. I stopped worrying about it.

"Are you interested in dessert?" he asked after our dishes had been whisked away.

"I'm interested in some sweet indulgence," I said, trying to be witty. "And I'm not referring to the sugary kind."

He grinned. "I enjoy indulging you." He took out his phone and thumbed a text message one-handed. "Go visit the restroom, which is right through there." He pointed somewhere behind me and withdrew his foot from my crotch. "I'll wait here for you."

In the restroom I wiped the juices off my thighs. There wasn't much I could do about the damp spot on the skirt, though. Thank goodness the fabric was black and the place was dimly lit. I neatened up as best I could.

He stood as I approached the table, then escorted me to

the front door, walking behind me the whole way and obscuring the damp spot from any curious onlookers. As far as I could tell, no one batted an eyelash at us.

The driver remained in the car and a valet opened the door. I went in first, and he followed me. Once the door closed behind him, I let out a sigh of relief. I hadn't even realized how tense I had been.

He merely chuckled. "Being in the public eye can be hard work," he said, and gestured around the car, which began to move. "Ah, sanctuary. A safe little cocoon."

I nodded, wondering what was going to happen next. I remembered my manners, though. "Thank you for dinner," I said.

"Thank you for accompanying me," he replied, in the same rote tone I had used. "Now tell me what you were thinking as far as sweet indulgences go?"

On the spot again. "I'm really not sure. I mean, I don't think I've ever wanted someone as much as I want you right now. But you don't seem the type to just do it in the backseat."

He chuckled. "I'm tempted to, but no. Even seeing my cock is a privilege you will have to earn."

"Really?" I sat up a bit straighter, trying to wrap my head around the idea. A man whose number-one goal wasn't to get off was still a foreign concept to me. "Is it that gorgeous? Or is it deformed or something?"

He put a hand over his eyes and I grinned in triumph. Cracking him up with laughter seemed to be one of my best skills. It took him a moment to get himself together and he cleared his throat. "When the time comes," he said, trying to sound serious, "it'll be up to you to decide whether you think it's gorgeous or not." His cheeks were pink.

It struck me then that it wasn't merely that he was playing a "hard to get" sex game with me. He really wasn't ready for me to see him exposed.

"All right," I said soberly. "I won't be pushy about that."

He gave me a small nod of acknowledgment. "Now. The question for tonight is whether you have earned an orgasm."

"You mean, without a time limit?"

He laughed and his moment of vulnerability seemed to have passed, or maybe I had imagined it. "Yes, without a time limit. Not every orgasm is a reward, of course, but this one could be."

"What do you want me to do?"

"I want you to take off your skirt and show me how you masturbate. As long as you keep answering my questions, you can keep touching yourself. Go on, take off your skirt." While I slipped out of the skirt, he took his necktie off. He tied the skinny end around my wrist and held the other end in his hand. I leaned back against the door to give him the best view and began to circle my clit with one finger.

"My first question," he began. "Let's start with an easy one. What's your favorite dish when you go out for Thai food?"

That he'd remembered what I said earlier made me laugh a little, and I switched to running two fingers up and down my seam, getting them slippery and then running one to either side of my clit. "What I love most are all the appetizers. Curry, noodles, they're okay, but the appetizers! Fried tofu with meat in it, crab rangoons, all those little fried things."

It felt decadent and dirty to be touching myself in front of him, and yet he seemed so genuinely interested in my answers.

"And what did you mean by 'real' ice cream?"

"Oh, you know, there is the soft-serve stuff that comes out of a machine, but you can barely call that ice cream. I mean the kind you have to scoop out of a tub, made with real cream. When I was little, there were small dairies that would each have their own stand that would open for the summer."

"Where was that?"

"Columbus, Ohio. They would make hot fudge so thick that it would stick to your teeth." As I drew my fingertips across my clit, my muscles tightened and I felt the glass Ben Wa ball again.

"Tell me what upset you earlier."

"Something upset me?" I asked. He tugged a little on the tie as if threatening to pull my hand away from where I was touching myself. "Oh, the bit about my thesis advisor."

"Indeed. Would that have anything to do with why you called me, somewhat upset, earlier this week?"

The thought was enough to dampen my mood. I stopped moving my hand of my own accord. The thoughts I had been obsessing over regarding Renault all week came spilling forth. "Yes. I want to graduate in May. My thesis is done. My advisor has been sitting on it for a few weeks. He's not even my real advisor, but my old one got sick. He's a jerk. A total and complete jerk."

"What sort of jerk?"

"The sort of jerk who says I'm not fit to graduate unless I . . . I wear a dress . . . and . . . Get this. He hasn't even read the thesis, but he told me the other day that if I sucked his cock, he'd pass me."

"What!" His spine straightened as his eyebrows flew together in a frown. "That's ridiculous."

"See! Even you don't believe me." I drew my legs together and turned away from him.

"No, no, don't misconstrue what I said," he said quickly. "His behavior is what's ridiculous, not your story! Of course I believe you."

I looked over my shoulder at him. He was biting his lip and frowning.

"You do?"

"Yes. Please tell me you didn't agree to go along with him!"

"Oh, I certainly didn't! I flat-out refused, and he tossed my dissertation into the trash. Went on and on about how I had proven myself unfit to graduate because I didn't dress up nice and didn't kowtow and suck his cock, like apparently I'll be expected to in the corporate world or something."

He made a disgusted noise. "I like to think there is less of that these days, but his very existence proves the attitude lives on." He shook his head. "What do you plan to do?"

"I don't know. I'm pretty sure I'm far from the only student he's demanded favors from." My voice was starting to shake. "I mean, how sick is this? He has a little pillow on the book-shelf by his desk that people can put under their knees when they . . . you know."

"Disgusting." He seemed to fall into thought for a few moments. "Tell me. How important is it to you to graduate?"

"Well, I've got student loans. It would be pretty stupid to have paid all that money for nothing."

"I see why you wanted to save that topic of conversation for later," he said. "That's a very serious matter."

"I'm sorry. I didn't mean to kill the mood with it."

He bent his head, looking at the end of the tie that was still in his hand; then he looked up at me through his lashes.

"Never apologize for being honest with me. Please, come here."

I didn't say anything but fairly threw myself into his embrace. He was all rigid muscle under his fine dress shirt, stiff and masculine, but one of his hands was gentle as he rubbed my shoulder comfortingly. The sound of the road under the wheels of the limo was soothing, even as we slowed and sped up, moving through the ever-present traffic.

After a while I raised my head. Through the dark-tinted window it looked like we were probably on the West Side Highway. The warmth of his body and the scent of him seemed to seep into me, driving Renault out of my mind and rekindling the arousal that had roared during dinner.

"I'm ready to continue," I said, "if you still want me to."

He brushed a bit of hair away from my eyes. "Want you to what?"

"Well, your command was for me to touch myself."

"That's true."

"And you were asking me questions."

"Yes, I was." He shifted on the seat so that we faced each other.

"And I think you were stopping me from pleasuring myself when you didn't like the answers I gave."

He clucked his tongue. "The only answers I don't like are dishonest ones."

"All right." I lay back against the door again and propped my feet up on the seat, my knees spread. "May I try again?"

"Yes, once you answer a question. Let's see." He readied his end of the tie in one hand. "Tell me about your first date."

"Well, first actual date that counted as a date?"

"You can count it however you wish."

"All right." I slid a little farther down. His gaze was making me feel warm all over. "I count my first official date from junior high school, because I wrote about it in my diary. I went to the mall with Frank West, with his father and my mother tagging along about twenty yards behind us the entire time."

"As chaperones?"

"I guess. And it counts as a date because instead of getting separate ice cream sundaes, we got one big one to share."

"So there is an ice cream connection after all?"

"Maybe?" I laughed and moved my fingers in a circle, not in any hurry, merely enjoying the sensation and the game we were playing. "It occurs to me now that my mother probably considered that a date with Mr. West." Perhaps that's why she had been so bitterly disappointed that I wasn't interested in going out with Frank again. The reason I wasn't interested was that the "date" had released a torrent of criticism from my mother about how I walked, talked, dressed, laughed, and even breathed while on the date. Like I was supposed to become someone else to keep Frank interested. Frank was plenty interested, but I wasn't anymore.

He tugged on the tie and I realized I had fallen silent. "Yes?" I asked.

He licked his lips. "Pre-Raphaelite art, was it?"

"Yes."

"Why?"

"It seemed like a good idea at the time?"

He tugged on the tie. "Lying to me counts as not speaking. In fact, it's worse. Five-second stop."

"I'm not lying!" I moved my hand to my thigh and squirmed.

"Then you are lying to yourself. You don't spend years studying something just on a casual interest."

I slumped. "You do if you're me."

"You're telling me you think graduate school was a waste of time, then?"

"No! I mean, well, I don't know." I sighed. "That's the truth. I don't know what I want."

He must have believed me because he let the tie go slack again. My clit was suddenly too eager for touch to care that my mind was in turmoil.

"Tell me about your favorite painting," he said as I began to pant.

"So many of them are gorgeous," I answered. "I love how beautiful the women are. *Sappho* by Mengin. Edward Burne-Jones has *King Cophetua and the Beggar Maid.*"

"Ah, yes, I've seen it. At the Tate in London."

"Have you? I've never seen it in person. I really want to, though." I moaned a little.

"Is that painting special to you?"

I paused to think for a moment and he let me. It was only one of many paintings I'd included in my thesis, but part of me wished I'd concentrated on it a bit more. "Well, it's kind of my Cinderella story again, isn't it?"

"Tell me the story," he said.

"Well, there are various versions of the legend, of course. Basically, the king looks out his window one day and sees a beggar maid so poor that she has no clothes. He falls in love with her at first sight and vows to wed her."

"Ah. Love at first sight." He licked his lips. "Are you close?"

"Very."

He leaned in. "I'm going to make a rule, Karina. I don't just mean for right now. I mean a general rule. Lie, and I'll deny you. Speak the truth and I'll reward you. Does that sound simple enough?"

"Yes. How will you know if I'm lying?"

"You'll tell me yourself because if you don't, then we have nothing here but smoke and false promises."

I licked my lips, completely lush with desire and taut with near-peak arousal, but I wasn't so drunk with lust that I didn't realize he'd said we had something more than a kinky game. Something he cared enough about to demand the truth over. "Yes," I said. "That sounds right."

He leaned closer and put a hand on each of my thighs. "I'm going to suck you now."

"Oh—" At that moment, my phone started to beep. "Ack, my alarm."

"Alarm?" He raised one eyebrow.

"I'm supposed to call my moth—I mean, my roommate—at eleven. To assure her you're not an ax murderer."

That made him snort. "Your roommate is savvy."

"Is she? She's actually kind of a dork."

He slapped me lightly on the thigh. "Call her."

"I could just send her a text."

"I said to call her. And remember, no lies."

"What? To anyone?"

"To anyone." He brushed his thumb over my clit and I sucked in a breath.

It took a moment to dig my phone from my purse. Even though I had Becky on speed dial, it seemed to take forever to get the call to go through. He looked up at me from between my legs, licking his lips and trying not to smirk. She picked up right away. "Rina?"

"Hey, Becks. Just calling in like I said I would."

"So everything's okay?"

"Everything's great." I yelped suddenly as he planted a kiss right onto my clit.

"Rina? You okay?"

"Yes, yes! Sorry, he's tickling me."

"Tickling you."

"Yes!" His tongue darted out and swiped across my clit. "Yes, it tickles a lot!"

"Oh, jeez, are you, like, in the middle of something?"

"Yes, of course I am. Hey, you're the one who insisted I call!"

"Okay, you're right. Look, do you know when you'll be home?"

He raised his head and mouthed, "Under an hour." I repeated it to her. She said she'd wait up and then disconnected the call.

I couldn't stop giggling as he licked all around my clit. The laughter stopped suddenly when he took my clit in his mouth—sucking like he said he would. That made me gasp and jerk my hips.

He sucked and teased with his tongue at the same time. I'd never felt anything like it, and my arousal shot right to the peak and then held there while the tip of his tongue did wicked things.

"So close," I said, and it came out a high whisper, like even my vocal cords were stretched to the max.

He hummed then, as if agreeing with me, and did something I didn't expect.

He bit down, not hard, but firmly. I probably would have been outraged, except that I started to come instantly. And his tongue kept milking my orgasm, my hips bucking but his teeth holding me fast as he drew the explosion of pleasure out longer than any orgasm I'd ever had before. When at last I went limp, he let go but continued to lick me, very gently now, as if he knew how sensitive I might be.

It was only as my mind cleared I realized his fingers were inside me, too. I made a surprised noise and squeezed.

He lifted his head and grinned, then moved inside me. Quite suddenly I was on the verge of a second orgasm and I sucked in a breath.

"Again, Karina?"

"Please! Oh God, yes, please!" I was squeezing his fingers with everything I had and I rocked my hips forward.

And then he fucked me with his fingers and a deep pulse of an orgasm rippled through me, getting stronger with each thrust of his hand, until I cried out again, pressing my head back against the door of the car. All I could feel was pleasure, expanding outward like a sun going nova. I went limp. He sat back and pulled his hand away slowly, and I saw he had the Ben Wa ball hooked in his two fingers. He took a handkerchief from his pocket. He wiped his face and mouth with it, then the marble and his fingers, and then handed the cloth to me. I wiped up as best I could.

The car came to a stop, and with a jolt I realized we were outside my building again. "Wow," I said. "Good timing."

He chuckled. "Give yourself a minute if you need to."

"That's a good idea because I think that orgasm turned my legs to jelly. And it's not easy to walk on jelly."

He laughed again. "No, indeed."

I picked up the skirt. "Oh jeez, I'm going to have to wash this. Well, she knew I was wearing it on a date, anyway."

"*She* being your roommate?"

"Yes, it's hers. I borrowed it."

He cocked his head. "Were you unable to find a suitable skirt at the store?"

"Oh, I never got to one. I asked Becky where the best thrift stores were and..." I trailed off as I realized how sharp his gaze was. "Oh no, I didn't do what I was told. Is that what it is?"

He nodded slowly. "That is exactly what it is."

I knew I was in trouble, but for some reason I couldn't stop smiling. Maybe because I'd had the best orgasm of my life.

He rubbed his chin. "Hmm. You'll have to be punished. Are you available Wednesday night?"

His seriousness finally sobered me, and I began to wonder what the punishment would be. "Yes. Yes, I'm free Wednesday."

He pulled a business card from inside his jacket, wrote something on the back of it with an expensive-looking pen, and handed it to me. I saw an address on the Upper East Side, Suite 324, and nothing else. "Eight o'clock sharp. Be late and the penalty will double. Wear whatever you like. You won't be in it long."

I swallowed, hating the feeling that I'd disappointed him. "I'm sorr—"

He cut off my apology with a flat hand to my lips. "No apologies are necessary, my sweet. You will make it up to me entirely on Wednesday. And I look forward to it."

"Oh." For some reason that made it feel quite different. I mean, I was in trouble, but it wasn't like he hated me for getting it wrong. In fact, I had the feeling he was holding in a smile. "Oh, then so do I." My own smile crept back a little.

"Good girl. Now, I think getting back into that skirt in the car is a challenge not worth attempting." He took several things out of his jacket pocket and set them aside, then slipped the jacket off. His shoulders looked lean and sculpted through his dress shirt, and I wanted to slide the shirt off and run my hands over his skin. "Here."

He wrapped me in the jacket and then knocked on the window. The driver got out and came around to open my door. I looked back at my date, the warmth of his body inside the jacket enveloping me.

"Good night," he said as I exited the car. "I enjoyed myself thoroughly tonight."

I leaned back in slightly. "What do I have to do to earn a good night kiss?"

He laughed again, a laugh that sounded like I'd surprised him. "Just lean over a little farther."

His lips met mine firmly, deliciously, like one small bite from a bursting ripe fruit, and then he pulled back. He sucked in a breath and quite suddenly the driver ushered me away from the car.

The driver accompanied me to the door while I fumbled for my keys. "Listen," he said, and I nearly jumped. I hadn't been expecting him to speak. "Be careful."

"Careful about what?" I whispered back as I found the right key at last.

"Hurt him and you'll have a lot to answer for," he said.

It was yet another thing that was completely backward from what I expected. "Wait, me hurt *him*?"

"Just be careful," he repeated, then stepped away as I turned the key in the lock and went inside.

As if that weren't enough like something out of a spy

movie, as I reached the elevator, a text came through on my phone. I checked it while waiting, wondering if I'd left something in the car. The message was from him and read, *When we are alone, call me James.*

When I got upstairs, I was carrying the damp skirt in one hand, still had his tie bound around the other, I was wearing his jacket buttoned shut, and the heel broke off one of the pumps as I tried to hurry down the hall from the elevator to the apartment. Becks took one look at me as I limped to the couch and collapsed there, and then we both burst out laughing.

"Would you say you had a good time?" she asked with a touch of skepticism.

"Yes! I would say I had a good time." I held up the bound wrist. "Could you help me with this? Um, and sorry about your skirt. It's kind of soiled."

She sat down next to me on the futon and picked at the pale green and silver necktie until it came loose. "But you had a good time."

"Yes. I had a *great* time," I said, putting the emphasis on *great.* "That is, he was extremely good to me. We had a fancy dinner and then, well, then some kinky action in the limo on the way back here."

Becky's skepticism deepened.

"It's not what you think!"

"What do I think?"

"You know, that he's treating me like a whore and just trying to get his rocks off."

"He's not?"

"He hasn't even let me touch him below the waist yet. Well, except once, accidentally." I didn't tell her it was with my face. "I know he's hot for me. He just...when I'm with him, all the attention is on me. It's all about my needs, my desires. I'm the one who gets off. He said I'm going to have to earn the privilege of his cock." I could barely say it without giggling. No, that's a lie. Once Becky started giggling, I did, too. I know, we were twenty-six, not six, but you wouldn't know it at that moment. We'd both had pretty sheltered up-bringings.

"So he's like a big-time BDSM dom, then?" she asked when the giggles subsided.

"Maybe? I don't know that much about it," I admitted.

"Well, do you call him *master*?" She wrinkled her nose at this new mystery.

"No."

"Daddy?"

"Definitely not!" I remembered his halfhearted suggestion of it. "Nothing like that."

"You said you were playing the part of sleazy secretary."

"For about five minutes," I said. I wondered about the name James. Was it his real name or an alias? "Role-playing doesn't stick with us."

"That isn't like any BDSM I've ever heard." She stood up and got her laptop from the tiny kitchen counter.

"Becks, don't do a Google search on BDSM right now. Please. All I can tell you is, it's complicated but feels right." I took a longer look at her now that she sat in the one armchair we had in the living room/bedroom. She was in electric-blue spandex tights and an oversized shirt with the British flag lined with sequins. It looked like she had been wearing blue mascara and scrubbed it off only partially. "So where have *you* been lately? You said you'd fill me in."

She looked up from the computer, which added a bluish glow to her face. "Oh yeah, I finally met some other Lord's Ladies right here in the city! I was kind of afraid to meet them at first, but it turns out they're not weird at all. They're really nice."

My impression of them from that night at the bar hadn't been so nice, but I was sure Becky had found the good ones. "Are the fan clubs going to keep going now that the guy is retired?"

"Well, see, that's what I wondered. I read about some groups that were having their last meet-ups the day of the concert, but of course that turned into like a three-day party. The women I met took me over to a scholarly conference where people were presenting pop culture analyses, and then we went to someone's loft and . . . what I'm trying to say is that the fan clubs will keep going. In December there's going to be a release of the concert film and a conceptual film and documentary to go with it. People are so excited for that!"

I yawned. I'd missed part of what she said. "Wait, why are people so psyched for this documentary?"

"Because he's always been so secretive! No one knows his real identity, like a superhero or something. You know how he always wears a mask or is heavily made up on stage and in his videos? And the concert film, they're going to do it as a theatrical release, so that'll be huge. And people aren't done talking about him." She closed the laptop and hugged it to her chest. "It means I'm not too late! I thought maybe I was but I'm not!"

"That's awesome, Becks. I'm so glad for you."

"I'm thinking of changing my dissertation topic, in fact."

"Really?"

"Really. This is what came to me while listening to his last album a few days ago. While tipsy." She blushed at that admission, which I thought was cute. Becky didn't have any tolerance for alcohol. "The entire thing can be interpreted as representative of a feminist utopia."

I yawned again. "Becks, I think I'm too tired to wrap my brain around how a bunch of pop songs by a white male billionaire equate to feminist utopia."

"Okay. I'm going to bed now, too. I'll explain it to you over breakfast and see if it makes sense then." She bobbed up. "Good night!" She went into her room. I could hear her singing along to her MP3 player as she got ready for bed.

I popped into the bathroom to do my bedtime regimen and then stumbled back out to the futon. I was too tired to flatten it out into a bed, so I just fluffed my pillow and lay down with my back against it, like lying across a car seat. I kept the jacket on, wrapped around me, surrounded by his scent. She was right. The way he talked didn't sound like any BDSM how-to article I'd ever seen on the Internet. They were all about how to tie people up safely and master/slave contract negotiations. What we had was a lot simpler than a contract, wasn't it? It was only a couple of rules. By following them, we could express our interest in each other, as well as desire, respect, and loyalty. I couldn't care less whether he measured up to some bogus online standard or not. I swallowed, a deep thrill running through me as I remembered the next time I saw him would be to make it up to him. To take my punishment, whatever that would be. Spanking? Flogging? Something else? I slipped easily into vivid dreams of his arms around me, his hands seeking my soft places, for both pleasure and pain.

Six

Just Be Still

I almost didn't go. By the time Wednesday came, I had done the following: researched sexual harassment cases at the university, hidden in the apartment the whole day afterward, called Jill to tell her about it, chickened out and didn't tell her anything about Renault, and gone to my part-time job working in the alumni relations office.

The university website had very clear information on how an *employee* of the school should report sexual harassment, but almost nothing about students other than listing lots and lots of places to report it. I could go to the campus police or any one of ten different agencies, but none of them provided any information at all about what "reporting" entailed. Nothing about anonymity, nothing about protection from repercussions or retribution, nothing about how investigations would be conducted or by whom. That was not confidence-inspiring. There were lots of detailed procedures for when the student was the one being charged with any kind of misconduct, but zero about how students could go about charging a faculty member.

I ended up on the rape crisis center page and found it even more frightening: It sounded like if I didn't have a semen sample, I was up a creek. Looking at the employee guide didn't inspire hope, either. If grad students were treated like employees, then I'd first have to schedule an interview with an investigator, then wait 30 days after the interview while they conducted a review, which could be extended for another 30 days if inconclusive. Ugh. By 30 days from now, I'd have missed my window to file for graduation. And really, what would the investigator find? I'd say Renault made inappropriate comments, and he'd say he didn't. I'd say he threw out my thesis, he'd say it was no good. I'd be right back where I was, with no leg to stand on and needing another semester of thesis seminar credits to graduate.

You can see why I hid for a whole day after reading all that. I imagined the procedures could easily be more victimizing than the original comments.

I finally decided to call Jill. My sister was a take-no-nonsense sort. I really didn't feel comfortable talking to her about this kind of thing, but I at least got up the courage to dial her phone number. Becky was out. I sat on the one rickety stool we had in the kitchen, at the end of the tiny countertop, and put the phone to my ear.

"Jill Casper," my sister answered. I could hear the sound of something metal banging into something else in the background: kitchen noises.

"Jill, it's me."

"Oh, hey, Karina, calling for your job back?"

"Hah, you wish."

"No, seriously, where the hell did you run off to the other night? The only reason I didn't worry is Luis told me you came in the next day when I wasn't here to pick up your envelope. I worry when people flake out, you know." By *people* she meant our brother. Troy was a stoner who sometimes got so high he forgot the day of the week. He hadn't lasted a month working for Jill before he moved out West.

"No, nothing like that. I just got fed up and I've got a lot to do," I said.

"Well, Mom's worried about you, anyway."

"Oh no, tell me you didn't rat me out to her."

"Well, I wouldn't call it 'ratted out...'"

"What did you tell her?"

"Nothing, really. All I do is deflect her from obsessing over me by talking about you," she said.

"So she obsesses over me instead!"

"Of course she does. Come on, Karina, you're her one real girl-child. She dreams about that church wedding in June. Your dyke big sister here isn't going to wear her wedding dress, and Troy sure as hell isn't either."

"Where is he now? Still in Boulder?"

"He's beach-bumming in Santa Cruz, at least according to his Facebook. The cell phone number I had for him in Colorado is dead, but at least I know he's not." She must've shrugged; something made the phone crackle. "Seriously, Karina, you know what Mom wants, but it doesn't have to be what you want. She wants you to have the perfect man because she doesn't. You have to learn to ignore it."

"Ugh, that isn't even it," I said. "She wants me to be perfect, because if I were, that's how I'd get the perfect man. Except her stupid definition of me being perfect is having the right man! It's like nothing I do matters unless I have a man. What happens if I don't want a man?"

"That's the argument I've been having with her since I came out, sweetie pie."

"Okay, okay, you win. But you know what? I bet even if I do get married, she still won't be happy."

"Well, duh, I know that and you know that, but Mom doesn't. We can't make her happy, Kar. The best we can do is try to make ourselves happy and hope she comes around to seeing what's good in our lives. Speaking of which, I'm thinking about popping the question to Pauline."

"No way! You've been together how long? Two years?"

"It'll be our third anniversary. I'm saving up for the ring. I'm thinking I'll take her out to dinner for our anniversary and then do it in a horse carriage ride through Central Park."

"Fairy-tale style!" I hopped off the stool and gave a little twirl. "Oh, you have to make me a bridesmaid then! Oh, except wait, are you the groom in this case?"

Jill's laugh was low and slow. "We'll figure it out. For all I know, Pauli will want to wear a tux, too. We'll have some of each kind of attendant maybe. I've got a couple months of saving up to do first anyway, and . . . let's not count our chickens before they hatch, okay? You're the only person I've told."

"Oh my God, Jill, that's so exciting! Wait, you haven't told Mom?"

"I haven't told Mom." She lapsed into a worried silence.

"You don't think she'd approve?"

"I'm not sure. She made some comments last Christmas—I don't even think she knew I could hear—saying things like same-sex marriage is a travesty, a parody of the real thing. I don't know. She might have been just talking to talk, though, you know? Trying to say what she thinks people want to hear."

"She does that. She might not have really meant it," I said, though my heart was breaking a little. I'd never heard Jill sound so nervous before. This must really mean a lot to her.

"I want to ask you a favor."

"What kind of a favor?"

"I want you to feel her out about the issue. Try to find out what she actually thinks."

I groaned.

"It doesn't have to be right away. We've got time."

"Jill—"

"You're the one on her good side, so you—"

"I am *not* on her good side! Everything I do is wrong as far as she's concerned!"

"Karina, please. You're the only one who has a chance at this."

She was right. And it wasn't like I'd have trouble bringing up the subject since my love life and marriage were my mother's two favorite topics when she spoke to me. "All right. I'll try to see if I can get it to come up in conversation in a couple of weeks. I'll have to be super casual about it or she's going to guess."

"Crap. I know. It's just that if we're going to go through with it, I need to know how she feels."

"Look, if you're going to marry Pauline, you have to do it for you and her, not Mom. Aren't you the one who not five minutes ago told me to ignore her?"

"I guess. Look, I've got to go. I've got a trainee server to deal with."

"Okay. Bye." I hung up knowing I had chickened out by

not telling her about Renault, but she had other things to worry about. I didn't want to be the basket-case sibling. That was Troy's job. I would have to figure out what to do about Renault on my own.

After what she'd said, I was dreading the inevitable call from my mother.

While walking home after my shift, my cell phone rang and I picked it up. The weather had turned chilly again, and I held the phone to my ear inside the hood of my sweatshirt.

"Your sister's worried about you," my mother said, which was her way of saying *she* was worried, but my mother wasn't very good about expressing anything directly except disappointment.

"That's funny. I just talked to Jill and everything was fine," I said. "What's happened to me since then?"

"I don't appreciate your jokes." My mother sniffed. "Save them for your fabulous career as a sitcom writer." That was just like my mother: to tell me not to use sarcasm and then turn around and use it herself. "She said there's a lot you're not telling her."

"Oh, really? Like what? Enlighten me." I stopped at a crosswalk and jogged in place a little bit to keep warm. The sun was already getting low in the sky and the streets were full of evening commuters.

"She said you didn't say a word about your thesis."

"She didn't ask."

"Well, I'm asking."

"Mother, what am I supposed to say? It's in my advisor's hands currently. He's had it for weeks. There's really nothing to do until he gives me feedback on it." All of which was true, I thought.

She made a disgruntled noise and changed the topic. "So you can call your sister but not me? You must have loads of time if you're not working on that dissertation anymore."

I didn't even want to dignify that one with an answer. She was baiting me and looking for an excuse to scold me over something. "Jill only calls me when she needs something," I said.

My mother brushed that aside. "Have you heard from Brad lately? I got a birthday card from him." She sounded unbearably smug.

"No, Mom, I haven't heard from Brad. I dumped him six months ago, remember?" I crossed the street with the crowd and then walked along the edge of the park.

"Well, I don't see why. He's perfectly nice, polite, a good provider, and he'd take you back in a heartbeat. He's not a closet alcoholic or something, is he?"

"No, Mom, he's not an alcoholic. I'm not in love with him."

"You were in the beginning." Her voice had the same accusing tone she used to use when I'd lied about whether I did my homework or not.

"And I wasn't at the end, okay? Why is that so hard to understand?"

"Karina, don't you take that tone with me."

"What tone? You're acting like you're angry that my infatuation didn't last." The problem was I was never really that infatuated with him to begin with, and after a year had lost all interest. "If you think he's so great, *you* date him. You should be happy I'm not making myself miserable with that self-absorbed loser."

"Name-calling is uncalled for, young lady."

"Call me back when you want to talk to me like a real

person and not like a dress-up doll you can spout parental clichés at."

I have to admit it felt really good to hang up on her. Then I wondered if maybe I hadn't hit too close to the bone: My mother probably would love to date Brad. Since my father left when I was a child, she'd had a constant string of boyfriends, and even one very brief second marriage to a guy named Jerry she now refused to talk about. I met him only once; that's how brief it was. They had eloped to Vegas in June and were separated by Christmas. I never, ever brought up the fact that she didn't stay with any of her guys, even when she was getting on me for the same thing. It felt like that would be too low a blow. It wasn't like she wasn't trying. And that was the thing: She accused me of not trying hard enough to keep them. It wasn't about Brad at all—it was about keeping a guy, *any* guy, at any cost. The thing is, if it hadn't worked for her, why did she expect it to work for me?

By the time I got back to the apartment, I was feeling depressed and angry. My mother never took my side in any argument, whether it was with one of my siblings or with the outside world. Anyone who had a problem with me she took as evidence that I wasn't good enough or that I'd done something wrong. That was a tough pill to swallow.

For about an hour I tromped around the apartment thinking the last thing I was in the mood for after being scolded by my mother was to be scolded by some guy. But the anger wore off in time for me to think it over a bit more. He didn't actually scold me. He expressed his feelings about certain matters and then gave me the choice of doing something about it. He told me what he liked, what he expected...

So unlike my mother, who seemed to think I should "just

know" what shoes went with an outfit and the right reply to when a man said something at a party, like the X chromosome was supposed to convey inherent knowledge. He wasn't like that. He told me what his expectations were. And I felt like I could meet them. More important, I could meet them without feeling fake or insincere about it. That was ironic, and I knew it. Even Becky expected us to be doing some kind of role-playing thing, daddy/girl, boss/secretary, *something*. But like I'd told her, it just didn't stick. When I was with him, I could really be myself.

I wondered if that was why he didn't want to tell me his name. Because with me, he'd found he could be who he wanted to be, too. Isn't that what he said at the bar, the night we met? He was finishing a big project and could finally devote some time to himself. And he'd wanted to be alone...

Until he met me. Was James his real name or the name of the man he wanted to be? Maybe in the world we created between the two of us, it didn't matter. James was who he *was*, I decided, regardless of what the world called him.

Each time we got together, he issued me an invitation to have an erotic adventure with him. An invitation I could decline, if I wanted to.

But I definitely didn't want to decline. It felt too good. And despite what my mother, sister, and roommate might think, it felt good for me. Whatever this "punishment" was going to be, I wanted to find out. I wanted to pass whatever test he put before me.

I stopped moping around and decided to get dressed. I picked up the card and looked at the address: the Upper East Side. He said not to worry about what to wear, since I wouldn't be in the outfit long, but there was always someone looking, wasn't there? What did people see when they saw Karina Casper? I hoped no one really noticed me at all when I took the subway. I put on my urban street armor: black jeans, a turtleneck, plain black waitress sneakers, and my somewhat beat-up leather jacket. I pulled a baseball cap over my hair. If someone wasn't looking carefully, they might mistake me for a messenger.

I took the subway uptown in plenty of time to scope out the place. I didn't want to chance being late. At one point the train got stuck, and I started rehearsing in my mind what I was going to say if I was late. As I ran the words through my mind, it felt lame. It wasn't a lie but it would sound like an excuse. My nerves bubbled during the wait and I wondered again what kind of punishment awaited me. He had given no hints. Thankfully, the train didn't sit long and got moving again. As it was, I was only about ten minutes early instead of the half hour I'd expected to be.

The building was two blocks over from the park and didn't look like anything special. It was on the corner, but the entrance was from the side street, not the avenue, and looked to be ten or twelve stories tall. The facade was a bluish gray stone like marble or granite, and the vestibule was tiled in the same stuff, highly polished. In the vestibule sat a security guard at a high desk, his viciously precise cornrows taking the place of a hat.

I spent a few minutes working up the nerve to approach him, checking the address a few times, and then finally going in. Beside the desk was one of those old-fashioned directories made of black rows of foam, with white letters pushed into it to spell out the names of companies and people on each floor.

The only thing listed on the third floor, where I presumed I was going from the suite number, was a place called Viva Associates.

"You have an appointment?" the guard asked me.

"Um, yeah. Third floor."

He nodded and waved his hand toward the elevators behind him. I gave him a smile and a nod as I went by and then pressed the button between the two sets of doors.

Upstairs, the elevator let me out into a small hallway. A windowless door at one end said VIVA in small silver letters. There was a doorbell. I pressed it.

A moment later the door buzzed and I pushed it open to find myself in a large, brightly lit waiting room. There were only five or six chairs, but it was spacious, with potted plants and magazines sprinkled liberally throughout. The carpet was white and lush under my sneakers and all the lighting seemed to be coming from hidden sources near the ceiling and behind frosted glass. I approached the sleek Lucite curve of the reception desk, but there was no one there. I had the feeling I was in a dentist's office, but a dentist for incredibly rich people.

After a moment a woman came from the back. She was dressed like a fashion model and was as tall as one, too, her brown skin and high cheekbones reminding me of Whitney Houston. It struck me then that this might be some kind of a beauty clinic, or maybe an office for plastic surgery?

I was even more surprised when the woman took the seat behind the reception desk. I'd assumed she was a client. "Karina?" she asked, eyeing me up and down.

"Yes. I guess that means I found the right place."

"Yes, dear." She gave me a nod and a pleasant look that

didn't quite become a smile. "Your appointment is for eight, so you still have a few minutes, but if you don't mind, I can show you to a room right away."

"Actually, could I visit the restroom quickly?"

"Of course. Right through there." She pointed at what I had assumed was a wall decorated with frosted glass, but once I took a better look I realized the chrome thing on one side was a door handle.

The bathroom was just as high-tech-looking as the rest. The sink was a white slab of porcelain like a miniature edge-less swimming pool. I didn't linger, even though I wanted to, and went back to the waiting room. I was obviously in the right place, and surprising me with what was going on was clearly part of the test. This was all about whether I could follow directions, wasn't it? Like with that first marble.

She ushered me into some kind of exam room. At least the medical exam table, complete with stirrups, was unmistakable, even if the room was much more posh than what I was used to seeing. "You can undress completely," she said as she laid what looked like a white terry-cloth robe on the counter. "Here's a robe for now."

"All right."

She closed the door behind me and I stripped quickly, putting my clothes onto a chair and slipping my arms into the soft bathrobe. Having the robe made this seem like a spa. I looked around, trying to gauge my surroundings, when I spotted a pamphlet on the counter. I couldn't see specifics but I could tell it was advertising some kind of skin treatment.

A knock at the door made me jump. "Come in."

A woman in a white lab coat entered. "Karina, I'm Doctor Powers." Her hand was warm and smooth as she shook mine.

"I realize we are meeting under somewhat unusual circumstances, but my employer would like to be sure that you are getting the best medical care. You can refuse my services if you want to—that is entirely your choice. I am prepared to give you a full gynecological and STD exam if you need one. At the very least, I would like to give a thorough dermatological check to your skin."

I swallowed. "Is this part of the deal?" I asked, trying to figure out what I was allowed to say.

She thought for a moment, perhaps trying to determine the same dance around privacy in her own head. "As I said, I know these are unusual circumstances. What transpires between you and him after I am done is your own business. My job is merely to offer you medical services."

"Oh. Okay." So she wasn't part of the punishment. "I actually had a gynecological exam at university health services recently, so I'd rather not do it again, you know?"

She gave me a knowing smile. "That's fine. And I know modern intimacy can create awkward situations. If you do need anything, now or in the future, you can call me, completely confidentially."

"Completely?"

"Completely," she repeated as she took a card out of her jacket pocket and handed it to me. "Someone just wants to be sure you're in the best of health."

I placed the card on top of my folded clothes. "Well, tell someone I've had all the tests. I don't mind if you get a copy of my record from my school."

She nodded. "You can tell him yourself, later. I have a release form you can sign so we can get your records. Now, what do you think about giving your skin a full check?"

"You mean like for skin cancer and stuff?"

"Exactly."

"Okay."

What followed was nothing out of the ordinary except for the fact that I hadn't exactly been expecting a medical exam tonight. She looked me over, every inch of me, but it was strictly professional except for maybe one thing. At the very end, she laid the robe over a chair instead of handing it back to me, so I was sitting there on the exam table completely naked. "Everything looks good," she pronounced, and then left the room, closing the door behind her.

I sat in the silence that followed, wondering what I was supposed to do next. During the exam, the doctor's pleasant manner had put me completely at ease, but now the thought that I was there to make up for my lapse and collect my punishment suddenly surged back in. What was he going to do?

And then came a soft knock on the door and I was glad I hadn't put the robe back on.

"Yes?"

The door opened and there he was, shutting the door quickly behind him. His smile was warm and he seemed genuinely happy to see me. As usual, he was dressed in a suit jacket and trousers, but no tie this time. In the bright glow of the exam room, he looked gorgeous, his skin and hair flawless, and I caught a whiff of his scent over the sterile background. Being in the room with him made me feel warm all over and I craved his touch. "Hello, Karina. I hope that Doctor Powers wasn't too rough on you."

I chuckled nervously. "Well, she wasn't rough at all."

"I know. I just wanted to be sure your skin was in healthy

shape before I consider doing anything to it." He stepped closer while I pondered the meaning of the word *anything*.

"What are you considering?" I heard myself ask. I could already feel my insides melting, even though what we were discussing right now was my punishment, not my pleasure.

His hand traced the edge of my collarbone and my shoulder caringly, an indulgent look on his face, and it surely seemed more like we were discussing pleasure than pain. Even though his words could have been scary-sounding, his tone was anything but.

"I don't intend to leave permanent marks," he said. "But accidents can happen. Bruises, burns, scratches—"

"Burns?" I burst out, scenes of prisoners being tortured with hot pokers in old movies leaping into my head.

He ran a gentle hand up my thigh, soothing me. "As I was saying, only by accident. Lie back."

I settled back against the exam table, which was tilted so that I could keep looking at him. He pulled the stirrups from the corners of the table and asked me to settle my heels into them. He stood between my legs and rubbed his hands lightly up and down my inner thighs, making my clit throb in the open air, yearning for touch.

"Tell me, Karina. Do you experience pain as pleasure?"

"I don't know. I mean, what pain I've experienced during sex has been the unintentional kind."

"Unintentional?"

"You know, like B—my ex-boyfriend knocking my head into the headboard accidentally."

"So no spanking, no tickling to the point of collapse, no love bites?"

"He bit me once," I said with a bit of an eye roll. "You

know, I haven't found guys to be that creative. I'm willing to try anything once, though."

"Your adventurousness is one of the things I enjoy most about you," he said with a toothy grin. "There are plenty of things we can try—just not all at once. Tonight I need to pick something suitable to punish you with. How do you feel about hot wax?"

"I've always heard wax jobs were excruciating," I said.

That made him laugh, and at first I wasn't sure why. "I wasn't thinking of it as a depilatory, but you have given me an idea."

His touch on my legs was making me want more. Being naked in front of him like this was, too. I tried to stay focused on what we were talking about. "What kind of hot wax did you mean, then?"

"Sweet girl. I'm trying to figure out a punishment for you. Something more sophisticated than just pinching your nipples. Next question: Are you afraid of razors?"

"Not that I know of."

"Then I won't need to tie you down, will I? You'll lie still like a good girl?"

"I'll at least try."

"Good. If you decide you'd rather be tied down, just tell me."

"Okay." The thrill in my blood was rising. This wasn't anything like what I'd done before.

He turned away, opening a cabinet and setting out numerous things I couldn't see. He then removed his jacket and hung it on a hook on the wall.

When he faced me again, he had a pair of barber scissors in his hand. "Hold still. I don't wish to cut you accidentally."

I took a deep breath while he put on a pair of exam gloves and then began to pet my pubic hair. Well, not really pet it, but get it all going the same direction so he could trim it. He was trimming for a while, and I could feel the occasional cold touch of the scissors as they made contact with my skin. When he was done with that, he blew on my crotch and I involuntarily thrust my hips upward.

"I thought you said you'd lie still," he chided.

"S-sorry! Just . . . mmm, very aroused now."

He gave another one of those indulgent smiles and then turned away and began sharpening the straight razor.

Oh, so that's what he meant by razor.

He rolled the stool into place so he could sit between my splayed legs. The moment he placed his hand on my thigh, he knew something was up.

"You've gotten very tense, my sweet." His face was framed by my thighs and stomach like the sun rising between mountains. In this light, his short blond hair looked very shiny and I wanted to run my hands over it.

"I might be about to change my mind about razors."

His grin was mischievous. "This isn't the punishment, Karina. It's just a luxury. I'm going to shave you."

"You rat!" I wanted to throw something at him. "You've been winding me up all this time!"

"Winding you up is my job," he said, settling a warm, gloved hand on my hip. "Isn't it?"

"Oh, I suppose!" The butterflies in my stomach had settled in my groin. I was so turned on. He was so gorgeous and the feeling of being entirely in his hands was intoxicating.

"I promise I'll tell you when it's time for the punishment. There shouldn't be any doubt in your mind," he said more seriously. "Shaving should feel nice, at least given what some women tell me. I've had a barber shave my face. The first time might be a little nerve-wracking, but...do you trust me?"

"I trust you," I said.

I tried to relax while he shaved me bare. At first the sensation was unfamiliar, a sort of tug and then a scrape, but his hands were warm, and he kept dipping the razor into what must have been a bowl of warm water. Now I understood why he'd said I had to keep still. His hands tickled sometimes, and there were other times when I was sure he brushed my clit on purpose, even though his face was serious and intent on his work. When he was done, he applied a warm washcloth and gently cleaned every inch between my legs, then dried me with a towel.

When he ran his hands over the area he had bared, I could feel how nude it was. I hadn't expected the skin would be tingling with sensation there, but it was, and as his palm grazed my protruding clit, it sparked another wave of arousal in my belly.

"When you come," he said, "you'll know you're forgiven. Before we begin, I should ask if there are any other infractions I should add to your tally. Any lies?"

"Any other...? Oh." I had to stop and think whether I'd kept to his instructions about honesty all week. "Does not telling my mother about my advisor being a pervert count as lying?"

"Only if she asked specifically about it," he said.

"Then, no. I think we've only got the previous stuff. I didn't follow your directions about buying the skirt and shoes."

"We should begin, then." He went to the cabinet and I heard a snapping sound. When he turned back to me, I could see he had lit a candle in a small glass jar, like a votive only it was purple.

"Aha. This is what you meant by hot wax," I said.

"Yes. It's a special candle, safe for this."

"Not something they have in most doctor's offices, is it?" I joked nervously.

"No." He ran a hand over my stomach and leaned down to plant a gentle kiss below my belly button. "But I've had days to get ready for your visit."

Knowing that he'd been thinking about it as much as I had sent a thrill through me. "Is it going to hurt?"

"Would it be a punishment if it didn't?"

"Good point." I bit my lip as he stood between my knees again and held the jar above me with one gloved hand. With the other he reached out and massaged my clit and the shaved area. That didn't hurt at all, and I wriggled into his touch.

The first drop fell right where he had kissed my stomach, and I gasped, expecting excruciating pain, but it wasn't like that at all. The burn seemed to spread across my skin much more like the burn of desire than pain.

The next drop fell next to that one, and the sensation intensified, making me gasp again. On the third drop, I pressed my head back against the table and my heels shook in the stirrups. Oh, that wasn't like anything I'd felt before.

"Does it hurt?" he asked.

"Not exactly?" I couldn't describe it.

"Hmm, it's possible you're so aroused that you really feel no pain," he said. "Let's see." And with that he let a drop fall onto my inner thigh near my knee.

I screamed. I didn't care that we were in some hoity-toity doctor's office. I didn't care that the fashion-model-like receptionist might still be sitting out there. That burned! But as before, it slacked off quickly as the wax cooled, transforming to pleasure, and the sensation of his fingers circling loosely near my clit became the center of my attention. I wriggled my hips. Just like the time he'd pinched my nipple, as the pain ebbed away, it left arousal in its wake.

"Remember to hold still," he said in a quiet voice. "Jostle me too much and I might pour more than I intend. . . . Let's see if your nipple is more or less sensitive than your thigh," he said, as if he didn't already know.

He increased the pressure on my clit before letting the drop fall to my left nipple, so what began as a scream became more of a gasp. Before I recovered from that one, he poured another drop onto my leg, beside the first. And then another as I bucked my hips into his touch, soothing the pain with more pleasure.

"Your clit is so engorged," he said, a hungry look on his face.

I looked down but I couldn't see it without sitting up on my elbows a bit. "I guess it is."

"Have you not looked at yourself before?"

"Not much. I've been more into what it feels like than what it looks like."

"Do you like what you see?"

"Yeah, I suppose. All pussies are kind of funny-looking, don't you think? I mean, you probably have more points of comparison than I do."

"Perhaps. Yours is quite lovely, though. Some women are convinced theirs is ugly—women who probably don't have much point of comparison, by the way, unless they count the shaved and docked beauties in the porn magazines."

"Docked?"

He slid a finger up and down my seam, spreading the slippery liquid. "It's one of the procedures they perform at this practice. Trimming the folds of the labia so they're neater." He switched to using two fingers and surrounding my clit as they skated past. "I do not find neatness to be a priority when it comes to a woman's parts," he said. "Their sensitivity, the way they respond to touch, is much more important."

I could only moan in answer to that. He let more wax fall and it made me writhe. He started letting more of it drip at a time, which meant it took longer to cool, but I was too aroused to feel pain anymore. My screams sometimes turned to long, helpless wails. He moved to the other leg, again starting near the knee and working inward.

His fingers seemed to find further ways to stroke me, to keep pushing me higher, until I was close.

"Now, tell me what you're going to do to improve in the future," he said, the jar again held high, like some kinky Statue of Liberty.

"Um...I'm going to pay closer attention to your actual instructions, not just what I think you might want."

"That was a highly coherent statement, Karina. I think maybe you still haven't had enough." And with that, he pinched one of my thighs where the wax had built up. I didn't scream. Instead I clamped down on the discomfort of the pinch. Then he did the other side.

But when he stopped, oh goodness I felt good. "I'm so close!" I warned him.

"Very well. Remember, when you come, the punishment is done." He settled his thumb against my clit, then flicked it back and forth and I tightened up, anticipating an orgasm.

He began to drip the wax directly onto my newly shaved areas, and even hot droplets onto my clit, one side, then the other, as he moved his thumb. My scream turned to a wail that turned to the sound I had made that first time I'd come in the back seat of his limo, a kind of full-body groan that I doubted I could ever fake. I was coming, the pleasure blooming like an explosion. Suddenly all other sensations faded, and the orgasm was still going. He had two fingers inside me again, and each time he pushed them, a new wave of pleasure burst through me.

He backed off slowly, my body shuddering less and less with each softer thrust, until he pulled out of me completely. I made a disappointed, almost petulant sound, then put my hand over my mouth. Was that me?

"Sorry," I said. "I don't think I've ever made a sound like a kicked puppy before."

He laughed. "You make the most beautiful sounds, Karina. I like hearing how needy you are. I love that I can make you like this." He ran his hands up and down my sides and I fantasized about his full weight on top of me. Any other guy would have fucked me already. Then again, he wasn't like any other guy. "Please tell me you don't want to get into puppy play?"

I let my head fall back. "No. But doggy wants a bone," I said, then put my hand over my mouth again. "Apparently I can't stop myself from making horrible puns either. So sorry!"

"It's all right. Endorphins can really send you for a loop." He patted me on the stomach. "Lie still while I clean you up."

I lay there in a haze while he cleaned me. I'm not even sure how he got the wax off—hot towels, I think? It was a good thing that I had no hair down there now, which of course was the point, so the wax peeled off of my sensitive parts easily.

When it was all done, he pressed my knees together and rolled me onto my side. Then he leaned over and kissed me.

I seized his head with both hands and pulled him in, my tongue trying to draw his out, wanting him, wanting to feel his desire flaring.

He pulled back suddenly and blinked like a man who has taken too deep a drink from the moonshine jug, exactly like he had after I'd kissed him in the car. He seemed stunned speechless. I spoke and filled the gap. I sat up. "What do I have to do to earn your cock?"

He shook his head slowly, a bit glassy-eyed. "Not yet," he said, then shook himself again.

"Seriously. I . . . I do love the attention, but"—*Fuck, I want you!*—"I won't feel complete until you at least come, too." I don't know where I found the chutzpah to say that, but the moment the words were out of my mouth, I knew I meant them.

He cleared his throat and spoke a bit louder. "Next time, if you're good, I might let you touch it."

"I'd like that," I heard myself say. I didn't even feel particularly dirty saying it. It just felt honest. And I could see his erection tenting his trousers. I didn't want it next time. I wanted it now, and he had to, too, didn't he? The bulge twitched when I said, "*Please* tell me what a good girl has to do to earn that."

To my surprise, he put his face in his hands and rubbed his eyes. Then he looked up. His willpower was stronger than mine, I guess. "I'll let you know," he said.

"Are you okay?" I asked.

"Fine," he said with a nod, and then cleared his throat.

He wasn't fine, but I wouldn't push him. I felt like the little cracks that had begun to show on our date were beginning to widen. I still couldn't see what he was holding so tight inside him, or why, but I remembered the driver's warning. Maybe he had a reason to take things so slowly. "Well, then, any instructions before I see you next?"

That seemed to bring him back to the moment. He put a finger to his chin. "As a matter of fact, yes. Are you free Saturday afternoon and evening?"

"Certainly!"

He paused for a moment, thinking further. "You'll receive a package. On Saturday at four o'clock, take the package, unopened, with you when you leave the apartment. Call me from the street and I'll give you further instructions. Are we clear you're not to open or look in the package? It's meant to be a surprise, of course."

"Of course. Yes."

"Good. Now. If you really desire this"—he hefted his own package in his slacks—"get down on your knees and kiss it."

I grinned. "Like you do the queen's ring?"

"Any sovereign's ring," he agreed, much more solemnly than I expected. I climbed down from the table, got to my knees, and leaned forward until I could press my mouth against the obvious hardness behind his fly. I swear I felt it throb.

He brushed his hand over my hair and stepped away from me hastily. "I must go. Four o'clock Saturday. I must go." And with that, he practically ran from the room.

Normally when a guy ran out of the room after fooling around with me, it was a bad sign. It usually left me feeling like I was worthless and a horrible lay. But that definitely was not the feeling I had this time. This time I was fairly sure if I pushed hard enough, I might get him to give in, to break his own rules and fuck my brains out. That was a powerful feeling. A good feeling.

What I didn't know was if doing so would actually be a good thing. Would it mean I won the game or that the game was over? I didn't want this to end so soon, not when every time I saw him I found out more about myself I had missed, experienced more than I ever had before.

"Saturday," I said aloud to the empty room, and then got up to get dressed.

Out in the reception area, the woman who had met me was sitting in one of the waiting room chairs, reading a magazine.

"Excuse me, can I use the restroom one more time?" I asked.

"Sure," she said, though she looked like she couldn't wait to leave.

I made it quick and then scooted out the door toward the elevator. Too quick, apparently. As the office door shut behind me, I realized I had toilet paper still stuck to my newly shaved parts, a bit of it showing over the top of my waistband.

I ducked into the stairwell beside the elevator to dislodge it. That's where I heard their voices. His and hers.

"Seriously, Byron, was that necessary?"

"Careful, Chandra. You're coming dangerously close to what's not your business."

"When you're endangering yourself, it's my business. At least you had the good sense to meet her here and not at home, but honestly—"

His laugh was forced. "She's not dangerous. I enjoy her. She enjoys me. Does it have to be more complicated than that?"

"That's what you said about Lucinda."

"Lucinda is many years in the past."

"You're sure she has no idea who you are?"

"Yes. Now if you're done mother-henning me..."

And that was the last I heard as they stepped into the elevator. My heart was hammering in my ears. I'd eavesdropped on what was clearly meant to be a private, maybe even secret, conversation. Now how could I be sure they were gone? They thought I had left already, obviously.

I counted to sixty and then pushed the elevator button. I had a fifty-fifty chance to get a different one from them. I did: the elevator was empty. I got in and pushed the button for the ground floor. What if they were lingering in the lobby? If they asked me what took so long, I could claim someone was moving something from floor to floor and it had taken time...

Except that would be a lie, and I wasn't supposed to do that.

Before I had time to think about that much more, the doors were opening. No one was in the lobby except the same security guard as before. He didn't even look up as I went out of the building. There was no sign of them on the sidewalk, either. They were gone.

There was a familiar face waiting for me, though. The driver. He was leaning against the car, which was parked at a hydrant near the corner with its blinkers on. His shoulders were hunched and he was scanning up and down the street.

He straightened the moment he saw me and gestured to the car, pulling open the back door.

"Are you here for me?" I asked, a little surprised.

"To take you wherever you would like to go," he said with a bow. "Well, within reason."

"Home's fine," I said, laughing a little.

"Very good, madam," he said, like a butler from a movie, and then closed the door after I got in.

In the backseat it was dark and quiet with the glass separating me from the driver. I knocked on it. There was no response, so I knocked again.

This time the glass slid slowly down. "Do you need something, miss?" he asked. I couldn't quite place his accent. Russian, maybe.

"How about your name?" I asked. "It seems like I'm going to be running into you a lot."

He squinted at me in the rearview mirror but said, "Stefan." He pronounced it with a long last syllable and almost a lisp: shte-FAHN.

"Pleased to meet you, Stefan," I said. "I'm Ka—"

"Karina Casper. I know," he said with a curt nod, his eyes on the traffic now and not on my reflection.

I was thinking about his warning to me and realized Stefan was probably more than just a driver. He was probably a bodyguard, too. "Did you have to check me out to make sure I was okay for your boss to see?" I asked him.

He glanced back at me, looking a little surprised. "Yes," he said curtly.

"Does he always do that? Or only when he meets random waitresses?"

Stefan rolled his eyes a little. "He has to be very careful. Women are sometimes after his money. Don't think you've been singled out unfairly."

"Have there been a lot of women after his money?"

Stefan snorted. "Women, men, long-lost relatives—fake, of course—you name it."

"So he's careful."

"Very careful."

"I'm not the slightest bit interested in his money," I said.

"Which is one reason he's still interested in you," Stefan replied.

Then I heard the sound of a phone ringing.

"I'm sorry, miss," he said. "I must pick that up." He closed the window between us. I could make out the murmur of his voice, but I couldn't tell who he was talking to. After a few minutes, it didn't seem like he was going to open the window again, so I settled back against the seat in the dark. That gave me some time to think. Byron. His name was Byron? Was I sure she said Byron and not Brian? Not completely. Was James a last name? For that matter Byron could be a last name, too. But the way she had said it sounded intimate and familiar. I thought about his lesson in reading people and I wondered what her body language had been like when she said the name.

He had to be some kind of plastic surgeon, I thought. One who only worked on the super-rich. Maybe that was why he had to be so secretive. Could that also be why every trace of a name was gone from the office upstairs? And yet the woman doctor, Powers, had introduced herself. I took out her card and looked at it. No address, just a phone number. I wonder if she did house calls. Things didn't quite add up. Maybe he was a super-skilled doctor who had lost his license to practice for some reason.

Maybe for tying up his patients and dripping hot wax on

them. I nearly laughed out loud when I thought that. Not too likely. He had been scrupulously careful never to force me into anything. He'd even asked if I wanted to be tied up or not, as if being tied up were some kind of special treat. With him, maybe it was.

I felt a little like I'd found the world on the other side of the looking glass or something. Everything was familiar and yet backward from what I expected. I couldn't help but feel like backward was an improvement, though. Maybe I'd been looking at love, sex, and relationships wrong all along.

Seven

She's Got Everything

The package arrived when I wasn't home. Becky brought it in and was intensely curious about what was in it.

"I'm not supposed to look," I told her while we sat on the futon eating takeout. "He said it's a surprise."

"I told you he was a big-time BDSM dom," she said. "I bet it's like a dildo or something. Don't you think?"

"I don't know what to think. Every time I think I know what's going to happen, I'm wrong." I was eating fried rice with a spoon straight from the container. Becky was pulling a bunch of noodles from another with chopsticks into a bowl.

"What do you mean?"

"I mean, he's not like the other guys I've known. Seriously. It's like...everything's backwards. Girls are supposed to be the ones playing hard to get and giving the guys oral sex in the back of cars, not the other way around, right?" I put down my spoon. "Oh my God, I wonder if that's what's going on?"

"What's going on?" she asked, confused.

"I mean, is that it? He's playing hard to get?"

"I thought you said you have to earn his you-know-what," she said, slurping up a noodle.

"Well, yeah."

"Maybe he's afraid to let you see it. What if he's disfigured?"

"I asked him that and he laughed it off. Seems unlikely." Then again, what did I know? I thought about how hurriedly he'd left me last time. "I think he's kind of freaked out by how much he wants me. It's like he's testing himself to see how long he can hold out."

"And that isn't driving you crazy?"

"Well, it is, but in a good way. I mean, he's already proved he's way better with his hands and his mouth than any guy I've ever dated. Not that I have a large sample size, but still." I clamped my knees together. "I think about him constantly. I've never been so into a guy like this one before. He's completely different. I don't even know his real name."

"Well, that's why. Every other guy whips his pants off and wants you to take care of him and be his new mom the second you agree to go on a date. This one, you really have to work to get to know."

"Does that make sense?"

"I don't know. I'm probably the wrong person to ask." Becky sighed. "Did I tell you about the guy my parents fixed me up with for my high school prom?"

"No."

"Okay, so I wasn't allowed to date when I was in high school, right? But my parents wanted me to be normal. So they knew I should go to my prom because that's like a big deal, like a rite of passage, right?"

"Right."

"They were always doing stuff like that. They didn't want

me to talk funny so they wouldn't teach me Chinese and never spoke it in the house."

"So you *are* Chinese!"

"Yeah, I am. Didn't you know that?"

"I wasn't sure which nationality you were."

"You could've asked, you know."

"I didn't want to be rude..."

"So it was better to be confused?"

"Yes?" I said, but I didn't sound too sure about that. "What about the prom?"

"Right. So they had this phobia that I wasn't going to fit in, as if not fitting in would ruin my life or my chances for success in American society. My mother actually said that. That I had to try harder to fit in or I wouldn't 'succeed in American society.' But at the same time they wouldn't actually let me do a lot of the things other girls did. They would let me go to the mall with my friends and try things on, but I wasn't allowed to buy anything."

"Okay, yeah, I get the picture."

"Now prom. They picked out this kid, a doctor's son from a couple of towns over, so we didn't know each other. Apparently we'd met when we were like ten or something, but I didn't remember him. And here's where you get the clash of expectations." She put down the bowl. "There I am in this ball gown that's all covered in lace and stuff, with a bouquet of flowers. It's exactly like a wedding dress, except it's powder blue, but you get the idea."

"Like Cinderella," I said.

"Exactly. And here comes Prince Charming, driving his father's Mercedes. We took a million photos and then off we go to this big banquet. He was even in a powder-blue tuxedo.

We were, like, a perfect match." She was looking at her hands instead of at me.

"Except it wasn't perfect?"

"Well, no. I mean, we danced, and lots of people took pictures, and it was kind of fairy-tale perfect in that way. I mean, I looked beautiful—my mother even put my makeup on, you know? And the dancing was nice. But he had the personality of a piece of broccoli."

That made me laugh, even though she was clearly getting to the serious part of the story.

"When it was over, we get back in his car, and he tells me he got permission from my parents to take me to an after-party at some other kid's house. I didn't even blink. I just said okay. I knew my father had given him this big talking-to, so I figured they had discussed it. It wouldn't be the first time no one told me anything, right? So we go to this party, and we're not there five minutes before he takes me by the hand and leads me upstairs into a bedroom and tells me he's so glad my parents wanted me to have this classic prom experience."

"Wait, what? You don't mean he thought you were going to have sex?"

"That's exactly what he meant. Now, I'm one hundred percent sure that is *not* what my parents meant by 'classic prom experience.'"

"Oh my God, Becky! What happened?" If I had pearls, I would have been clutching them. Seriously.

"He was such a stupid dork. He pushed me up against a wall and pushed my dress over my head, and put his thing between my legs and came in like ten seconds."

"He raped you!"

"Not really. I mean, he didn't come close to getting it in anywhere. What a loser, right?"

"Why did he push you up against a wall?"

"He couldn't figure out the dress."

"But..."

"But what? That was that. I cleaned up and then we left right away. I don't think he had a clue we didn't have actual sex."

"It was against your consent!"

"Well, I didn't actually say no. I mean, I've thought about it a lot since then. I don't really consider it rape, because he was too stupid and clueless for that."

"Becky!"

"Hey, it's my story. I get to think what I want about it." She gave me a stern look. "His parents did the same stupid shit to him that mine did to me. Neither of us knew anything about sex. It was never talked about. It occurred to me he probably was under the impression that I liked it, like the penis is a magic wand and it merely has to touch the girl for her to like it, you know?"

That made me laugh again.

"Anyway, he dropped me off at home and I never saw him after that. I kind of half-worried my parents were going to try to fix me up with him again, but they never said a word, which suited me fine." She shrugged. "Anyway, why was I telling you this?"

"I don't know," I said. "But...wow. He was even lamer than my lamest boyfriend. Though not by much."

"Oh, I know. I was going to say I blamed my parents for picking such a lame guy. Obviously they thought they were choosing someone safe for me."

"Except that he—"

"Well, I mean, obviously they didn't know he was going to try anything. But the point is, I thought, when I picked a guy to date, it wouldn't be like that. I promised myself when I went to college I was going to stop letting them rule my life, and if they wanted me to be successful and normal, then I was going to do what normal girls did."

"Why do I hear a 'but' coming?"

"Well, my first weekend at school I got horribly drunk, puked my guts out, and woke up in bed with a guy."

"What!"

"We both had all our clothes on, and the other girls said I was puking too much for anything to happen. But then the guy kept calling me, so I figured, okay, if he could handle seeing me like that, maybe he really likes me. Well, it wasn't any better. So I swore off guys for a while. I tried again around Thanksgiving, picked out a guy, flirted with him, asked him out, and oh my God, same basic thing. I mean, this time he actually got it in, you know, for real, but ugh. Such a waste of time. I literally had to pretend I didn't know him after that because we were both so embarrassed at how bad it was." She sighed. "I decided love must be the difference. Sex isn't worth it otherwise. Explain this to me—every woman's magazine has a ton of articles on sex tips and how to please a man. Where the hell are the articles like that for men?"

She had a point. I assumed those same kinds of articles were in men's magazines, too, but I didn't know for sure, having not read them myself. "Well, even if they do have those articles, maybe a magazine article isn't the best way to learn anyway."

"True." Now we were both down about the opposite sex. Well, with one exception. Then she asked me, "So what was your prom like?"

"I didn't go to my prom. I had no date and I didn't want to go solo."

"Oh." Becky blinked and changed the subject. "When do you get to open the package?"

"I'm supposed to go out Saturday and call him and then he'll tell me what to do with it."

"Really? That's so interesting. It's like James Bond or something."

"He's really secretive."

"Do you think he's married? Are you his *mistress*?"

"I have no idea." I'd wondered the same thing that night at the bar when we met, but the idea hadn't stuck. He seemed very solitary to me. Stefan made it sound like he was almost isolated by his money. "All I have to go on is what we do with each other, you know? It's like the rest of the world stops mattering when we're together." I sighed. It was more accurate to say the rest of the world's judgments about sex stopped mattering. But maybe that was the same thing. "You know what I think? I think he's lonely."

"Hmmm." She took a dumpling out of another container with her chopsticks and nibbled it. "Well, people in loveless marriages can be lonely."

"I don't think it's that. I'm not sure what it is. He's really secretive, but..."

"But what? Do you think he's like a mob guy or something?"

"I doubt it. I don't know. I thought maybe he was a plastic surgeon for the rich and famous, but that doesn't really explain it. Maybe he just wants us to know each other on our own terms and not focus on who he is or whatever it is he does for a living." I thought about that. The most romantic thing to me in the world was that two people could love each other purely for each other and not because of money or status. It didn't matter where we were—the back of the car, a restaurant, an office—when we were together, it was like we were in a bubble that contained nothing but us two.

Becky broke into my reverie. "Could he be a politician?"

"Wouldn't people recognize him?"

"True." She sighed. "You're really not going to open it now?"

"I'm really not going to open it now."

"Drat. You'll tell me what it is later?"

"Maybe."

"Hey, I told you about my horrible prom date! It couldn't be more personal than that, could it?"

"Probably not, but I can't make any promises, Becks. Seriously."

"Oh, all right. You're an awesome roomie, though, Rina." She bounced up then. "Hey, guess where I'm going tonight?"

"Where?"

"A club! To see a band play."

"With some of the fan club women?"

"Yeah. One of the guys who played guitar with Lord Lightning on his second album started a band, and that's who we're going to see."

"That sounds like fun. Have a good time. I'll clean this up when I'm done eating."

She went to get dressed and I looked at the package sitting on the futon. It was in a Tyvek envelope, impossible to open and seal again.

Despite how much I wanted to open it, I was good and waited until Saturday. Becky was out again: this time at the library trying to catch up after she'd been out a couple of times that week.

I put on a pair of jeans and a clean scoop-neck T-shirt, a cardigan sweater, and my sneakers. I put the envelope in a tote bag and went downstairs. The weather was warming up, a nice day for a walk. Once I was out on the street, I called his number.

To my surprise, I got his voice mail, but it wasn't the usual message. The message said: "Thank you for calling. If you once pretended to be a girl named Ashley, proceed to the used-clothing shop on Eighth Street." He rattled off some other details so that I knew which one he meant. "When you arrive, the clerk has something for you." Then came the beep.

I was so surprised I left a message. "I'm on my way."

It didn't take me long to get there. The shop was down a few steps from street level, and I ducked inside. No clerk was immediately visible, and there was no one behind the register, only loud music playing.

I walked up and down the aisles for a while. There were a few other people browsing. The shop was long and narrow, with two changing stalls with shuttered doors at the back that were open at the top and bottom.

A guy came out of the back room then, carrying a pile of things on hangers. I followed him as he moved to the register and laid them on the counter.

"Hi," I said.

"Hi." He looked me up and down. "Are you Ashley?" He had a piercing through the middle of his lip and another one in his tongue. The two piercings clicked when he talked, which seemed like bad planning to me.

"Yes, do you have something for me?"

"Yeah, one sec." He went around behind the register and rummaged through something I couldn't see behind the counter. He came up with a small envelope and handed it to me.

I opened it to find a gift certificate and a note. The note read, *Use this to buy something you like, something you'd never buy for yourself usually. Try it on, take a photo, and text it to me. You may also open the other package now.* At the bottom were four numbers: 3-2-4-0.

I grinned. The gift certificate was for a lot more money than I'd spent on clothes at one time in years.

"Got a sugar daddy?" the clerk asked.

"I guess so," I said. "Hey, what do you know about the guy who left this?"

He shrugged. "Wasn't me here. Regular manager told me to be looking for you, though."

"Oh." I was disappointed. "This is really good on anything in the store?" I showed him the gift certificate.

"Good as cash," he said. "I should warn you, though, we don't give more than twenty bucks in change. So you better spend the whole thing."

"Good to know." I began walking up and down the aisles a bit more enthusiastically, bopping along to the Ramones. This was a funky sort of shop, with all kinds of crazy clothes, hippie stuff, punk stuff, leather, feather boas, secondhand boots, and costume jewelry. I took my time, investigating the nooks and crannies.

I laughed when I came to the prom dresses. I hadn't told

Becks the whole story, probably because I wanted to forget about it myself. I'd had a boyfriend my senior year of high school. My first real one, I guess. I think he and I were thinking the same thing: that if we were going to have sex, prom would be the time. Making out with him was exciting for a few minutes and then got dull. When I complained, he told me it was because we were supposed to progress from kissing to "other stuff." The next time we made out, I let him put his hands in my pants and it hurt. I broke up with him a week later so he wouldn't think it was about that, but it was.

And here I was eight years later, and I'd finally found a man who could touch me without disgusting me, boring me, or hurting me. Well, without hurting me in a bad way, I should say. Just thinking about the hot wax spreading over my skin made me go melty inside. I didn't remember it as painful at all now.

I ran my hand over the lacy frills of the prom dresses. "Can I try these on?" I asked aloud, mostly to myself.

"I think so," the random woman at the other end of the rack said with a shrug. "As long as you don't get them dirty or snag anything."

I grinned. I took a dress off the rack and held it against my body. It was peach-colored satin, covered in a layer of frothy lace. It felt kind of nice.

Then I saw the one that had been hidden on the over-stuffed rack behind that. It was a mixture of blue and purple, floor length, covered in a net of crystal beads, with a lacy jacket with more crystals woven in.

"Oooh," the woman said, coming closer. "That looks like it would fit me."

Looking at her, I didn't think she had a chance to fit into

it. She was shorter than me and a little chubby, with ample boobs. I suddenly didn't want to give her the chance to try. "I'm going to give it a shot."

I took it back to the changing stall and went inside. I hung the dress on the hook there and then sat on the small bench to dig out the package and open it.

After what Becky had said, I was expecting a sex toy. I was surprised to find a cell phone, a much fancier one than mine. I turned it on and saw it needed a security code. Could that be what the 3-2-4-0 was? I typed it in.

The phone unlocked and opened to the speed-dial menu. There was only one number in it.

I set the phone aside, took my clothes off, and turned my attention to the dress. I carefully removed the jacket from the hanger, then started taking the dress off. My breath caught in my throat a little as I realized what was hiding inside the bodice. Stuck through a loop was a gorgeous silver tiara, hung with matching crystals.

I put the tiara on first. I wasn't sure how to do it, but as it turned out, it fit on my head and didn't seem to need to be attached in any way. The dress had several layers, some of which were attached, while some were separate. I put the under-layer on first, then pulled the rest over my head. It took some straightening, but I got everything where it was supposed to go, then zipped it up the back most of the way. It helps to have really flexible arms sometimes. The fabric reminded me of an expensive sports car: From one angle it looked blue, from another purple. The jacket, which was completely see-through lace, dotted with more glass, went over the whole thing. The sleeves weren't even full sleeves, more like forearm covers attached to ruffled shoulders.

I looked in the mirror and was amazed. Half the reason I didn't buy skirts and dresses is because I always looked stupid in them.

I didn't look stupid this time. I looked elegant. Different. Like I'd just stepped out of another world. Or was about to step into one.

I patted myself, trying to find the price tag. Then I realized it was on the hanger.

The gift certificate would cover it. My heart beat ridiculously. I wondered if he knew the dress was there and if he'd left the amount on purpose? Or even hid it there? No, couldn't be. First of all, how did he know my size, and how would he have known I'd flip over a dress like this? Even I hadn't known I would.

I twirled in a circle and the layers of underskirts brushed my bare legs. I picked up the new phone and looked for the camera. I held it up and took a photo of myself in the mirror. Hmm, looked okay, but...

I took a second one with the skirts hiked up to reveal my inner thigh, where there was still a hint of a bruise where he'd pinched me the other night.

I texted the photo to the one number in the phone.

A text came back immediately: *Beautiful. Send another.*

I grinned and leaned back against the mirror, holding the phone up high and taking another with it aimed downward. The tiara looked extra sparkly in the photo and I sent it.

Stunning. Another.

I texted back. *A naughty one?*

I could almost hear his voice in his reply. *I will not place limits on your creativity.*

I smiled as I slipped my panties off, too, and then fiddled

with the phone. Yes, there was a timer setting on the camera. I set it for ten seconds, placed the phone on the floor, then straddled it. I saw the bright flash under the edge of the skirt.

I had never seen a photo of my pussy before. The lips were puffy, the interior a dark red, glistening in the bright flash. The hair had just started to grow back.

I texted it without comment.

There was a long delay before his answer. I heard a woman's voice. "You doing okay in there?"

I stood on tiptoe to see over the top of the saloon-style shutter doors. "Sorry, do you need the changing room?"

She had an armful of stuff but said, "No rush. Take your time." She obviously didn't mean it.

"Just a second," I told her. "This dress is a little tricky to get in and out of."

I had to be careful not to tangle or catch the lace getting it off, then pulled everything else back on hurriedly. I came out carrying my shoes in one hand.

The phone chimed. I stayed against the back wall to check it.

Here's your next destination.

A graphic appeared that looked like a little Rolodex card attached to the message. I opened the contact and it showed me an address a few blocks east of where I was.

I still had some of the gift certificate to use, so I got a skirt for Becky to replace the one I wrecked, and a garter and stockings for myself to go with the dress. I got $19 in change back and a laugh from the clerk as he counted it out. He put everything in an immense shopping bag and gave me a little salute on my way out the door.

I was walking to the address he gave when another text came.

They'll offer you a few treatments. Choose one.

Treatments? Where was he sending me?

As I turned the corner onto the block where my next destination was, I saw a dark limousine pulling away from a fire hydrant. Was it his? I didn't recognize the license plate, but I wasn't sure I'd actually looked at that before.

I found the place easily enough, a few doors down. Inside it had the look of a salon or a spa, everything tastefully done in beige and sage. Two women were saying good-bye to the one at the front counter and I got the impression they were coworkers. They went out and a rather tall woman with voluminous golden locks locked the door behind them.

She turned to me. "You must be Ashley."

"Oh." Wait, if I said yes, did that count as a lie? "I answer to it sometimes. I was sent here to pick a treatment?"

Her lipsticked smile was wide. "Come have a look at the menu."

She led me back to the glass counter, which I noticed was full of silver and gold rings. "We do body piercing," she said when she saw me looking, "but I don't think that's what you're here for today." She handed me a small list of spa treatments.

The Goddess was a full-body and head massage with essential oils. The Priestess was a hot-stone treatment. The Earth Mother was a mud facial.

The Princess was a foot massage and pedicure. I knew immediately that was what I would choose, and I put my finger on it without even reading the rest of the list.

"Well, that seems fitting," she said. I wasn't sure why, but I smiled at her. "I'm Mandinka. Now come with me to a changing room where you can leave your things."

I followed her into the back where there were changing stalls. Inside each one was a locker, and I was putting the tote bag and both my phones into it when the new phone chimed again.

The message read, *Bring the phone with you.*

I looked around, wondering if he had some way of knowing what I was doing. Perhaps the phone had GPS tracking on it, so he knew when I arrived at the spa? I wasn't sure how that would work, but it seemed possible with a phone this fancy. I locked up everything else and left the prom dress on the bench while I got out of my clothes. I stripped down to my underwear and put on the short robe provided for me.

When I came out, Mandinka was waiting by a chair. At the foot of the chair was a small tub with flowers floating in it. She invited me to soak my feet as I sat. While I did that, she ducked behind the chair and said, "I'll give you a little scalp massage if you remove your crown, Your Highness."

"Oh!" I reached up in surprise. I'd completely forgotten about the tiara and had been wearing it ever since taking the photos in the clothing shop. No wonder she'd said the Princess treatment seemed appropriate. I slid it free and she set it aside.

Her fingers were strong and muscular. She did not only my scalp but also my neck, making me half wish I'd opted for the full-body oil rub. Then she switched her attention to my feet, setting aside the flowery soak, raising my chair, and settling herself on a small stool. As she worked my feet, it was almost like she was doing my whole body, releasing tensions I didn't realize I had. I nearly fell asleep, floating in a kind of reverie.

My mind wandered to the dress and when I was going to wear it. Maybe it was going to be nothing more than something for him to tear off me in the back of the limo at some future point. I sort of hoped not. He took me out in public dressed terribly; wouldn't it make sense to take me out dressed nicely? Where did one go in formal wear besides proms, anyway?

Once I was completely relaxed, she did a bunch of things to my toenails and the sole of my foot, scrubbing and filing and so on. When that was done, she spoke, and I startled a little: I'd forgotten what her voice sounded like. A bit lower than I expected. "You've got hardly any calluses, and your cuticles are in great shape," she said. "Now, I can put a coat of clear polish on them, or we can get fancy."

"What kind of fancy?"

"Oh, any color under the rainbow, your initials, the Yankees logo, you name it."

I'd never had painted toenails before. I don't even think I had any open-toed shoes at the moment, other than the flip-flops I hadn't seen since last summer. And of course under a ball gown, no one would even see my feet.

Well, except James. "Could you do them sort of bluish purple with a kind of sparkle to it?" I asked.

She gave me that wide smile again. "You mean to match that dress you came in carrying? I can't see much of it but some of it peeks out of that bag, you know."

I don't know why that made me blush, but it did. "Um, yeah. Is that too silly?"

"Darling, I've painted women's toes to look like ladybugs and typewriter keys, and I've spelled out the words *No Way José*. I assure you this is not silly." She got up and came back with some bottles and a soft thing that kept my toes spaced apart.

She had to apply multiple coats, first a purple background, then a light blue, then a layer with silver sparkles, and finally a clear topcoat of some kind. As she was finishing that up, she said, "It'll be a few minutes to dry. There is one more special treatment I've been told to offer you, though."

"Oh? What's that?"

She looked up from her improbably made-up eyes and blinked her long lashes at me. "A pubic shave."

I swallowed. "I'm already shaved."

"A touch-up, then. Are you starting to get stubble?"

"I guess, a little."

She nodded knowingly at me and then said, "Call him."

I suddenly remembered his text, telling me to bring the phone. I dialed the number.

"Hello, my sweet," he said. "Put the phone into video mode."

"There's a video mode?"

"Yes."

I looked at the screen and sure enough, there was a little icon that looked like an old camcorder. I tapped it and his face appeared. He looked a bit tired, with circles under his eyes, but he smiled.

"Can you see me, too?" I asked.

"I can, and you look gorgeous."

"Silly. Mandinka hasn't done a thing to my face."

"You look relaxed and happy, and that is the best makeup there is," he said. "I'd like you to hold the phone so I can watch."

Aha. "All right . . . I mean, yes." I held it out from my body, pulling back the edges of the robe and aiming it at my crotch. There was something thrilling about exposing myself right there in the spa, and even more the feeling that he was watching from afar.

"Here we go, then," Mandinka said. "Oh, someone did a very nice job on you. Did you do it yourself?" she asked.

"Um, no, that would be the fellow on the other end of the phone," I said.

"Uh-huh. Well, I will just touch up these little bits and then..."

His voice came through the phone. "Don't forget the last part."

"Oh, I won't, darling. I have it right here."

"Good."

Now my curiosity was really piqued. What did she have? I had to stay still, though, while she finished the shave and then gently washed off the shaving cream and dried me. She kept brushing against my clit while doing that, and I was quite aroused by the time she was done toweling me off. I'd never been touched by a woman like that before, but my mind was less on her and more on the voice on the phone.

"Why don't you go on and stroke her for me, Dinka," he said.

"With pleasure." She ran her thumb up and down my clit, going through the moisture that formed there and up over the sensitive bump.

"Is she wet enough?" he asked.

"Yes."

"Good. Put it in, please."

She grinned at me and I nearly lost my grip on the phone when she said, "Tada!" and held up a glass statuette of a penis.

A glass dildo, I realized a moment later. I hadn't even

known you could make that sort of thing from glass. If I had seen it on a shelf, I would have thought it was a piece of art. Like the marbles, it was clear glass with swirls of color inside it. It was about five inches long, gracefully slender, and slightly curved, with a somewhat realistic shape to the head.

"Here you go, darling," Mandinka said, rubbing it up and down my slit, covering it in my own slickness and moving past my clit over and over. I'd never felt anything like it. Cold and smooth, no friction at all, just pure delicious sensation.

"Enough teasing," he said. "Put it in now."

And then she pushed. I cried out a little as the bulbous head moved past the tightest part of my vagina, sliding right in.

"Fuck her with it," he hissed.

I moaned as she moved it in and out of me five or six times.

"Good. Don't hurt her."

"I wish you were here!" I cried out, breathless, my hand shaking so much I had trouble holding the phone steady.

"Show me your face again," he said. I turned the cell over to see him smiling at me. "I'll see you soon. I have one more thing for you, though."

Mandinka set the dildo aside and lifted up another box. She opened the lid and showed me what was inside: something shaped like a butterfly with short stubby wings and elastic straps.

"Oh," was all I could say. I'd seen them in a catalog Becky had in her room. "It's a vibrator, isn't it?"

"Custom made."

It was beautiful, even more gorgeous than the Ben Wa balls, with glittery specks inside it. "You can make these out of glass?"

"If you're talented, I suppose," Mandinka said with a chuckle. "Stand up and I'll help you get it on."

I stood up and she loosened the elastics. The straps were to go around my legs and hips, so the butterfly would nestle between my freshly shaved lips. A thin cord went from the body of the butterfly to a small control box that looked like an old-style phone pager.

It *was* a phone pager. As I got the butterfly into place, it began to vibrate without warning. I yelped in surprise at first, but then, just as my voice was dropping into a moan of pleasure, it stopped. I heard his chuckle.

"You're controlling it!" I grabbed the phone and confronted him.

"Yes. A bit more sophisticated than my foot under the table."

I sucked in a breath as the vibrations started again, but they only went for a few seconds.

"And now you're more gorgeous than ever," he said, his expression a bit wistful. "I can't wait to see you. When you exit the shop, the car should be waiting. Stefan will take you somewhere to grab a bite to eat and then bring you to me. I have some business that can't wait, but I'll see you in an hour."

"I understand. Should I wear the dress?"

"Oh, definitely not. That's for a special occasion," he said, and I could hear the smile in his voice before he hung up.

Mandinka was grinning at me. I couldn't help myself. I had to ask. "Have you known him long?"

"Yes, dear. Years," she said as she picked up one more thing and showed it to me. It was a pair of black briefs, more like a Speedo bathing suit than panties. "These will keep that from moving around."

"Like, how many years?" I asked as I pulled them up, sucking in a breath as the toy rubbed against me. Even though the vibrator wasn't turned on, it was right against my clit.

"Enough years to know that I shouldn't discuss him with you," she said. She patted me on the knee. "I will tell you one thing. If you're worried, there's no need to be. He won't hurt you, except in the most wickedly delicious ways."

There were a million questions I wanted to ask, but it seemed obvious she was under a gag order, too. Had he sent other women here? How did she meet him? Had he always been rich? Was she an ex-girlfriend? They seemed to know each other intimately, anyway. What had he told her about me? Apparently she knew of his wicked ways. How?

"Are you sure he won't hurt me?" I asked, hungry for any crumb of information I could get.

"Well, not intentionally," she said. "He's very fond of you, darling. That much I can see. Now go on. Don't keep poor Stefan waiting." She picked up the glass dildo. "Get dressed while I clean up. The bill is all taken care of, of course."

I went back to the dressing room and pulled my jeans on over the black underwear, stuffing my previous pair into the shopping bag. I put my T-shirt and sweater back on, wondering where Stefan was going to take me and whether I was appropriately dressed. I'd never thought about clothes as much as I had since the night we met.

Mandinka handed me a bag with the boxes for the sex toys in it and unlocked the front door for me, and I waved goodbye as I went out to the curb. It was just starting to rain and I ran to the dark car at the fire hydrant.

As I opened the back door and tossed my bags inside, I had a sudden idea. I closed the door and opened the front door instead, slipping quickly into the seat and slamming the door behind me.

Stefan looked at me in surprise. He had switched the stereo off suddenly when I'd pulled open the door; he'd been blasting one of the Lord Lightning songs I often heard coming from Becky's bedroom. I supposed he was allowed to listen to whatever he wanted when he wasn't actually ferrying someone around. He seemed a little embarrassed about it and a bit perturbed that I was in the front seat.

"You shouldn't sit up here," he said, a frown curving his thin brown eyebrows.

"Why not? You're not a taxi. I told you, I think we should get to know each other better."

He made a dismissive noise and pulled the car away from the curb. "If you think I'm going to tell you anything about him, you're wrong."

"Did you not hear what I said? I want to get to know *you* better."

"Don't bother," he growled. "It's not going to last, you know. The second you step out of line, you'll be gone."

"Who says I'm going to step out of line?" Besides, James had said if I made mistakes, it was just a chance to punish me, right?

"When he tires of you, same thing," the driver said as we pulled to a stop at a traffic light. "As soon as he gets bored, he has no reason to keep you around."

"Well, I'll just have to keep it interesting, then."

"I predict he's going to fuck you right in the back of this car. You'll see." He gunned the engine waiting for the light to change. Then as the light turned green, the car rolled forward. "When he can't hold back any longer, he's going to do it, and once he blows his wad, he'll kick you to the curb wherever we are. He'll leave you lying on the sidewalk with his come leaking onto your thighs and forget you ever existed."

Stefan's face was bright pink as he said this. I got the feeling he was supposed to be shocking me, but instead he was only succeeding in embarrassing himself.

I folded my arms. Would James really end things when we finally had sex? "Did he tell you to say that? Why would you say such a thing?"

"Because it's true!"

"That really doesn't seem his style."

"You don't know him."

If Mandinka hadn't told me what she had, I might have been more worried. "How many women has he done it to?" I asked.

"I've seen it," Stefan insisted, but he seemed to be wavering.

"If it's a game and that's how it ends, presumably you weren't supposed to tell me that." I looked at him out of the corner of my eye and kept my voice light.

He didn't answer.

"So does that go for you, too? Will you be gone if you step out of line? How many rules did you just break, talking to me like that?"

His knuckles went white on the steering wheel.

"Come on, Stefan. What's this all about? I won't tell him if you—"

He jerked the car to the curb and slammed on the brakes, jarring me but bringing the car to a complete stop. "You need to break it off with him. Tell him you can't see him anymore."

"Why? If he's going to dump me anyway, then why not let it run its course?"

He cursed in a language I didn't know and pressed his forehead against his hands, which were still gripping the steering wheel. He was hyperventilating but after a few moments seemed to gather himself. He let his hands fall to his lap and hung his head. He murmured something I couldn't hear over the sound of the rain on the car roof.

"What did you say?" I asked, somewhat cautiously.

"Please don't tell him," he said, his voice rough with emotion. "Please."

"Tell me what this is about and I won't tell him unless he asks me directly," I said. "You know I can't lie to him."

Stefan took a deep, steadying breath. "You know that I'm not just a driver," he said. "Part of my job is to protect him."

"I know."

"And we think you're dangerous. I was...I'm supposed to try to scare you away. If you went away on your own, he wouldn't question it. Things would go back to how they were."

I was fairly sure James would question it. And I wondered who "we" was. Did he have other bodyguards? Other staff? Had my presence changed a lot in their lives?

All I could say was, "I'm not dangerous. I'm just a grad student. I'm letting him set the rules, right? You guys know all about me and who I am, apparently, but I don't have a clue who he is. How could I be the dangerous one? There are lots of rich guys in the world. It can't be only because of the money. That's not what you're worried about."

"We all suffer when he—" He broke off, folding his lips between his teeth.

"I apologize for saying upsetting things and trying to scare you. I'm not good at this sort of thing."

"He must mean a lot to you." Was his staff trying to protect him from getting hurt? From heartbreak? If so, that was kind of endearing. "It sounds like you were trying to do what you felt was your duty," I said. I felt a little sorry for him.

"Thank you for understanding." He took another breath and then looked around. "I'll have to pretend none of this happened."

"So will"—I sucked in a gasp as the vibrator began to buzz without warning—"I." My cheeks flushed instantly as I tried to sit very still.

Stefan did not seem to notice anything was happening to me. He put us back on the road, moving easily into light avenue traffic again. "Would you rather have Chinese food, pizza, or something else?"

"Are you eating, too?" I asked, one hand gripping the handle on the door tightly as the vibrator wound my arousal up.

"No, just you."

"Then, um, let's pull over at Ray's and I'll grab a slice or two," I said. "There's one up there."

He pulled to the curb and made as if to get out.

"No, wait." I stopped him with a hand on his wrist. "I have an idea."

He turned to look at me.

"You want him to think we're getting along? Do this. Take the phone and video me walking over there to get the pizza and coming back."

Stefan took the phone. "Why?"

"Because he's...he's buzzing me right now. I think he'll enjoy watching me try to do it while I'm like this."

"Oh." His eyes widened as he understood what I meant. He handed me some money and took the phone. "Okay." He tapped on the phone screen a few times until the camera came up. "Go ahead."

He filmed me getting gingerly out of the car, then leaned out the window to follow me getting two slices to go. I had to walk slowly, trying for a sexy saunter, but really all I wanted to do was curl into a ball and let the sensation wash over me. The speed on the vibrator kicked into a higher gear while I was trying to give my order to the man at the service window on the sidewalk. He must've thought I was on Ecstasy or something as I gasped and threw my head back.

"Mmm, I *really* love pizza," I said in a comical attempt to cover the true reason for my rapturous expression as he handed me the slices on a paper plate.

He took the money with a "whatever, honey" sort of look. As he handed me my change, the vibrator suddenly quit and I sighed in both frustration and relief.

When I returned to the car, I was flushed and horny. Stefan continued filming me as I took the first cheesy, luscious bite of the pizza and then he stopped. Between bites I told him how he could send the video. Then we got on the road again, this time headed uptown.

"Where are we going?"

"A hotel," Stefan answered. "Which reminds me, I'm to tell you to go to room 324. I hope he's pleased by the video."

"I have a strong feeling he will be."

Stefan laughed nervously. "It's a good thing you enjoy doing such things. If he asked me to, I'm sure I would fail."

"He doesn't?" I had one brief moment of wondering if the

reason his staff was so loyal to him was because they'd been
seduced like I was.

"Oh no, thank God, no," Stefan said. "He's very demanding
of me, but not for *that*." His cheeks reddened visibly as he
said it. That made me wonder what else Stefan did, though.
He had been behind the wheel every time—could he hear
anything that was going on in the back? Did he get aroused
knowing what was happening? It occurred to me that based
on what he said, he knew that we hadn't had sex yet. If he
took his job protecting his employer seriously, then I had to
assume he heard everything that went on in the car. If he got
turned on by what he heard, did he go home and jerk off?
Did he have a girlfriend, or a boyfriend, for that matter?

He pulled over on a side street in front of an unremarkable
brownstone. "You should move to the backseat," he said.
"Here, I'll get the door."

He came around to my side and opened both doors, just as
the vibrator turned on again. He held out his hand to steady
me. I slipped into the backseat with my shopping bags, trying
to keep my breathing even.

In the next block we pulled up to a small, old hotel, and
two bellmen in long coats with impressive rows of gold buttons helped me from the backseat, one taking the shopping
bags while the other opened the door to the lobby.

The place may have been small, but it was opulent in an
Old World way, velvet and mirrors and marble. I made my
way through slowly, trying to act as if I weren't about to come
all over the rug, to the back where the elevators were. By the
time I reached the third floor, the vibrator had stopped again.

The hallway was thickly carpeted and completely silent.

I knocked on the door of room 324.

He opened it and the sight of him nearly took my breath away. He was barefoot, in blue jeans and a white dress shirt, untucked, half buttoned, the sleeves undone. Sounds crazy, I know, but every other time I'd seen him, he'd been in a suit jacket and tie, and seeing him like this—so casual—it made him seem more real, more flesh and blood and less a figment of my imagination. He looked edible.

Before I could rush in and hug him or something equally foolish, he stepped back, saying, "Karina, I'd like you to meet a friend of mine, Reginald Martindale. He's a curator at the Tate Britain. I thought you might join us in a discussion of art."

Eight

Possessing and Caressing

I took a few steps into the room, and an older gentleman in a full suit and tie stood up from a table and shook my hand. "Pleased to make your acquaintance," he said. He sounded like a butler from a BBC TV show.

"Likewise," I said, then turned to the man who loved surprising me. "Am I interrupting anything?"

"Please have a seat and join us while we finish the wine," he said, directing me to a chair at the table with a light, surreptitious caress along my back. Now that I was inside, I could see the room was a suite, with a sitting room and a bedroom. "I think you and Mr. Martindale have some interests in common."

The table was set for two, but most of what I saw was the remnants of fruit and cheese. I wondered if the wine had come in a gift basket. At the center of the table was a swooping glass sculpture, classy and expensive-looking.

"Isn't the Tate about to open a major exhibition of the pre-

Raphaelites?" I asked as I sat down. I knew perfectly well they were, but it seemed very British to me to open the conversation with a question.

"Oh yes, a hundred and fifty works, a major undertaking," Martindale said. That set him off talking about how tricky it had been to assemble them all, and somehow we got from there to the relationship between the pre-Raphaelite painters and the pre-Raphaelite poets, which I didn't know that much about. I was pleased to hear Martindale describe the pre-Raphaelites as "art punks," though, which was one of the points I made in my thesis. They were shocking and in-your-face in the oh-so-genteel Victorian age.

James poured the last drop of the wine into Martindale's glass and said, "Let us not forget what a complicated time period that was to express any form of sexuality." When he said the word *sexuality*, his foot slid against my ankle. He didn't activate the vibrator, but I could feel it pressing against me as surely as if his hand had been there.

Martindale sniffed. "People today think the Victorians didn't have sex. In fact, they produced more words of pornography per literate adult than any other culture with printed publications. The difference is that they had many more reasons to hide it."

"My point exactly," James said. "It was the expression, not the action, that was complicated. One could do a lot as long as it was not known about, not talked about. Art, on the other hand, is about making ideas visible."

"People look at some of these paintings now and see a pretty picture. But I agree with you wholeheartedly, Karina. The audience of the day might have been shocked. Scandalized."

"What do you think of *King Cophetua and the Beggar Maid?*" I asked him.

"Oh, it's practically pornographic, isn't it?"

"Is it, Reg?" James finished his own wine, tipping back his head and showing his long, smooth neck.

"Well, you can debate it," Martindale said, "but I think putting her in the garments he has, Burne-Jones didn't clothe her to appease Victorian sensibilities. He puts her in some form of underclothes. If he had done her nude, it would have merely been seen as a commentary on the Renaissance nudes. Instead, he had her in something the Victorians would have viewed as half-clothed. Not quite stockings and garters, but suggestive just the same."

"Especially since everyone else in the painting is completely covered," I said. "She's supposed to be exalted by the king at that moment, and yet you see two spectators whispering to each other as if it's scandalous for them to be looking down on it."

"You grasp it exactly. Were they depicted alone, as in the Leighton version, one might be able to interpret it differently," Martindale said.

"I only saw it once," my mystery man said, "so I don't remember it with such clarity."

"Well, come back and visit again sometime soon," Martindale said as he got to his feet. We both stood as well, and he shook my hand. "Miss Casper, I do look forward to reading your dissertation when you finish it. Please take my card and e-mail me." He took a business card out of a case and handed it to me.

"I'll do that." I was flattered that he was interested enough to actually give me his card. Were the Tate museums only in England? I wondered. Not that I thought there was much chance to get a job there, but Martindale could be a good person to know. I wondered if James had arranged for us to meet on purpose.

The two men sort of clapped one another on the upper arms, and then out he went.

James pressed his back against the door with a sigh. "I thought he'd never leave."

"Weren't you the one who invited him?" I asked, standing next to my chair and wondering how to ask if part of that meeting had been for my benefit.

"Yes, and I wanted you to have a chance to talk with him, but God, from the moment I saw you at the door, I wanted nothing more than to be alone with you." He looked at me, tilting his head downward as if glancing over the tops of nonexistent glasses. "You ought to be more impatient than I am, shouldn't you?"

I pressed my knees together. "Well, I am...rather... aroused."

"Rather," he echoed quietly, and stepped close, running his finger along the scoop neck of my T-shirt. His accent was more pronounced than usual. I wondered if Martindale had affected him or if he was putting on airs for fun. "I find glass to be such an exquisite material."

"Gorgeous, smooth, and unforgiving?" I said. I could have been describing him, perhaps, thinking about what Stefan had said.

He raised an eyebrow, as if daring me to go on, to say more. But I kept still. With him standing this close, I could feel the heat of his body, and my heart rate soared. He was taller than I remembered. Had we ever stood face-to-face like this? Once. That night at the bar when we met.

One of his hands rested on my hip, while the other slid under my chin, tilting my face upward.

"Would you mind terribly if I kissed you?" he asked.

That almost made me laugh. After all he'd done to me so far, the idea that he would ask me for permission to *kiss* me seemed comical. "Be my guest."

He made contact gently, lips parted and soft, exploring mine and my response. My breath caught as he nibbled at my mouth, his tongue darting out to moisten the way a little and daring mine to do the same. The hand under my chin slid into my hair then, encouraging me to bend back and open my mouth to a fuller exploration. His tongue was teasing and coaxed mine into playing. My whole body seemed to melt against him, and he pulled me closer, his tongue now plundering and claiming my mouth for his own.

I'd never been kissed like that. It left me breathless and even wetter than before.

"What time is your safe call?" he asked.

"Hmm, what?"

"Call your roommate and tell her you'll check in at eight-thirty," he said as he nuzzled my hair. "Because you're about to let a strange man tie you up."

The words sent a thrill running through me and made my voice shake. "O-okay. I'll just text her, all right?"

"All right. Join me in the bedroom, naked, when you're done with that, and bring the other thing Mandinka gave you," he said, and went through the double doors into the bedroom. I heard music begin to play softly. Violins.

My hands were shaking so much I could barely text. It was from excitement, not fear, but the result was the same. My breathing was fast and I trembled a bit.

I took off my clothes and left them draped over the chair where I'd been sitting. He'd said naked, so I needed to take the vibrator and the black underwear off, too. They were soaked. I left them on the table, picked up the small shopping bag, and tiptoed to the bedroom door.

He was standing there with a coil of black rope in his hand. He was still wearing the white Oxford shirt, jeans, and no socks. His hair had grown a bit since the night we met, and I wanted to run my fingers through it. The blackout curtains were shut and the reading lights on either side of the king-sized bed lit the room softly.

He beckoned me to come closer. "Have you ever been tied up before?"

"Only in a game of cowboys and Indians," I said. "Never for sex."

"Tell me if anything goes numb," he said, pulling me close to him again and running his lips against my hair. "Or if anything hurts. I want to know. Sometimes it might be intentional."

"Okay."

"You know you're not supposed to say that."

"Agh! You're right. I'm sorry."

"Bend over and place your hands flat on the bed. I'll give you one swat on each cheek for each lapse."

"Yes, *yes*," I forced myself to say. I bent over with my hands on the bed.

I heard the rustle of the bag behind me. I couldn't see what he was doing back there, but the next thing I felt was the rounded tip of the glass dildo, touching the spot where I was wettest. He moved it back and forth. "You're very slick," he said as he coated the glass with my juices. "This should go in easy."

It did. He slid it in and then I felt his thigh press against my backside, between my legs, holding it in place. "One spank on each side," he reminded me, and then let a heavy smack fall on the right cheek. I yelped in surprise. Before the sting from the first one could fade, he struck the other side and I yelped again, resisting the urge to reach back and rub the sore skin.

"Now, let's put you in something to keep this in place," he said, steadying me with one hand on my tailbone and pushing on the glass dildo with the other. I could only groan with pleasure as the bulb of glass moved back and forth inside me. "Crawl forward onto the bed."

I did as he asked, and he looped the rope around one leg and then the other. The rope was much smoother than I expected, no rough spots at all, almost like satin. I couldn't quite follow what he did, but he wrapped it this way and that, knotted it here and there, and when he was done, my lower lips were spread by crisscrossing lines, while a knot sat right under the base of the glass dildo. He showed me with a mirror so I could see the ropes and how spread open I was. I was much more interested in looking at him. His shirt was mostly unbuttoned, giving me glimpses of the toned muscle of his chest and abs.

"Gorgeous," he said, with a light and loving touch of his lips against my hair. "You look incredible. Now get up on your knees, and I'll make a matching top to go with your bottoms."

He climbed onto the bed behind me and this time crisscrossed the ropes between my breasts and around my torso. He worked methodically, brushing his fingers up and down my skin between setting knots and running his lips down my neck or over my shoulder, often telling me to lift my arm or move a certain way. The music had changed from violins to some kind of world music—African drums with Celtic-sounding harps—and I swayed almost like we were dancing.

When that was done, my breasts were framed by the rope and squeezed enough to make each one come to a point. He retrieved the mirror again and held it for me to see his handiwork. "It matches like a bikini," he joked.

I giggled at that. "It's very stylish." The black of the rope stood out against my skin.

"Bondage is art," he said as he set the mirror down.

"And art is..." I tried to recall his exact words. "Art is making ideas visible."

He climbed behind me again and ran his hands over my stomach, from the edge of the ropes around my hips to the ropes across my chest, making me tremble. "Ideas and feelings."

"And which is this?" I asked, reaching my arms up and back, hoping to pull him down for a kiss.

He growled a bit as he gave in, kissing me harder than before, then ran his hands down my front again, sucking on the back of my neck as he brushed over the tips of my nipples, down past my belly button, and then to flick lightly over my very exposed clit. "What's visible here?" he asked, flicking again and making me jump. "What's visible is my desire to control you. My desire to pleasure you. My desire to beautify you. Not necessarily in that order. Lie down. On your back."

Rather than answer, I did as he asked. He wasn't finished tying me yet. The next step was wrapping and knotting rope around my right wrist and attaching it to my right ankle, then my left wrist and my left ankle. My knees were mostly bent.

"Now, show me if you can get to your knees," he said, standing back and watching.

It was a bit tricky, but I managed to roll to one side and then get up without using my arms.

"Good. Now face down and show me your ass."

That was easier to do. Flopping over onto my side wasn't that difficult, and then it was just a matter of rolling and getting my arm out from under me.

"Very good. Now on your back again."

I returned to the first position, a little out of breath and throbbing from the constant movement of the glass inside me as I moved around. My breasts felt extra sensitive as well, brushing against the duvet and my skin as I moved.

"How do you feel?" he asked.

"Horny as hell," I answered.

He grinned. "Make your desire visible to me. Make art."

I looked at him, hesitating while I thought about that. Could I sing? Recite poetry? Dance? Well, I couldn't exactly dance while tied up like this, but I could move a bit. The music was unfamiliar but beautiful, some kind of flute playing a melody over the drums and strings.

I was self-conscious as could be, but he was waiting. He crossed his arms.

I kept my eyes locked with his and folded one knee across my body, hiding my bare crotch from him.

Then I extended one leg toward him. I had to sit partway up so my arm, which was tethered to it, could also move. I pointed my toe like a ballet dancer and moved my leg and arm in a circle, turning and exposing myself to him again.

I continued to move like that, the world's slowest burlesque, except that I was already naked before him. I arched my back, thrusting my breasts upward, my hair crackling against the pillowcase as I moved.

Then suddenly his hands were there, sweeping over my breasts and pinching the nipples. I gasped at the sudden flood of sensation, sharp and hot, then again as his tongue soothed the hurt he'd made. His hips were between my legs and I could feel the hard length of his erection against my pubic bone, through the denim of his jeans.

I whimpered, wanting it. Wanting him. He moved his mouth to the other nipple. I tried to squeeze him with my thighs but that was pretty much all I could do besides whimper.

Or beg. "Please, oh please, oh please," is what came out.

He reared up, holding himself on his arms, and thrust himself against the knot, pushing the glass phallus into me. His voice was as deep as I'd ever heard it. "Is that what you want?"

"Fuck, yes, no, I mean...yes."

He chuckled. "It was a simple question," he teased, thrusting again. "Was such a complicated answer necessary?"

"Well, it depends what you mean by *that*," I whined. "I...oh...why won't you fuck me, James?"

"Mmm, when you beg like that, it nearly makes me give in and do it," he said.

He pushed in a rhythm that felt so much like sex, and yet not like the mediocre, sometimes painful intercourse I'd had before. It felt like what I'd imagined sex would be like when I was younger. Being overwhelmed, filled up, and ready to burst with my own pleasure. That it took a pound of glass, a hundred feet of rope, and this eccentric man to feel that way? I tried not to think about that. Instead, I pushed back, my hips moving in time with his.

My clit felt raw and exposed against the denim ridge of his fly, but suddenly that was exactly what I wanted, and I sped up a little, rubbing myself against him.

"Uh-uh," he warned, and pulled back. "Did I give you permission to come?"

"I didn't come," I said. "I only wanted to get closer to you."

He leaned over and kissed my neck, then breathed in my ear. "I'm going to make you wait for it, Karina."

"Oh!"

"Unless you can come from the thrusts inside you. Turn over, ass in the air." He pulled back quickly, all the way off the bed to watch me reposition myself. "Move back until your feet are over the edge of the bed."

He came up behind me and I heard the sound of cloth rustling. He was taking off his shirt. I felt his warm hands on my hips. "Here we go."

He rubbed himself against the knot, thrusting slowly at first, dragging his bulge up and down. But he quickly moved to a sharper push, one that drove the head of his cock against the base of the dildo, pushing the glass into me again and again.

Deep and heavy and sparking something on every motion. I couldn't help but push back against it, wanting more, needing that feeling so deep inside me. As he picked up the pace, I could feel my arousal sharpening, focusing, even though my clit was rocking against nothing but the empty air.

"Oh my God," I heard myself say. "Oh my God, I'm...almost there."

"Only if you get there before me," he said through gritted teeth. Then he cried out, an animal bellow, thrusting wildly and his hands jerking me toward him even as he spasmed hard. A second cry followed the first as he held still, pressing hard against me, and then finally one last groan, and the tension left his body limp.

I listened to his rough breathing for long seconds, the music in the background having changed again to something with spacey violins. Then he patted me on the rump and said, "Thank you. I'll take the glass out now."

"Must you?" I asked.

"Will you feel terribly unfulfilled without it?"

"Maybe. If I can't have *you*..."

"I promise you, dear Karina, that if you let me, I'll place many more things into your body that will bring you pleasure in the future. My cock included." He tugged a bit on the ropes, moving them aside, and drew the dildo out of me.

I let out a long sound as he did, a cry of longing. He kissed me on the hair, patted my back, and told me to turn over again. I shifted, the ropes still tethering my wrists to my ankles, as I moved onto my back.

He lay beside me, and I turned my head to take in the sight of his bare chest, glowing with a slight sheen of sweat from his exertions. I wanted to lick the sweat from the sculpted planes of his torso. There was a sodden spot on his jeans, but he ignored it. He held up a few feet of the silky black rope. "Your clit seemed to like the friction of cloth. Let's see how it does with this."

I let my legs fall all the way open, the bottoms of my feet touching and my wrists at my sides. He suckled one of my nipples and I pressed toward him, eager for more.

He drew back to watch my reaction as he tossed the rope down by my feet and then began to drag it slowly upward, touching my clit the entire time. So slowly, a fraction of an inch every second, his hand climbing up my body and then past my lips, my forehead. I kissed the rope as it went by, and it was damp from my juices.

Then the knot on the end jolted me as it grazed over my clit. He kissed me and it felt like a reward. His lips looked as deliciously swollen as mine felt.

And then he repeated the traverse of the rope again, the length traveling up the center of my body, a constant source of friction right where I was most sensitive. He massaged my clit a little with his knuckle and I ground against him, groaning with need, until he quieted me with a look and began another slow, upward journey of the rope over my nerve endings. By the time it had gone all the way up my body a third time, I was panting and short of breath, which made the kiss at the end heady and dizzying.

"I have something even better than rope for this," he murmured, and climbed off the bed. When he returned, he held whatever it was where I couldn't see it. He nestled close, his body touching mine along my side. I felt something cold and smooth touch my thigh lightly; then he laid something long and cool along my clit and down the center of my labia where the rope had been. What was it?

He drew it up my body like he had the rope, and I felt smooth nub after smooth nub bump over my clit. I thrust my hips up, trying to get more friction, but instead of friction this new toy tweaked my nerve endings in an even more delicious way.

His hand slid low again, one finger massaging my clit for a moment before he once again dragged whatever it was—a string of beads?—upward.

I was trembling by the time he had finished. "What is that?" I asked, breathless. "Can I see?"

"Can you guess what it is?"

"It feels like a string of beads," I said. "Glass beads?"

"A good guess," he said with a pleased smirk. "You know me well, but no, sweetness, it's a string of pearls. A very long string of pearls." He began the next pass, dragging them through my juices and over the center of my pleasure.

And again. And again. After the seventh or eighth time I lost count, and by then I was letting out a series of whimpers and moans as the pearls climbed. It was too much and not enough at the same time. I tried to close my legs reflexively and he trapped one knee under his own and spanked me on the cunt, making me squeal.

"Lie still," he whispered. "You seem to enjoy a very light touch, Karina. Would you like me to try something even lighter?"

"Yes, please," I whispered, forcing myself to relax.

He kissed my cheek, climbed off the bed, and came back with something I didn't expect. A paint brush, the artist's kind, not the kind you paint a house with.

He settled at the foot of the bed, and I felt the bristles tickle at the opening of my vagina. He wet the brush with my juices and then, very gently, painted a swipe on my clit.

I made a noise of surprise. I barely felt it and yet the sensation made my arousal jump.

He did it again, lightly brushing around my vagina, and then crisscrossing my clit with the barely there bristles. "What do you suppose went through the painter's mind when he painted King Cophetua?" he asked casually, as if he were painting my toenails and not my most intimate place.

"I...well..." I couldn't form a coherent sentence.

"You and Martindale both believe the painting borders on the pornographic. Do you suppose Burne-Jones was aroused while painting?"

"I...I'm sure he was."

"Indeed? What do you suppose turned him on so much that he created such a masterpiece?"

"The...the idea..." He was flicking the brush back and forth now, up and down, a moth wing making me so very, very close and yet still not enough. "The idea that the beggar maid was so available to him. Naked, the king falls for her."

"Helplessly in love, one might say?"

"Yes."

"But then he exalts her?"

"Yes. He has to. Because if he truly loves her and doesn't view her as gutter trash that he can fuck and discard, he has to."

"Fascinating. And you think Burne-Jones was aroused by this idea? The idea that a highborn man could pick a naked peon from the gutter and not just fuck her but also have such feelings for her that he puts her on a pedestal? Do you suppose the artist fucked the model he had sit for the portrait of the beggar maid?"

"Maybe." The idea was a heady one, that Burne-Jones might have been embodying his own lusts and perversions into that piece of great art. "One of his models was his mistress. But not that one. I wonder...?" Was the woman in King Cophetua someone he lusted after but could never have?

"Yes, one has to wonder," he said, and I felt his other hand tug at the ropes, spreading me even wider. "Come for me now, Karina."

"Now?"

"Now, before I rescind the offer."

I cried out then as he switched the flutter of the brush from up and down to side to side, and it was somehow, inexplicably, just enough to trigger my climax. That should have been even less stimulation, but maybe that was the secret, as my body seemed to reach for the orgasm, needing it so much after the entire long afternoon of the teasing, the shaving, the glass, the conversation, and the bondage. I started screaming before I was even there, and it was as if I willed myself over the edge, screaming even more as I took the plunge into a long, slow-motion explosion. I felt it all the way to my fingers and toes, the sensation taking its time to flood me so fully that it reached my extremities.

And then, as it was tapering off, he slid the glass inside of me, and this time the explosion came in real time, another orgasm blasting through me, and then a third as he jiggled the glass inside me with his hand in a wholly unfamiliar but incredible sensation.

When he pulled the glass free, I was too spent to protest. He pressed a gentle kiss against my ravaged clit. "I'll free you in a moment," he said, then draped the pearls across my body and climbed off the bed.

Nine

Face the Strange

He returned with a warm, wet cloth and a dry towel and tended to me gently, without removing the ropes. Then he began to let them go, loosening the ones around my hips first. That allowed him to wipe me down completely between my legs, and then he kissed my shaven mound reverently before folding one of my knees over to touch the other, like closing the covers of a book.

"You are a gorgeous tangle of rope and limbs," he said, framing the imaginary shot with finger Ls.

"Take a picture," I said, too spent to do anything but smirk.

"Are you serious?"

"I am. I mean, not a dirty one. You know."

He chuckled and retrieved his phone from the parlor. His fingers brushed softly at my hair, hiding my face, and then he snapped the photo. "There. And I've texted it to you."

I heard the chime of the new phone. "Is that for me to keep?"

"The photograph?" he asked as he sat on the edge of the bed.

"The phone, silly."

"Ah. Didn't you say you wanted to get rid of your piece-of-junk phone?" He grinned. "It's all yours... if you'll answer it when I call."

I raised my head to look at him, shaking the hair from my eyes. "Why wouldn't I answer it?"

He picked up the pearls and set them aside, then rubbed my calf tenderly. "I didn't say it would be a difficult price to pay, necessarily."

"We have a deal, then." I giggled suddenly as he touched a ticklish place on my leg.

He grinned but laid his hand, firm and warm, over the spot. "Did you enjoy your shopping trip?"

"Yes, definitely," I said, lots of questions fluttering up in my mind, about Mandinka, Stefan, money, and nicknames. "Why did you leave the envelope made out to 'Ashley' instead of 'Karina'? Even Mandinka had 'Ashley' in her appointment book."

His other hand joined the first, kneading and massaging my leg. "I wasn't sure if you would want your real name being used."

"Why wouldn't I?"

"In case you were embarrassed about something, or changed your mind, or some other privacy concern came up," he said, very nonchalant. "You never know. Maybe you have a cousin I don't know about who works at that store, and if she saw your name you'd have to answer a lot of nosy questions. Using a name that only you and I know protects you from anything like that. It makes it your choice whether to tell people or not."

"You did it to protect me." I suddenly wondered what

name he had made the reservation at the restaurant in. Did he use an alias for that? He must have.

"Yes. Now tell me about this dress you bought. I admit I wasn't expecting that." He moved his hands to my wrist, massaging it gently where the ropes had been.

"What were you expecting? Wasn't the whole point that you'd find out what I picked?"

He chuckled. "True. You're right."

"And you said in the note to get something I wouldn't usually buy for myself."

"But you like the dress? You didn't buy it because you thought I would like it?"

I raised my head to look at his face. "I don't know what came over me. I just fell in love as soon as I saw it."

He smiled. "Good. I was going to ask why you picked it, but it sounds like you didn't think it over very much."

I rested my head again as he switched to my other wrist. "No, I didn't think at all. Though thinking about it now, I guess I kind of had Cinderella on my mind."

"Did you?"

"Yes. My roommate was telling me the horror story of her high school prom, plus I told you my fantasy, and talking about that painting, which keeps coming up." Even after I'd bought the dress. "Hmm, I just thought of something—there's a bit about anonymity and names in Cinderella, too. In the story, she knows who the prince is, but he doesn't know who she is."

"Yet he falls for her anyway," James said, lifting my hand to his mouth and kissing the underside of my wrist. "The version of the story I know is it's something like her pureness of heart that captivates him."

"Well, of course, she wasn't part of his world of royalty, which you figure was all politics and the backbiting of the court, right? It was the kind of place where the wicked step-mother would cut off her own daughters' feet for a chance at it. And she came from outside all that."

"You have a point," he said. I hadn't been intending it as a big metaphor for him and me, but, well, I was the one from outside his world. He drew a deep breath and said, "Let me ask you something."

My ears pricked up at that. Anyone else saying it wouldn't have caught my attention so much, but as I was learning, he took issues of permission and boundaries quite seriously. "What is it?"

"Would you say you have an exhibitionist streak?"

"Come up here if you're going to ask me questions like that." I have no idea where I got the guts to be that sassy. When a man tells you you're gorgeous and looks at you all misty-eyed, though, it's probably a help.

"All right." He shifted to sit closer to the headboard, where he could comb the hair back from my face with his fingertips. "Well?"

"Well, what?"

He grinned as his hand slid behind my neck and gripped not forcefully but firmly. "Would you say you have an exhibitionist streak?"

"If you asked me that a few weeks ago, I would have said no. Now I'm not so sure."

His thumb caressed the soft spot under my ear as he listened. In the dim light, his eyes looked dark amber.

"There's something very exciting about the possibility of being seen. Or heard. Doesn't everyone feel that way?"

"Perhaps."

"And then there's being seen, but people not knowing what they're seeing." Like in the restaurant. "When people say *exhibitionism*, don't they usually mean being seen?"

He bent a little closer. "How would you feel about that? Actually being seen?"

I felt a thrill run through me, and the spot between my legs began to warm, even though I was spent. "It might depend," I said. "I wouldn't want people on the street to recognize me, you know?"

He nodded slowly. "You wouldn't want someone who saw you exhibit yourself to walk into the bar and leer at you when you were at work, for example."

"Exactly."

"So, imagine this, exhibiting your body but not your face."

"It might depend on who was doing the looking but... well, if there's really no chance of anyone seeing my face, then maybe it doesn't depend on who's looking." I caught hold of his hand with mine suddenly. "You'd be there, right?"

"Of course." He touched his forehead to mine lovingly. "You're leaping ahead a bit, but I would never put you on display without watching you carefully. Besides, I wouldn't want to miss a moment."

"Then the answer to your question is yes, I have developed an exhibitionist streak, but only for you. I have no interest in doing it for the general thrill." I turned one finger in a sarcastic "whoop whoop" gesture.

He kissed the spot where our foreheads had touched. "You're excellent. And I'm a mess. I'm going to get in the shower."

He drew away as if to leave me lying there, but I kept hold of his hand. "Am I excellent enough to, um...to..."

There was that eyebrow again, exhorting me to finish my damn sentence.

"To wash you the way you washed me?" I finished with a slight squeak.

He took my other hand and pulled me to my feet, coils of loose ropes pooling around my ankles. "Yes," he said simply. He fastened the pearls around my neck, the long strand hanging low between my breasts, and led me into the bathroom.

The bathroom attached to the suite wasn't huge, but it was lavish, with marble everywhere. The shower was a large, glassed-in stall with ample room for two.

I faced him, standing on the soft, thick bath mat, and had an idea. I put my hands at the button of his jeans. "If the king would allow this beggar maid?" I said as I sank to my knees.

His voice came out a bit breathless. "Of course."

I wasn't quite as deft at getting his fly open as I would have liked, but it was good enough. As I eased his jeans off his sharp hips, I could see the tremendous wet spot in his shorts. He wore dark blue briefs, somewhat silky. I lowered the briefs to his ankles, keeping my eyes down as I helped him step out of his clothes. His feet were more slender than I expected, and on a whim I bent down and kissed them.

His breath caught. I kissed one, planting a short line of kisses from his toes toward his ankle, and then went down the other instep from ankle to toes.

I raised my head slowly then, letting my eyes travel up his legs to his...and then *my* breath caught. He was rampant, his cock jutting out from his pubic hair. Having his feet kissed aroused him that much? I looked up at him as I pressed one almost-chaste peck on the tip of it and saw that he was biting his lip.

"Stay here," I said, and went to the sink to soak a washcloth with warm water. I watched him in the mirror as I did, and he watched me the same way.

When I returned to kneel at his feet again, he was no longer chewing his lip, but his eyes were dark with lust.

I bent to my task, sopping and wiping the come from his pubic hair and gently washing his balls before turning my attention to the shaft. I got a second cloth to do the shaft and head.

His entire body was long and muscled like a dancer's, matching the impressive length of his cock, every inch of him sculpted and firm. I squeezed the washcloth, dribbling warm water over the shaft, then set to trying to scrub it gently. I worried I was being too rough, but every time I glanced up, he was looking down intently.

Until the time I looked up and saw he had closed his eyes. He reached out a hand and steadied himself against the tiled wall. I took that as a sign to keep going.

You've heard that expression "to have someone by the short and curlies"? I'd always pictured it as one person having grabbed a fistful. But now I wondered. I was the one on my knees. I was the one who had been tied up. He was the one in charge.

Yet right now, I had him, literally, by the short and curlies. He was clean now, and my attentions continued for the sheer pleasure of it. I loved seeing him so captured.

I had a feeling that if I sucked him into my mouth right now, I might get him to give in. And then I thought about what Stefan had said and wondered if that was what I actually wanted. Would that be the final move? I wasn't ready for this game to end.

I patted him dry with a towel and kissed his balls the way he had kissed me when he'd untied me. Then I sat back on my heels. "I hope the king is pleased with his maid."

His eyes fluttered open and he took a deep breath, but didn't seem ready to speak.

I decided I had to let him make the next move, if there was going to be one. That was how this dance went, how this game was played. "Is there anything else I can do for..." What were the right words? Your Majesty? Your Highness? It turned out I couldn't say either with a straight face and I had to try to hide a laugh, which of course failed completely and made him laugh, too.

He pulled me up into a kiss, chuckling against my mouth. "Ha, Your *Majesty*." He released me with a light swat upon my shoulder. "Isn't it about time for your check-in?"

"Is it?"

"I think so. And I have another appointment."

"On a Saturday night?" I squeaked out before I realized I sounded jealous.

"I assure you, sweetness, it will be a far more tiresome meeting than ours was." He pulled me close again and planted a kiss on the top of my hair. "Now, enough. Go tell your friend all is well."

As I went back into the bedroom, I heard the sound of the shower turning on.

I found my old phone and sure enough, it was almost eight-thirty. I called Becky.

"Wow, you were serious about calling me," she said. I

could hear music in the background, one of the Lord Lightning songs she played often.

"Are you at home?"

"Yeah. How was it?"

"Awesome. Oh my God, I really mean that."

"Really?"

"Really. And now he's in the shower and I guess I'm about to head back downtown."

"Well, good, then you can tell me all about it when you get home."

"What's to tell?"

"You just said it was awesome! Are you really going to leave me hanging with no details at all? Rina, that's so unfair."

"Well, you know, the details are kind of intimate."

She made an exasperated noise. "Seriously, Karina, how am I supposed to live vicariously through you if you won't give me the details?"

That made me laugh, but then I said, "Wait. Are you joking or serious?"

"Both. See you at home."

She was crazy, but I was really starting to like her as a friend, not just a roommate.

I looked up to see him toweling his hair in the doorway of the bathroom. He was wearing a bathrobe with the hotel's crest embroidered on it.

"That was quick," I said.

"Years of practice. I might be close to the Guinness World Record for fastest shower, in fact," he joked. He hung the towel over his neck and gestured toward the shower. "Your turn?"

"Probably a good idea." I went up to him and ran my

hands up and down the softness of the luxurious robe covering his chest. "You'll be gone by the time I get out, won't you," I said, making my guess a statement, not a question.

"You're learning my ways," he said, and pressed a kiss to my head. "Feel free to order room service if you're hungry."

"I doubt I will. No matter how good the food is, it's not much fun to eat alone."

"Well, the offer is there, in case you get hungry. Oh, and here's the number to summon Stefan to take you back downtown." He moved past me and picked up his phone, which was the twin of the one he had given me. A few moments later I heard it chime.

"Thank you," I said. "Stefan won't be busy with you?"

"He'll be available shortly." He pulled open the closet door and I saw he had a clean shirt and a suit hanging there.

I turned to go into the bathroom, but he stopped me with my name.

"Karina. One more thing. What are you doing Friday?"

"Nothing right now, why?"

"There is . . . a private gallery show. Modern art. Your presence would enliven things considerably."

"Well, then I would be honored to accompany you, Your Grace." I made an exaggerated bow.

He covered his eyes as he laughed. "I think *Your Grace* is for clergy, my sweet, the way *Your Honor* is for judges."

"Great," I said. "I can pretend you're the Pope." I ducked into the bathroom then, laughing, as he threw the towel at me.

I got into the shower. There was a small array of bath products on a glass shelf. At first I thought they were the hotel's, but some of them were unlabeled bottles. Here was another mystery about him. He clearly lived in the city somewhere, but he didn't live *here*. Then why was he in this room? It wasn't only to have sex with me, I didn't think. The meeting with Reginald Martindale? Who else was he hiding his identity from?

A sudden idea struck me. What if he was some kind of royalty? He was obviously well off and had a chauffeur bodyguard with a kind of fanatical loyalty about him.

I opened one of the bottles and sniffed it, then felt a sudden rush of desire. Yes, that was how his skin smelled. The only thing missing was the masculine musk that was uniquely his. I washed with it, which meant when I got out of the shower my skin was still steaming with that gorgeous scent. Friday? That was almost a whole week to go without seeing him.

After I dried off my body and the pearls and combed my hair, I snooped around the room a bit. There wasn't much to find. An extra pair of socks sat in one drawer. He really was here for only one night, it seemed.

As I left the room, I noticed one thing out of place. The glass sculpture that had sat on the table where we'd shared the wine with Martindale was gone.

I pondered that and other mysteries—like how much trouble our discussion of exhibitionism was going to get me in, and when I was going to get a chance to wear the ball gown—while I waited just inside the front entrance for Stefan to pick me up. I could feel the string of pearls next to my skin under my shirt. He hadn't said so, but I had to assume they were a gift, too. Certainly I couldn't imagine another woman wearing them after what we'd done with them. And he'd fastened the necklace on me. That seemed definitive.

When the car came, the bellman held an umbrella over my

head, opened the rear passenger door, and then closed it behind me. Stefan was completely silent as he drove down the side street, though the window separating us was open.

I leaned forward. "Can I move up front?"

He seemed startled at the sound of my voice. "Oh, do you want to? I'm sorry. I apologize for my behavior earlier. I was terribly rude to you."

"Stefan, seriously, you don't have to be all manners and politeness. You're not *my* driver."

We stopped at a red light and he turned to look at me. "I don't know what to think of you," he said.

"What do you mean?"

"What you are to me depends on what you are to him," he said. "Are you more like me? Or are you more like him?"

I'm the beggar maid who is being exalted, I realized. *No wonder it's confusing.* "I don't know," I said. "I think we're still figuring that out."

"Okay." He shrugged. "In that case, just to be on the safe side, I should probably treat you like a princess."

"I'd rather you treated me like a friend, though."

"Ha! All right." He looked behind us. There was no one. Even though the light turned green, he said, "Then get your ass up here."

I hopped out into the rain and jumped into the front seat.

"Just don't tell the boss," he said as he turned the limo onto the avenue.

* * *

Stefan dropped me off in front of my apartment and waited until I had gone inside to pull away. Becky was in the shower. I laid out the dress on the futon couch and put the tiara on, then sat down next to it to play with my new phone. It only occurred to me as I set up my e-mail that although he had given me the phone, he hadn't said a word about who was paying for the monthly charges. Part of me wanted to keep it as a special phone that was only for us. The more I thought about it, the more I realized that wasn't merely a romantic notion. I didn't want to give my mother or my sister the number.

An ear-piercing squeal made me forget the phone for a moment. Becky stood in the door to the bathroom looking at the dress, her hair still soaking wet and coming loose from the towel she had wrapped around her head

"Oh my goodness, it's so beautiful!" She was practically jumping up and down from excitement. "Did he buy you this? I thought you said you were doing some kind of bondage scene!"

"That was later," I said. "This was what was in the mystery package." I held up the phone. "I went on a treasure hunt today. One of the places I went to was a clothing shop where he left a gift certificate for me."

"Oh, wow." She sat down carefully on the edge of the couch, coiling the towel again so that it would stay on her head. She had on a short bathrobe. "I think when most guys buy clothes for the girls they're sleeping with, it's usually lingerie and stuff."

"I think he wanted me to pick something as a way of learning about me," I said. "Also, by doing it this way he wouldn't have picked the wrong thing or the wrong size. Besides, I had fun shopping and texting him pictures from the dressing room."

"That's smart," she said, fingering the crystals woven in the netting. "And then bondage?"

"And then bondage," I said. I didn't bother to tell her about all the stuff with Stefan.

"Oh my God. Was it like being kidnapped?"

"No! It wasn't like that at all. It was more like being turned into a work of art. He used ropes and these." I showed her the long string of pearls. Each one was identical and perfect.

Becky whistled appreciatively at the pearls, but she was more interested in the bondage. "But he pretended to be forcing you to do it, right?"

"No, it wasn't like that, either." I stopped and thought about it. Wasn't that what all those fantasies from pirate movies and Westerns were about? About being captured and tied up so the captor could have his way with the victim? "You know, it really didn't feel like that at all. It was more like a game we were playing. Being tied so I couldn't use my hands was only one part of it."

"Is that what they mean by 'recreational sex,' then?" Becky asked.

I couldn't help it. That made me laugh and picture little old ladies who took macramé classes at the recreational center learning to tie different kinds of knots and ropes. "Um, I don't think so," I said when I stopped laughing. "I think recreational sex is any sex you have that's just for fun and not, I guess, for purposes of having a baby or developing a serious relationship."

Wait. By that definition, then, was the game that he and I played just for fun? I felt like it was much more serious than that. It was emotional, passionate. Stefan had tried to get rid of me by claiming I would get discarded because it wasn't a serious thing. Yet James's actions made it seem as if this was a serious thing. Why would Stefan have warned me away otherwise? The conversation I'd overheard uptown added to my point. The woman telling him not to make me into another Lucinda led me to believe she was afraid of him getting too involved as well. He had bought me a phone. He had also promised me a future of pleasure earlier tonight. He had even introduced me to someone who could be useful in a job hunt, someone way better than the jerk Renault had sent me to interview with.

When he was teaching me to read people, he had said to add up all the facts. It only takes a few points to define which way a line goes. Thinking about it, I realized I had more than a few points from him that pointed to how serious he was about me. He hadn't only been teaching me to read people: he'd also taught me to read himself.

Beyond all that, I felt it in my gut, in my heart. I shared an intimacy with him I had never had with another person, not only sex, but also a kind of knowing each other that was hard to put into words. I felt safe and protected when I was with him, safe enough to leap into one erotic adventure after another. I thought about how he held himself back, how armored he was, and how it seemed like I could pierce that armor anytime I put my mind to it, with a joke or with a kiss.

Stefan was right. I would be dangerous to him if I wanted to hurt him. That thought sent a delicious thrill through my belly as I realized it was good for both of us that I was starting to feel as protective of him as he did of me.

"Rina? Are you okay?"

"Oh, sorry. Yeah. Just thinking."

"I've been meaning to tell you. I found a piece of mail for

you on the stairs in the vestibule. I think it got put in one of the neighbors' mailboxes and they left it there, but it's postmarked like a week ago."

"Oh?"

"It's from the art history department. I put it on the kitchen counter." Becky then ran her fingers over the dress one last time. "When are you going to wear it?"

"I don't know. He sort of hinted I would be wearing it soon, but I'm not sure when." I reached up and took the tiara off.

"Well, you better find out, because you're going to need shoes to go with it, and we have to go out shopping for them," she said as she headed back to the bathroom to comb out her hair.

"I'm seeing him Friday. I'll ask then," I said.

It was going to be a long week.

Ten

A Man Who Wants to Rule the World

The letter from the art history department turned out to be from the head of the department, warning me that there were various pieces of paperwork that I had to turn in by certain dates in order to graduate. A few of them, in fact, were already late, but they were generously giving me an extension. Great. The papers were all things that required Renault's signature, of course. I wondered if I could catch him at one of his classes and get him to sign the documents in public, where he couldn't pull anything.

Surely he wouldn't be so brazen as to refuse in front of everyone. Of course, maybe he would take it as a sign I was giving in, but I didn't care as long as he signed them. That wouldn't solve the problem of him refusing to approve my thesis, but it was a step.

I walked from the department secretary's office to the building where his class was being held. It looked like it was snowing, but really it was just winter's last hurrah. The sidewalks were all slush and the streets were small rivers. Ah, springtime in New York. I clutched the folder of papers close to my chest and stomped through the wet weather.

I fumed about the incident all over again. It didn't matter that he threw the printout in the trash, I told myself. He could access the current version of the document in the department computer server any time he wanted to. He was only doing it to freak me out and fuck with me. Literally.

He didn't really mean to block me from graduating, did he? He'd made his bid to get his jollies and it had failed. He'd move on now, right? I tried to convince myself that if I pretended the scene at his house had never happened, then he would pretend, too.

That got me to thinking about the thesis. After talking with Martindale, I wondered if I shouldn't refocus the conclusion from a more general treatment of gender by the Pre-Raphaelite Brotherhood to one focused specifically on sexuality?

Oh, but Renault would surely see that as a come-on. Ugh. And besides, the previous work was surely good enough to deserve to get out of here, wasn't it?

The classroom was in a large building with an atrium entrance, where high echoes bounced off the glass and stone. I got into the elevator.

When I got out on the floor, I started walking slower and slower. I knew I needed to get there before class ended so there would be people around, but maybe I should try Thursday instead. Maybe it would be better to get there before class instead of after, so he'd be stuck there and more easily pressured.

I approached the door, my throat feeling dry. It had a tall, narrow window and I could see they were still in session.

Now what? Slip in and sit in the front and hope I didn't disturb the lecture too much? Or wait out here? But if I waited until people were already leaving, that might be too late.

I stood there too long dithering. By the time I decided I should slip in, people were starting to stand up from their seats. I opened the door and hurried over to the desk, where he was putting away the books he had brought with him. He was hunched over, placing them into a bag, while a student was asking him something, but she seemed to be the only one in line. Okay, maybe she would be quick.

I was standing behind Renault, but I could hear what he said clearly enough. "Well, Miss Sementello, I would strongly advise a revision meeting with me to pull your grade up." She had curly, dark red hair, round eyes, and very white cheeks. "If you could come by my office tomorrow at two—no, wait, I believe I have another appointment then. I have an hour in the morning before my office hours. Why don't you come by my house first thing tomorrow morning?"

I stared at her from behind him. I could barely hear what he was saying my heart was pounding so hard in my ears. *Don't do it! Don't go!* I tried to give her some kind of signal by staring extra hard. What else could I do?

She wasn't really paying attention to me, though. Although she agreed to meet him, she whined about the early hour, and he cut her off—exactly the way he did me.

Unbelievable. Not only did he do this to students regularly, but he also had an MO.

She flounced off and I nearly ran after her. It wasn't a large seminar, so the room had emptied out. He turned then and saw me.

"Miss Casper," he said, his expression severe.

"Professor Renault," I said, launching into my practiced speech. "I received a letter from the department this week insisting that I turn in these signed forms."

He didn't move for a moment, didn't breathe, and I wondered what thoughts were going on behind his narrowed eyes. He was probably trying to figure out how much he could get away with or whether signing any of the documents committed him to approving the thesis itself. "Let me see them."

I produced the sheaf of papers and he laid them out on the table, putting on his glasses to examine them. He made a "hmph" sort of sound and signed the first one, then the second. He picked up the third and looked it over, then signed it also.

He thrust them back at me without looking at me or saying anything more. I didn't push it. I just took the papers and nearly ran out the door.

Down in the atrium as I came out of the elevator, I saw her, the red-haired girl. She was going through the revolving doors to the outside. I hurried to catch up.

She was pausing to open her umbrella in the shelter of the building when I caught up.

"Um, excuse me, you don't know me, but..." Oh God, how could I tell her? What was I going to say? "Look, maybe it's just me or maybe it's nothing," I began. I looked both ways and then back at the doorway to make sure he wasn't sneaking up on us. "I've heard that being alone with Professor Renault is risky."

She gave me a look like I'd opened a smelly bag of shit. I guess in a metaphorical way, I had. "Who the hell told you that?"

"Look. It's talk that goes around the department. I'm a grad student. He's my thesis advisor."

She was still giving me that look.

"He's done it to me," I finally admitted. "The whole bit, asking me to come to his house instead of his office, first thing in the morning, and then . . ." My throat seemed to close up, and that finally cracked her expression. She went from disgusted to concerned. "Then . . ."

I couldn't even get the words out. She put a hand on my arm. "And then?"

"He's got a goddamned pillow on a shelf in his office that's for people to kneel on while they service him," I said. My face was beet red. "You're the first person I've told. Don't go to his home, please. Call and cancel the appointment. Make him meet you at his office."

She rubbed my arm. "Oh, honey, oh my God, you have to report it."

I shook my head. "It's useless. I'll only get myself into even more trouble. I want out, that's all. I don't even know if I can say it again."

"Here." She dug a tissue out of her purse and handed it to me.

I dabbed at my eyes and blew my nose. "I'm all right. I'm fine. That was just hard to say."

"I'm sure it was. Thank you so much for warning me. Let's exchange phone numbers." She dug her phone out while I wondered whether to use my new one or the old one. How about the new one? That was where all the secrets currently were.

"Right." Becky's idea suddenly popped into my head. "If you're in trouble and you need me to come ring the doorbell, you can call me. If you use the word *sunset*, I'll know you're in trouble. Tell him you have a conference call you can't miss or something." Oh, this wasn't making any sense.

"I have no intention of letting him do anything funny, no matter where I meet him," she said. "If he tries, my first call will be to nine-one-one. I'll definitely call you to let you know if anything happens, okay?"

"Okay. Thank you."

We parted and I went to a coffee shop for some ginger and chamomile tea to try to calm down. I sat with my mug and held it, breathing the steam without drinking and trying to unknot my frayed nerves.

I jumped when I felt James's phone chime. I took it out of my pocket to find a text from him that read, *Just thinking of you.*

I texted back, *What a coincidence. Thinking of you too.*

His answer was a smiley face and then: *In a meeting. Must go. My turn to speak.*

I sent back *Good luck* and then realized the time. I needed to get back to the department office to turn in the papers before anything could go wrong. They closed at five and I had five minutes to get there. I could make it.

I squeezed in the door around some deliverymen just before the clock on the church across the street struck five and was worried to see the secretary was not at her desk. I don't know how it is in other universities, but the person who has the true, ultimate power to make or break you in our art history department is the department secretary. Ours was an older woman with a formidable hairdo, sculpted of many curls and pins and dyed an improbable shade of burgundy, her hands heavy with gold rings.

I shifted nervously from foot to foot, then saw her. She was directing the deliverymen, who were wrestling a large crate over the lintel and into the main foyer. Once they made it over the hump of the lintel, she came over to the desk. I was grateful that she sat down instead of shooing me away.

"This is the paperwork I picked up earlier," I said timidly.

"Oh yes, hand it over. Nice work turning it around so quickly." She skimmed the things I handed her. "Oh, here, you sign this one, too." She handed me a pen and indicated the corner of her desk nearest me.

I signed and handed it back. "Yeah, I just tracked him down at a class he teaches and wouldn't let him go until he signed them," I joked.

She took all the papers and stamped them with a very Official-Looking Stamp and then filed them in two very Official-Looking Folders. "There. Did you need something else?"

"Yes, one other thing." I tried not to sound completely pathetic. "What's the date again by which I need my advisor's signature on the final draft of my dissertation?"

"Oh, well, technically he and the committee don't have to sign off until the date of your defense, but these days usually the defense is more of a formality, a chance to show everyone what you did. They can sign at any time leading up to it. But the last date would be twenty-four hours after your defense. Have you scheduled it yet?"

"No, but I'll get right on that." The makeup of my committee was the other thing besides the date that I needed to talk to Renault about and had been avoiding since the "pillow" appointment. "Thank you."

I turned around to see the workmen uncrating what they

had transported. An abstract glass sculpture, on a black pedestal. Something about it looked similar to the one that had been on the table at the hotel.

There was no plaque or sign yet. I hurried back to the desk, where the secretary was putting on her coat. "Excuse me, but do you know the name of the artist who did the glass piece there?"

"Oh, it's new," she said. "Let me think. John something, Jim something..."

Another woman came down the hallway then, also wearing her coat and taking an umbrella out of her bag.

The secretary turned to her. "Esther, what's the name of the artist who did the glass piece?"

"Oh, let me think." I realized then who she was, Esther Carmichael, the head of the department. She had short white hair and wire-framed glasses so round they looked almost like bicycle wheels. She snapped her fingers as she remembered. "Lester. J. B. Lester. American. From upstate, I believe?"

"Thank you," I said, and gave her a little nod. "It's very nice."

"Aren't you Karina Casper?" she said as we all moved toward the exit.

"I am." The one time we'd met before was when she'd told me my old advisor needed to be replaced. She seemed like a very nice woman, even if a little spacey sometimes.

"I'm looking forward to your graduation, my dear," she said as we stepped out onto the street. The snow/sleet/rain had stopped. "You'll be the only doctorate degree awarded from our department, I believe."

"What about Feisenhurst?" the secretary asked.

"Oh, he's hopeless," the professor said, making a hand mo-

tion like throwing something away. "Every time I think I'm
going to get rid of him, he ends up back for another year.
One more and we kick him out for good, I suppose." She patted me on the arm. "Good luck, dear. Are you still on your
first draft?"

"Er, yes. I'm a bit stuck there at the moment."

"You'll get past it. You have all the ideas in your head. You
just haven't thought them all yet." She looked up and wrinkled her nose at the pending bad weather. She put up an
umbrella and she and the secretary moved off together.

I went the other way, wondering what I was going to do if
Renault pushed the issue. Maybe dropping out and avoiding
Renault and the whole mess was the way to do it. But that
would leave people like Esther Carmichael disappointed.

He had signed the papers at least. And he had found someone else to harass. Maybe if I left him alone for another week
or so, he'd soften up and let me go.

He had to or I'd report him. Right? But then I thought, *Well,
you haven't reported him yet. Obviously* no one *has.* He's
probably got some way of dealing with that kind of threat.

My feet took me on autopilot back to my building. I
microwaved some macaroni and cheese and then got in
bed—or onto my futon, as the case may be. I could hear
Becky in her room, but I didn't even go to say hello. I put my
head under my pillow and lay there in the dark trying not to
think about it.

Then I remembered the snazzy new phone. My old laptop
computer was too creaky and ancient to run a current Web
browser. The only programs that worked were a word pro-
cessor and a few old games. I usually had to go to the library
to surf the Web or do research.

I did a search for "J.B. Lester Glass Artist" and immediately got a hit for a website. I clicked on it and up came an online gallery of photos of glass pieces. I tapped on the biography page, holding my breath while it loaded, hoping there was a photo. Could I have found him?

I was disappointed. The bio didn't say much, and the photo was of a man bending over a glass forge, with goggles on his face. It could have been anyone.

It would have fit so perfectly, I thought, if he was the glass artist and had made the marbles and the gorgeous glass butterfly and dildo himself. The thought excited me, but it didn't quite fit. He was friends with a high-ranking curator at one of England's most prestigious museums. He was filthy rich. It seemed more likely he was an art dealer or collector than an artist, didn't it?

What about the paintbrush? I thought. *Where did he get that from?* He must have brought it with him to the hotel room. That wasn't the sort of thing a non-artist had lying around, was it?

I searched a bit further for more about the glass sculptor. A few blogs and magazine articles called him a recluse. Did the J and B in J. B. stand for James and Byron? I eventually found a reference, and no, it was supposedly Jay Brian Lester.

That was too close to be a coincidence, I thought. Things still didn't quite add up, but just as my feelings for him were becoming more certain all the time, so was the feeling that I was coming closer to knowing who he was, not just in the ways that mattered to my heart, but to the rest of the world.

* * *

On Wednesday I got a text from him with a photograph. It showed a bedspread on which sat four items. A riding crop, a fraternity hazing paddle, a candle, and what looked like a miniature pizza cutter. I zoomed in and saw it was a small wheel with a handle that had needlelike spikes sticking out of it.

Pick one, came the next message.

I mulled it over. Were they to be used on me? If they were, which one looked best? I did a quick Internet search. I was already intimately familiar with the candle. The wheel was actually a medical object called a Wartenberg wheel. It was used to test people's nerves and reflexes. Nonetheless, I didn't think I'd enjoy it being used on me. The paddle looked large and heavy.

I texted back, *Riding crop*.

A smiley face came back, which felt like approval and glee, even though it was an emoticon. Then I heard nothing for the next twenty-four hours.

Becky, meanwhile, had made herself an expert on BDSM relationships by reading about them on the Internet. She had cooked a whole chicken and was exhorting me to help eat it for dinner. She had roasted it in a Chinese style so that the skin looked red and the house smelled like cinnamon. We sat in the living room eating on the steamer trunk we used as a coffee table. Becky had a bowl of rice in front of her but was gnawing on a wing with her hands. "Ooooh, he's probably trying to mind-fuck you," she said when I told her the latest.

"Mine-fuck?"

"Mind, as in, fuck with your mind."

"Oh, he's very good at that," I said. I was too embarrassed

to tell her about the whole "sex with words" thing in the restaurant.

"He's trying to get you all keyed up about it. Why did you pick the riding crop? In the stories I read, those always hurt the most!"

"Becks, in the stories, everything hurts. And all their dicks are huge, too."

She giggled and hid both the chicken wing and her mouth with her free hand. "Well, that's true."

"I'm not sure if what you read on the Internet and real life match up," I added.

"Well, some of it must. There are a lot of real people blogging, and you can talk with them on Bondbook."

"Bondbook?"

"It's kind of like Facebook but for kinky people only," she said. "A bunch of the fan club women are on there. There are even some guys on there who dress up as Lightning and enact scenes from his rock operas. Only with real sex and spanking." She giggled again. "They seem like they have a lot of fun!"

"Are you going to hook up with one of these guys?" I asked. "I mean, isn't that kind of your ultimate fantasy?"

She shrugged, setting down the bones and licking her fingers. "I don't know. Some of the people you meet on the Internet are kind of sketchy."

"The only people you've met from the Internet are your fan club ladies and you said they're great," I pointed out.

"Well, yeah, but they're women. Men are a whole different story. Although, a lot of the Lightning impersonators out there are actually women. I think some of the best ones are. But those are the ones making YouTube videos and stuff.

I'm not sure if any of them are putting up personal ads to meet fan girls like me." She seemed deflated by that admission.

"How do you know? I would think a woman who performs as a man might have a pretty high interest in fan girls."

"You think?"

"Well, don't you think some of them are lesbians, or even transgender?"

"Oh. I guess so." She got a wrinkle between her eyebrows as she thought about it. "I hadn't really thought about it that way. That totally makes sense. I'm still not sure I'm really interested in meeting someone like that, though."

"Not even for recreational sex? It sounds like it would be a lot more recreational and fun than the jocks and pre-meds you used to try."

"True. I guess I'll keep hanging around the online chats and see if I meet anyone interesting."

The phone from James chimed then, and Becky clapped her hands. "Oooh, new text! More pictures?"

I checked it. "Nope, just an address and a time for tomorrow."

"Oh, fun! Type the address into the online maps and see where it is!"

"Okay! Okay, hang on." I searched for it. Up came a map of a block not far from here, in SoHo. There was a little tag on the map of the building. "It's an art gallery," I said. "I guess I was expecting that. He said it would be a modern art show. His exact words were 'Your presence will enliven things considerably.'" There was a link to the gallery's Web page. I followed it.

"Aha!" The show featured the combined works of four

artists. One of them was J. B. Lester. "Oh, wow. According to this, the show doesn't open until next week."

"It must be a special preview, then, for top buyers and gallery supporters?"

"What do you think I should wear?"

"Maybe you should ask him?" Becky suggested.

"Good idea." I texted him: *Wardrobe instructions/suggestions?*

All that came back was a single word: *Shave.*

* * *

Becky convinced me to go in an Indonesian print top with blue and black designs on it and black jeans, saying that would be plenty artsy for any SoHo gallery crowd, especially modern art. I figured if he didn't like what I wore, I'd get some diabolical but fun punishment for it, and if he did, I'd be rewarded.

As it turned out, he had asked me to arrive before the rest of the invitees. I showed up at Gallery Three2Four at six-thirty and the door was still locked. The front windows were blacked out with heavy theatrical drapes. A skinny man in skinny jeans unlocked the door for me.

"And you are?" he said, looking me up and down.

I froze for a moment. Was my name on a guest list? Who should I say I was a guest of? Then I remembered the name he used for me that kept my real name a secret. "Ashley," I said.

His face went from guarded and skeptical to a brilliant smile. "Ah! Of course!"

James appeared at his elbow at that moment. "Right on

time," he said, and showed me in while the skinny man locked the door behind us. "I'll take you back to the installation." We went through another heavy drape, like the ones that keep out the cold at restaurant doorways, and into the gallery proper.

At the front were two tables set up with cheese platters, still covered in plastic, and a caterer was uncorking bottles of wine. There were very large canvases on the walls, with some industrial metal sculptures and glass pieces on pedestals here and there, but I wasn't paying attention to any of that.

My attention was on a large, softly glowing white construction that took up the whole back of the room. It looked almost like an igloo, except the bricks were glass, some opaque and some clear. In front of the igloo was a wall of glass bricks about three feet high. The front wall was like the fence around a yard and the igloo was like the house. The house had two openings in the front like oval windows, except that side by side they resembled nostrils in an enormous face.

Polishing the top of the glass wall with a piece of cloth was a man with unkempt brown hair, in a black T-shirt and ragged corduroys.

"Ashley, I'd like you to meet J. B. Lester," James said.

Oh. Well, I suppose that answered that. "Nice to meet you." I shook the artist's hand, which was calloused and rough.

"Likewise," he said in a gruff voice, then nodded at us both and walked off, leaving us standing alone.

"Not very comfortable with the public," he explained. "Come in back with me."

I followed him around a curtained off area and then into the igloo. From inside, only slivers of what was out in the gallery could be seen. I noticed there was what looked like a massage chair and a few other pieces of furniture inside, all completely white, so I hadn't seen them from the other side.

He put his hands on my upper arms, turning me to face him. "Karina, I would like to ask you if you are willing to take part in a bit of performance art."

"I'm willing to try just about anything once," I said. "With you, anyway."

"I'll be right here the whole time. You remember our discussion about exhibitionism?"

"Yes."

"The concept behind this piece, which is entitled *Performance Art*, is that art makes one naked to the world and subject to pain and exposure."

I gripped his wrists in my hands. "How much pain?"

"That will partly depend, but I promise if it's too much, I'll end it. It will only last five minutes."

Five minutes. "What do I get if I last more than five minutes? Another wish?"

He laughed as if I had surprised him. "Yes, you may have a wish. And a kiss, right now." He pulled me close. He was wearing a beige suit and tie, and his arms felt whipcord strong as he pressed my body against his and then bent me back for a kiss.

It was another one of those kisses that began slow and gentle but left me panting by the end. I pulled back from him somewhat reluctantly as the skinny man cleared his throat.

James introduced him to me as the gallery manager, who then showed me to the restroom.

I had butterflies in my stomach, just like before a dance performance when I was a teenager. When I returned to the igloo, James twirled me into his arms as if we were about to begin a waltz. "I haven't felt like this since junior high talent shows," I told him.

"What did you perform?" He rocked us back and forth as if to music, though there was none.

"Dance, mostly. I wasn't really that good a dancer, but I kind of liked getting up in front of everyone, and with dance, I didn't have to say anything. I tried one drama club play and didn't like having to memorize lines."

He brushed my hair back from my face with his fingertips. "You don't seem to enjoy pretending to be someone else."

"I have enough trouble figuring out how to be myself," I said.

He bent his head and kissed me again, this time tenderly. "For this performance, that's all you have to do. Be yourself. You won't even have to move."

"That sounds intriguing. Will I be tied up?"

"Not exactly. You will, however, be exposed."

"Naked?"

"Yes, though only I will see your face." He ran his fingers over my cheek as he looked into my eyes. I think he got a little lost because a long moment passed before he blinked and went on. "It will be a very exclusive crowd here tonight. It's nearly time, so we should get ready."

"Should I get undressed?"

"Yes, down to nothing. And here's a box to put your clothes and things into." He showed me a white bin. I hid my clothes inside it, and then he pulled me into another full-body hug, my bare skin against the soft, suede texture of his suit. "Now settle yourself here," he said when he let me go, pointing to the thing that looked like a massage chair right behind the "nostril" holes. It canted forward more than a massage chair did, so that my butt cheeks aimed right at the holes. There were straps that went over my back to keep me in place, a cradle to rest my forehead, and padded shelves for my arms.

He stroked my back with his hand, and then my backside. "You're very brave," he said.

"Am I?"

"Not everyone would let their rump be shown to a room full of strangers."

"Not everyone has their own personal genie to grant them wishes when they do," I pointed out.

"Ha! True. Now, sit up a moment and look at this." He released the straps and when I sat up, he handed me a black riding crop. "This is what you picked."

I had not held one of these since a Girl Scout riding class when I was ten. At the time, I'd been afraid to hit a horse, and fortunately didn't have to, since the horse they gave me was docile and didn't fight me.

I flexed it a few times and said, "Horses have much thicker skin than humans, don't they?"

He took it back and kissed my temple, whispering, "They do, but you'll do fine."

He gestured for me to get back into position, so I did, and then he ran the leather loop at the tip up and down my back, giving me goose bumps.

"It can give pleasure, too," he said, leaning close so that his voice was in my ear while he tightened the straps to keep me still. He ran the crop between my legs, dragging it over my clit lightly and making me pant with desire, then flicking my clit with the leather tip. I moaned.

"More of that later, perhaps," he said, and then rolled the

chair back until my buttocks were fitted into the two holes, my ass protruding into the gallery from the frosted glass wall. "Now, let's test this."

I could turn my head enough to see him, and he took a seat in a folding chair and put his arm through another hole I hadn't noticed. I felt the tip of the riding crop tracing its way up and down my rump.

"Distance is just about perfect," he said. "All right. Two more things to prepare." He reached into his pocket with his left hand and pulled out his phone. He must have been using it to control various things, because the lights around us changed, the glow of the wall brightening, and suddenly I could hear the voices of the people in the gallery much more clearly. "Directional microphones," he explained. "So we can hear what the people out there are saying when they come up to the wall."

The staff began letting people in. He leaned against the wall with his arm through a hole and hanging on the outside like a piece of art, I supposed. He was quite still and silent, but when I turned my head, his eyes met mine and he gave me a conspiratorial smile.

We could hear the voices clearly. "Oh, this one is weird. Is that real?"

"Real what? Oh my God, I think it is real. Or we're supposed to think so, at least. Are we supposed to be scandalized by seeing a woman's private parts?"

"It'd be much more subversive to see a man's. Female nudity is still standard in fine art."

"That's entirely because the female body is so objectified by the male-dominated art establishment, not because female nudity is acceptable."

"Well, that's clearly what the male arm here is about. Look at the business suit and the riding crop. Think someone's making a statement about what a slave driver their business manager is?"

"Is Lester here? I heard he was."

"That's him over there."

"That's him? I thought that was a homeless guy crashing the party!"

"It's not real. It's just as much of a statement if we think it is."

"Oh my God! He moved!"

The spectators fell quiet for a moment, watching. I looked at his face, and he winked at me.

"There! He moved again!"

"It could be animatronic."

He blew me a kiss. And then he struck me with the crop across both buttocks and I screamed.

"Holy shit! Did you see that!"

It burned and it hurt and in an instant I was panting, but I could hear him whisper, "Good girl."

The voices were still talking. Some male, some female. "Look at that! A welt is coming up!"

"That's crazy."

"That's proof it's real. She's real."

"Oh, come on. They're probably paid actors. No need to freak out."

"But she screamed!"

"I would've screamed, too!"

And then there were enough people trying to talk at once that I couldn't really make out what they were saying.

I felt the tip of the crop making a circle on my butt cheek and the crowd quieted again.

"Oh, this is so kinky," one woman whispered.

"Agreed, and we're all getting teased and tortured by that guy. Rawr."

He blew me another kiss. "This one won't be as hard," he said quietly.

He was right. He struck me so that the leather tip made a cracking noise, but compared to that first blow, it didn't hurt at all. I yelped a little. Then again he gave me that tap, tap tap tap, just light smacks with the leather. I wiggled my butt, and that had two effects. One was it rubbed my bare clit against the column of glass between my cheeks, and two, it made the audience giggle.

"Now let's see if they get bored," he said, and I felt nothing for a while. He didn't move. I didn't move. From the sound of things, people drifted away somewhat.

New voices came, many of which said similar things as the previous group.

"Oh, that's disgusting."

"I think it's rather brilliant."

"It's a cheap ploy."

"It's putting their money where their mouths are."

"Instead of art being a metaphor for all the sex we can't talk about, sex is a metaphor for art."

"But is it sex? It looks more like torture."

"Objectification."

"All of the above."

He was grinning. "I'm going to strike you again now, sweetness. Hard."

"Okay." I pressed my forehead into the cradle instead of looking at him, steeling myself for the blow.

I screamed when it hit, not in surprise since I knew it was

coming, but in sheer expression of pain, and maybe even a little outrage at being hit at all.

"That scream! I can't watch!"

"Eh, you can see a lot worse at the BDSM clubs on the West Side."

"I didn't know Lester was a pervert."

"That's not him back there. He was up front."

"Is this some kind of comment about people in glass houses?"

"If we're supposed to start throwing stones, I'm leaving."

Then came a voice that sounded a lot like Professor Renault's. "Oh, we don't need to look at this. It's probably just some slut."

A male voice answered him. "I don't know about you, but it's not every day I get to see a woman's bare ass."

"Turn on the television any day of the week," a woman said, "and you will. Yawn. Clearly desperate for publicity. Oh, what's this?"

James pulled out his phone and did something. I could hear a sort of hum, then a clatter.

"Karina," he said. "That's the sound of a pile of riding crops falling from the ceiling in front of the crowd. If they do what I think they will, please tell me if it gets to be too much."

"I will." Though I didn't feel anything at the moment.

It was several minutes before someone worked up the nerve to swat me with one, and then it was her who yelped "Oh!" and ran away. I tried not to laugh.

Several people picked up the crops and touched me with them, but very few were willing to hit. Then a female voice said, "I'll show you how it's done," and crack! A sharp blow landed right across my cheeks, not as hard as his, but enough to make me mouth a silent scream while I tried to absorb the pain.

"You're gorgeous," he whispered. "Absolutely stunning."

A few more tried to hit me, but they had the angle wrong, or they weren't trying very hard. I couldn't make out individual voices for a while. Then things began to thin out, the room sounding more empty.

"You did beautifully," he said softly. "Let's bring this to a close, then." He tapped on his phone and the lights shifted once more, as small but brilliant lights inside the glass came on. He withdrew his arm from the hole but left his jacket hanging there, and then rolled my chair back from the holes and put something into their place to seal them up.

He ran his hands down my back and over my backside. "The marks are bright and lovely," he said. "You might have two spots that bruise. Both my doing, I think."

"What does it look like?"

"Here, I'll take a photo." He took it with his phone and then texted it to me. "How it looks is entirely secondary to how it feels, though," he said, running his hand over the flesh again. He grabbed a handful of my cheek and I sucked a breath in through my teeth. Arousal and adrenaline were flowing through me in equal measures, and I wanted to hump his leg but couldn't since I was still strapped down.

"You are so brave. Sore?" he asked.

"Sore," I agreed.

"And how about here?" He moved his hand to my clit and labia, brushing his fingertips back and forth. "You're practically dripping."

"Does that mean I'm a masochist?"

"Perhaps an exhibitionist, too. All those people staring at your bare ass."

I felt myself gush at the thought.

He chuckled. "I wonder if you'll come more easily or more powerfully here."

"What do you mean?"

"They can't see us. All they can see is perhaps a flicker of movement through the glass and lights. But they can still hear you if you're loud enough."

"Oh, I—" I broke off as I felt his tongue licking one of the stripes left by the crop. He paused to kiss my cheeks in a few places, and then licked at the wetness dripping from me. Even though I had been shaved for more than two weeks now, I still felt extra sensitive and bare down there. His fingers spread my lips apart and his tongue went hunting for my clit.

The angle was all wrong this way, but that made it so very right, each darting lick of his tongue making my arousal leap and grow. And then he sucked my clit into his mouth and let my lips loose, sinking one finger deep into me. That made me wail with pleasure, and it wasn't long before the wail was one of release, as the suction and the flicking of his tongue brought on the inevitable orgasm. His finger inside me seemed to find more spots to trigger me with, and a second and third orgasm piled on top of the first, making me scream myself hoarse.

When at last he withdrew, he rested his cheek against my bare back and sighed as if he were as spent as I was.

"Do I get my wish now?" I asked.

"Mmm. First you get a glass of water for your poor, parched throat," he said. "And then you may have anything that is in my power to give."

I felt him stand and release the straps, and then move away. When he came around to the front of the chair, he had a bottle of water in his hands. I sat up and drank it greedily.

"You want to know what's ironic?" I asked when I paused for breath.

"What?"

"I didn't like sex with my early boyfriends because of how much it hurt."

"Is that so?"

"Yes. But it hurt in ways that proved they either didn't know what was going on with me or didn't care." I reached up for him and pulled him down into a kiss, then let him go just enough that I could still feel his breath on my face. "You, though, when you hurt me, you prove you know exactly what I like and how much you care."

He kissed me again, in total agreement, his tongue claiming me thoroughly. When he pulled back, he said, "The same is true when I pleasure you, isn't it?"

"Yes. And when you control me and test me."

"Mmm-hmm."

"So what about my wish, then?"

"Whatever you like, sweetness. Didn't I say that already?" He nuzzled his nose against mine.

"You did. I'm just making sure."

"Well, then, what is your wish?"

I was surprised by my reaction. "Tell me if you're the real J. B. Lester. I thought for a while that maybe you commissioned the glass works, but now I think you're the artist. Well?"

He jerked back but didn't let go of me, searching my eyes.

His voice was rough from emotion when he said, "You're right. I am."

I tightened my hold on him, my heart racing. "You made the marble and the other things." I felt my groin tighten as I pictured the glass butterfly. "The toys."

"I did," he admitted, closing his eyes.

I leaned up to kiss him on the cheek. I didn't know why he would pretend to be the buyer of the art instead of the creator, but maybe that was one more thing I would eventually come to know. "You're amazing."

He opened his eyes. "No, *you* are amazing, and I'd like to go somewhere more private to tell you so and celebrate your fabulous performance."

"All right."

He helped me to extricate myself from the chair. "Let me go and say good-bye to the others while you dress," he said. "I'll be back in a moment."

I got back into my clothes, wondering if "somewhere more private" meant another limo ride, or hotel room, or what. My jeans felt rough on the welts on my ass, even through my underwear, and I felt as relaxed as I had been after the foot massage except for the tight thrum of sexual tension between my legs. Somewhere private. Would tonight finally be the night? I was open to whatever intimacy came next, whether it was physical or emotional.

Eleven

Tremble Like a Flower

He returned wearing a floor-length coat, which seemed logical at first since I thought we were leaving the building. But he handed me a large cardboard box and led me out the back door of the gallery into a service staircase at the rear of the building. Up we went, two, three, four floors, to the top floor, where he opened the door into a haphazardly furnished loft apartment. The furniture looked like it had been assembled from other people's moving sales and castoffs. The corner nearest the door served as the kitchen, separated from the rest of the main room by a dining table with six unmatched chairs.

The box, it turned out, held canapés and pastries from the caterers, and under his coat he had a bottle of champagne.

Above the sink we found a few mismatched pieces of glassware, and he pulled out two and led me to the futon couch, much more stylish than mine, in the front window. The illumination from the streetlamps was bright, so he didn't turn on the lights. The coffee table was shaped like a glass kidney bean. I laid out the open box while he poured the champagne.

We clinked glasses. "To a successful performance," he said as he settled back on the couch. "And a stunning debut." He took a sip of the champagne.

"To my ass's debut," I agreed.

He almost spat his champagne when I said that, then gave me a dark look for a moment before he grinned and said, "That was cruel."

"Oh God, did it sting going up your nose? I'm sorry! I didn't actually think it was going to work!" I couldn't help but laugh. "No, really. I didn't think it would work."

"You, sweet, are the only one who can make me laugh like this."

"You mean Stefan's not much of a comedian?"

"He is sometimes unintentionally funny," James said. "Which means I have to hide that I'm laughing or he'd be mortified." He took another sip of his champagne, this time keeping a mock stern expression on his face as he did so. "Let's not talk about Stefan. Tell me. How did that compare to dancing?"

"I don't think I ever got a welt from dancing," I said, pretending to look back at my rear with concern. "But seriously, that was intense."

"Would you say you liked it?"

"What I liked best was that you were there," I said seriously. "I liked that you challenged me, dared me to do it. And I liked meeting that challenge." I moved closer to him on the couch, tucking my legs under me and holding the champagne glass with my arm hanging over the back.

"You know something?" he asked, his fingers coming to rest on my knee. "I like that you challenge me, too, Karina."

"I challenge you?"

"You do. To be my best. And to be . . . myself." He set down his half-empty glass and took my other hand in his. "I haven't felt this free in a long time. With most women, in fact, I can't."

"What do you mean, can't?" He picked up a canapé and held it out for me to eat.

I gratefully did, having almost forgotten about food in all the excitement. I had no idea what it was I had eaten, only that it was delicious. Something with ham? He popped one into his mouth and chewed thoughtfully.

"Most women," he said after swallowing, "want me to be a certain way. The ones I meet in the BDSM scene especially have very specific expectations. They want a master, or a dom, or a daddy, and they have very detailed ideas of what each of those roles should be. That can be fun, for a while, but like any role, it can get tiring to maintain all the time."

"And they want to be your slave girls?"

"Or pets, or loyal servants, or any number of other things. People's fantasies are very powerful. Sexual fantasies come from deep inside, sometimes so deep you can't even say what the origin is." He picked up another one of the hors d'oeuvres and fed it to me, then ate another himself. "But you? You didn't come out of the BDSM scene. I thought surely if I gave it time, some fantasy role would suggest itself, either for you or what you wanted me to be."

"But it wouldn't stick," I said, thinking about what I told Becky. "Every time we try some kind of 'let's pretend,' it falls apart."

"I know." He picked out another treat from the box, this

one cone-shaped and filled with deviled egg yolk. I licked my lips after swallowing. "I do wonder if we just haven't found the right thing yet," he said.

"Stefan calls you *boss* or *boss man*."

"Which is appropriate, since I'm his employer."

"Well, we know I can't handle *my lord* or *Your Highness* or any of that renaissance faire kind of stuff with a straight face." I picked up something wrapped in bacon and after eating one, held one out for him. It was crunchy, fatty, salty, and delicious. "I mean, maybe for the space of one scene or one night of fantasy, I could, but it would be hard to keep from laughing. Even if you got all dressed up as royalty. It simply wouldn't feel real."

He looked down at his hands, at his strong and graceful fingers. The hands that sculpted such beauty, drew such pleasures out of me with the surest touch. "Does it feel real to you, Karina? When we do what we do?"

I looked into his eyes, willing him to look up at me. "It does. Maybe I'm foolish for feeling that way, but it does. Wasn't it you who said if I didn't obey, I would be making a mockery out of it?"

"I did."

He took one of my hands in his and gently sucked on the tip of a finger. Then he said, "What do you suppose the prince called Cinderella, since he didn't know her name?"

"I suppose until he met her, he could call her anything he wanted in his head."

"Let me be more direct. Do you mind that I call you *sweetness* and *my sweet*?" He sucked on my next finger, as if checking it for chocolate sauce or powdered sugar.

"Why would I mind that?"

"Some women might find it demeaning to be considered delicious," he said.

"Well, I guess I'm not one of them. *Sweetness* is a helluva lot better than *baby.*" I giggled. "As for you, this might be too long for a pet name."

"What might be too long?"

"The Artist Formerly Known as Prince."

That set us both to snickering, but I didn't want to get distracted from the conversation.

I rubbed my cheek against his knuckles. "Perhaps that's the thing. Stefan calls you what he does because your relationship's defined. Maybe what I'm trying to figure out is something to call you that honors the reality of what we mean to each other, who you are *to me* and who I am to you."

He held out his arms, inviting me to snuggle and rest my head on his shoulder. "I haven't felt about anyone the way I feel about you," he said. "You astonish and delight me, and each time I see you only makes me wish the next time would arrive faster."

"Well, that's good, because that's pretty much word for word how I feel about you." With my body resting against his, I could feel how at ease he was. The tension that had filled him in the past was absent. I put my hand on his chest to feel his heart beating. "What's the word for that?"

"Lover?" he hazarded.

"Well, yeah, but that doesn't work so well as a nickname. Maybe once in a while, like 'Hey, lover, how was your day?' but not for all the time."

"What about when it comes to defining what I mean to you?" he asked.

"Hmm. Okay, yes, *lover* does seem to fit. *Boyfriend* really doesn't. That sounds so...beneath you somehow. *Boyfriend* sounds so mundane and dull. And loaded with mundane expectations."

"I could not agree more, sweetness," he said, kissing my forehead.

I snuggled even closer. "Maybe I'll just have to keep calling you James when we're together."

"That would suit me just fine."

"So how was the mind reading tonight? You could see the audience, couldn't you?"

"Yes, I could," he admitted. "It's a shame you couldn't see their faces, too. Truly a fascinating exposure of human vulnerability."

"Hah, for all concerned," I said. "Wait, was that the point? That they were as exposed as I was, in your eyes?"

"Maybe."

"That's the kind of voyeur you are," I teased. "It's not just watching girls like me touch themselves that gets you excited."

"Are you saying I'm more complicated than that?"

I sat up a little so I could look him in the eye. "You are the most complicated person I know."

"Is that a good thing?"

"It's neither good nor bad. It's just you." I settled back down. "I worry that I'm nowhere near complicated enough to keep you interested."

"Just because I am taking my time plumbing your depths doesn't mean I find them shallow," he said, running a finger along my neck.

"Was that a euphemism?" I teased.

"No, sweetness, though it was a double meaning. I plan to plumb both your physical and psychological depths." He shifted on the couch. "I want to play with your body right now. Will you let me?"

"Will I get another wish?"

"Hmm, I'm not sure I'm obligated to grant multiple wishes per night. You can look it up in the genie contract. For now, come here," he said, motioning for me to straddle him.

I stood to do as he'd asked but paused to look at him. "Clothed or unclothed?"

"Unclothed would be better," he said, stripping out of his shirt. That surprised me. I'd assumed I would be the only one removing my clothes.

He undressed halfway, leaving his pants on. I climbed onto his lap, my hands on his shoulders and my legs on either side of his. He reached between us, spreading my lips but not touching my clit.

"I never tire of looking at you," he said. "Shaven or unshaven, you are so easy to admire."

"Is my pussy really that cute?" I half whispered the word *pussy*.

"Don't compare yourself to other women," he said, looking me in the eye. "That's a losing game no matter who plays. But yes, yours is quite beautiful, and not merely because it's *mine* to do with as I wish." To emphasize the point, he slid a finger deep inside me without taking his eyes from mine.

I groaned. The orgasm from earlier had only heightened my appetite for him. "The real reason I can't call you *lover* is because we still haven't done it," I complained.

"Do you really feel that way?"

"I'm half kidding, but only half. When can I have you for real?"

"Define *for real*, sweetness. I thought we just decided it

was real?" he teased as his finger crooked inside me and made me see stars.

I leaned forward and whispered in his ear, "You know what I mean. Your cock in my pussy." My cheeks blazed with heat, but so did everywhere his fingers touched. "You said I had to earn it. What do I have to do to earn it?"

"There is a way you can win it, if you're game."

"What do I have to do?"

"You'll have to fight for it."

"Who will I fight?"

"Me." He grinned.

"Oh." This was a very intriguing twist to the game. "What kind of a fight would it be?"

"We would both be naked, with our wrists bound to each other, my right to your left and my left to your right. Your goal will be quite simply to get me inside you or to make me come. My goal will be to avoid letting you. Bound that way, I'll be unable to turn away from you, of course." He wiggled his finger inside me.

I thought about it. He was already aroused, between the entire scene in the gallery and now toying with me up here. "All right. I'm game. What happens if I lose?"

"You'll forfeit orgasm for a week."

"I can go a week without sex."

"Oh, I didn't say it would be a week without sex, my sweet." He pumped his finger in and out. "Only that you won't be allowed release."

"Well, I'll just have to win, then, won't I?"

"Let's move the futon to the floor," he murmured into my ear. "For a wrestling mat." He pulled his finger free abruptly and it was true: I could think again.

We flattened out the futon and dragged it onto the Persian rug that looked like it was where a dining table would go if anyone actually lived here. He went into the bathroom and came out with ACE bandages.

I, meanwhile, had set up my phone camera on the coffee table, aimed at our wrestling mat.

"What's this?" he asked. "So we'll have an instant replay if you think I cheat?"

"No," I said, leaning up and kissing him on the cheek. "It's that I think you'll be more turned on if you think someone might see it. I'm definitely not the only exhibitionist here."

"Ha-ha." He twirled me in a circle like we were waltzing. "You *do* know me."

I figured I had best start pressing my advantage early, so I helped him get out of his pants and into a condom, taking every opportunity I had to caress his balls and run my fingers down his shaft as I rolled the slick condom into place. He didn't protest and seemed quite confident that my ministrations weren't going to help.

Wrapping the bandages was a bit of a trick, but he inverted one of his hands in relation to mine and then after wrapping around both wrists, turned it right side up so that now the wrapping was in a figure eight. He repeated it on the left, though that meant my hand was a bit dragged along, too, while he wrapped the other.

"I didn't make the wrapping too tight," he said, "so let it be a rule that pulling free of the bindings is a forfeit."

"All right."

"Then let's go!"

We were standing on the flat futon and I pulled on him to see if I could get him to move. As I stepped back, he took a step forward like we were in some kind of ballroom dance.

I reached for his cock, but his arm tightened and kept me clear of him. We fought that way for a while, with me trying to get my hands inward and him trying to keep them stretched out. We circled a little as we did this. What I wanted was to get him on the ground. If I could get on top of him, I thought, I could get him inside me, and once that happened, he probably wouldn't be able to resist fucking me. I had to get him down somehow.

Then the idea hit me of how to get him to the floor. I bent my knees and fell slowly back, too quickly for him to completely compensate, but I was not sneaky enough that he lost control of himself. Instead he went to his knees.

Almost as good. I wrapped my legs around his thighs and twisted, and it worked. I had flipped us over so I was on top, my breasts in his face.

He took a nipple in his mouth immediately and suckled it. Distracting and pleasurable, but I needed to get my legs untangled and move my hips back to reach my goal. I tried to move and his teeth took hold, trapping me in place.

I was still on top. I mashed my breasts into his face so that he couldn't breathe out of his nose or mouth, and when he pushed at me and gasped, I was free. I wriggled back and felt his cock nestle between my legs. He tried to flip me off, but tied as we were, my weight stayed centered on top of him. What he hadn't counted on was all the wrestling me, Jill, and Troy had done as kids. I had quickly learned that the easiest way to win was not to pin them with an actual wrestling type of move but to spread myself out on top and make myself heavy so they couldn't do anything to me. This, they told me at the time, was no fun.

Now it was a lot of fun. He squirmed in frustration. "You're much smaller than I am. How are you so heavy?" he said.

"Lucky, I guess," I said, now rubbing my wet labia against his shaft. Having no pubic hair this time was a great advantage—nothing in the way and everything slick.

The wrestling began in earnest when I tried to maneuver him inside. He couldn't get free of me or out from under me, but I couldn't get the angle right to trap him. We fought that way for a while, both of us getting moist from the sweat of effort and his erection never flagging. This was definitely exciting him.

How could I up the ante even more? What else might arouse him?

"At the next art installation," I murmured into his ear as we struggled, "maybe my whole backside should be exposed or my whole lower half. I know! I can be in a cocktail dress, with strappy heels on my feet and maybe even a diamond anklet. The dress up around my waist and pantyhose torn down the crotch leaving my pussy completely exposed."

"And riding crops?" he asked.

"No. Perhaps dildos, though, artful glass ones, each representing something like hope or love or freedom."

"And what will you call this masterpiece?" His voice sounded breathless.

"How about *Fuck the Rich*?"

I'd got him again, and he couldn't help laughing, which distracted him enough for me to waggle myself into place and impale myself on him.

Oh my God, he was big. I wasn't prepared for it at all.

"Karina!" He held perfectly still, and so did I.

I hadn't realized, because of his length, that his girth was so wide. When I'd washed him that time at the hotel, he had seemed slender, but he was tall, and I didn't have a lot of experience gauging these things.

I tried to press myself down farther but it hurt too much. Even as aroused as I was, even after his finger had been inside, I wasn't prepared for something that big.

"Don't move," he whispered. "Don't hurt yourself."

"I'm...I'm..." I was trying to say I was okay, but apparently I wasn't.

He was making shushing sounds, soothing sounds, squeezing my fingers with his. "Touch yourself, or let me," he said in a quiet, serious voice. "It'll feel better."

I let him move his hand toward where our bodies met. My fingers were pressed against my stomach as his thumb sought out my very exposed, very naked clit. I jumped as he brushed over it—too sensitive. He switched to massaging what flesh he could reach around my opening, and that felt good. That made me want more. But the pain had made me tighten up and I couldn't let go.

In my mind's eye, I still had one goal: riding him like a cowgirl on a bull, my hips snapping until he couldn't hold back anymore.

There was no way. I couldn't even imagine sitting up straight right now.

"Slowly ease yourself off, okay?" he whispered. "Gently."

I nodded and whimpered in answer.

"Lean forward. I've got you." He arched his back at the same time and pulled free.

I sighed with relief. I was still nearly trembling with desire, but I knew I shouldn't push things and make it worse.

He twisted his wrist and the figure eight opened. I slid one hand out; then we did the other. "Good girl. Lie here a moment." He held me on top of him, chest to chest, his hand rubbing my back soothingly. "Good girl," he repeated.

"But I lost."

"A very valiant attempt, though," he said. "Had I known it would hurt you like that, I wouldn't have suggested it."

"I didn't know either," I said. I felt stupid. How could I not have known my own body? "You must think I was trying to dupe you or something."

"Not at all." He switched to the other hand, making circles between my shoulder blades. "Knowing one's own limits is a very good thing."

"I clearly didn't."

"Hush, that's not what I meant. I mean when finding one's limits, respecting them and backing off, instead of forcing yourself into a worse situation."

That made me think. I lifted my head a little so I could look at him. "How long did it take you to learn to respect your own limits?"

"Too long," he said very seriously, and then ran his thumb along my bottom lip. "Kiss me."

I did, tender toward him but still angry at myself. As we kissed, he rolled us over so that I was on my back.

Then he kissed his way down my front, all the way to the bareness below. His tongue snaked out gently to massage my clit.

"Ohh, that feels good."

He chuckled against my skin and settled down farther. His tongue continued its gentle undulations, supple and spongy and warm. Then he began tracing my opening with his fingers, teasing at the edges while his tongue continued to work.

He ran his hands and arms under my thighs and drove his tongue deep into me. There was no pain at all, no soreness, unless you counted the spots on my butt where I could still feel the welts from the riding crop. He wiggled his tongue inside me and then withdrew, only to dive in again. And again. Soon he was fucking me rhythmically with his tongue and I began to moan. It didn't go deep enough, unlike the glass dildo, which had fit so perfectly. His tongue felt amazing, so wonderful, but it ignited a deep ache for more.

I wondered if he could read that need on my face or in the line of my body. What he did next was settle his cock between my lips and rub the length along my clit. God, he felt huge, inches and inches of him rubbing up and down where I was so sensitive. Then he shifted again, and I looked down to see him holding his cock in his hand, the head protruding like a plum.

He rubbed the head up and down my wetness and groaned and shuddered as if it were painful to hold back. He teased at my opening with the fat head, and I wondered if he was going to take it slow, eventually working his way inside me. It felt so good I moaned aloud, my voice mixing with his groan. I wanted him, and he clearly wanted me every bit as much.

My groan only got louder as he pulled back, panting. He wiped his forehead on the ACE bandages and said, "I better not tempt myself any further."

I opened my mouth to beg, but he stopped me with a stern look. "That's enough for now. The week without orgasm has begun, after all."

"Oh, can't we start tomorrow?" I pleaded. "I know I lost, but—"

"Sweetness, you had a perfectly wonderful release in the gallery already," he said, swatting me on the thigh. "Don't be greedy."

"It's hard not to be when it comes to you!" I protested, but acquiesced. "All right. A week, then?"

"We should meet every day, at least once," he said, sitting up now and stretching.

"Afternoon? Evening?"

He went over to the phone and turned off the camera. "Send me all the times you're free throughout the week. I will give you notice of when and where, but a surprise visit is not out of the question."

"All right."

He pulled me to my feet and kissed me, and that kiss felt like it righted everything in the world.

"There's something else I should tell you," he said.

"Yes?"

"I got an invitation to a formal ball for this coming Saturday."

"A ball, you say?" I tried to sound teasingly aloof but it came out too excited.

"Yes. A highly formal affair among the ridiculously rich and influential." He nuzzled my hair. "I believe you have something appropriate to wear?"

I couldn't help it. I nearly squealed.

"Does that mean you'll come with me?"

"Yes, yes, yes!"

"Good," he said with a grin. "Your presence will enliven things considerably."

Twelve

Who Could Ask for More

The next day was Saturday and we went to the Metropolitan Museum of Art. On the way there in the back of the car, he pulled me tight against him, my back to his front, and wormed his hand into my panties to arouse me the whole way. I barely remember what we saw. He seemed to enjoy listening to me opine about the art, but my attention was on him. He would put a hand lightly on my shoulder and trace a zigzag with his finger, imitating the motion he'd used on my clit, and my toes would curl as if it were my clit he was touching. The museum was crowded, and he brushed against me whenever he got the chance.

We had a lovely meal at a Japanese restaurant near the museum. Then Stefan picked us up and headed downtown again. This time he made me strip below the waist and went at me with his mouth, artfully alternating the sensuous slide of his tongue with the nip of his teeth. When he kissed me good-bye, his upper lip was salty with my sweat and my head was spinning from unfulfilled need.

On Sunday our destination was the Museum of Modern Art.

In the car on the way there, James pulled out what looked like a small briefcase, except the leather was blue. Was it a jewelry box? He had that grin he got when he was giving me a gift, and he set it in my lap so I could open it.

I lifted the lid to find several gorgeous glass objects sitting in blue velvet niches. The first was a globe a little larger than the Ben Wa ball I had worn once before. It had a cord through the middle of it. Next to it was what could only be a dildo, but not as large or phallic-shaped as usual. This one was spiral and tapered like a unicorn horn, only rounded at the end. The next was like a series of spheres connected together into a rod. The one after that was more traditionally penis-shaped, with thin ripples down the sides. The final one was the longest in the case, widest not at the head, but in its bulbous middle. Each was a work of art by itself, while the whole set together was dazzling.

"Did you make them?" I asked.

"I did. Ideally they will help prepare you for me, sweetness."

I felt gushy between my legs thinking about that. Already the memory of how much the attempt had hurt was beginning to fade, and I was eager to try again. I felt like a wimp for not forging ahead with it. But he'd insisted. "So tell me how this is going to work."

"Each one is bigger. By the time you work up to the last one, it's nearly the size that I am. Now, strip. I want to put the ball inside of you before we go into the museum."

I slid my bottoms off and lay back against the seat. He paused to tease my clit from its hood and tickle it with maddeningly light touches. Then he coated the ball in my juices before pressing it against my opening. There was a moment when it felt too large, but then he brushed my clit again and in it went.

"Very good, my sweet," he breathed, and leaned down to lick my clit with deliberate slowness. It was delicious torture, knowing that he wasn't going to let me come, but it felt so good anyway.

He tugged on the cord and I put my hands on his shoulders in warning. "Don't!"

He looked alarmed for a moment, before I went on.

"I almost came," I explained.

"Ah. Good girl." His smile was warm and approving. "Goodness, you're gorgeous."

I wiggled my bottom. "I get the feeling you're suffering as much from deprivation as I am."

"I am," he affirmed, shifting back from me and straightening his clothes. "It'll make it that much sweeter when I can finally take you the way I want to. For now, I'll have to settle for fucking you by proxy. In public, just the way you like it." He grinned wickedly.

I got dressed again and we walked around the museum with the Ben Wa ball inside me. The last time there hadn't been so much walking, and the ball hadn't been as big. This time every step made it feel a bit like he was fucking me, and his loving touches and whispers as we went through the place only enhanced that feeling.

In the car on the way downtown, he pulled the globe free, using the cord and being careful not to touch my clit while he was teasing me with it.

"How do you feel?" he asked as he dangled the glass from its string.

"Like I want you," I said. "Like I really, really want you."

"Then it sounds like the training is working so far," he said with a grin. He wrapped it in a handkerchief and then pulled the piece shaped like the blunt unicorn horn out of the box.

It slid in easily, and instead of merely leaving it there, he held on to its base and fucked me with it, slowly at first, then faster, sometimes jiggling it up and down until I wailed with how close to orgasm I was. He never let me go over the edge. He fucked me with it all the way downtown.

When we got to the apartment, I was soaked in sweat and shaking from the need to come. He licked my clit again, slow and soft. "You are one of the most beautiful beings imaginable," he said as he sat up. "Your willingness and your sensuality make you even more amazing."

I could tell he was tempted again. But we were both going to be good and it was going to be worth it.

Monday I had to work, so Stefan picked me up at eight o'clock when I was done. When he pulled up in front of the alumni office, I saw he was alone and tried to get in the front, but he gestured to the backseat. In the back I found the case but no James.

I looked at Stefan in the rearview mirror to see if there were any other instructions.

"We'll be meeting him," Stefan said. "He said he didn't want you to get off schedule, whatever that means, and that you'd know what to do. He told me to point out that there is a cell phone holder attached to the back of the seat. I am to drive around until you tell me you're prepared for...ahem...prepared for him."

"All right." I closed the partition between us, figuring I knew what that meant. Then I set the phone to video and

waved at the camera before pulling the next of the pieces
from the case, the one shaped like a series of spheres connected together. I waved it in front of the camera and kissed
the round tip of it before I began working on trying to get it
inside me.

I aroused myself first, sliding two fingers down each side
of my lips. I wanted to get good and wet. At first I was turned
on, but I wasn't really lubricating a lot. Then I started pinching my nipples and the juices started to flow. Had he trained
my body to react that way? I wondered. Or was that always
something I would have responded to and he had been the
one to discover it? There was no way to know. I dipped my
fingers in and coated the toy, then slowly worked it in, one
sphere at a time.

When I had it all the way in, I held my thighs shut and
turned off the video, sending it to him through the phone.
I was about to knock on the window to ask Stefan if there
was anything else, thinking James might have sent more of
the heavy-duty briefs, when I noticed there was another bag
there.

The first thing I pulled out of the cloth bag was a pair of
leggings. They were like tights, only thicker and had no feet.
Under that was another pair of briefs and then...a cheer-
leader skirt? And under that...mittens? What kind of kinky
scene was this going to be?

I opened the partition again. "Where are we going?" I
asked Stefan.

"I believe I'm dropping you off at the skating rink at Rock-
efeller Center," he said with an amused tone.

"Oh! God, that makes so much sense." Getting the leggings
on was a bit of a trick. I remembered Becky's technique for

putting on stockings and that helped. The glass stayed inside me, just as I knew it would.

James was waiting there for me, and I gave him my shoe size so he could rent us skates. At that time of night, it wasn't crowded and we were soon on the ice.

I stepped out gingerly at first, not sure how much I'd remember of my childhood skating lessons. As it turned out, it came back to me quickly and I pushed forward, then stopped myself by pivoting on one toe. He followed me, gliding confidently on one foot.

"You can skate?" I asked. "Where did you learn that?"

"My mother had an affair with an Olympic medalist," he said rather matter-of-factly, "so I spent a year or two hanging around skating rinks. How about you?"

"There was one year all the girls in my town wanted to be Michelle Kwan, and my mother signed me up for lessons." I took his hand and we continued on so as not to block traffic for the dozen or so other skaters going around the small rink. "Was your mother...um..." I tried to think of how to ask without sounding judgmental.

He rescued me by answering the question for which I couldn't come up with words. "My mother always aimed quite high in her partners," he said. "Though she still hasn't found one good enough to keep for more than a few years."

He said this without bitterness. I wondered about that. "She didn't stay long with your father, then, I guess?"

"I never knew him at all," he said, sliding his hand across my back so that we were skating together, matching his stride to mine. "She claimed not to know who he was, in fact. For the first several years of my life she raised me by herself. Be-

fore you get any ideas about that, I'll just say she had plenty
of help, between a nanny, a driver, and a cook."

"You grew up wealthy?"

"For the most part. When we moved back to the States,
she got rid of all the servants except the driver. I didn't need
a nanny anymore since I was in school. She started dating
again around that time."

"It's funny. My mother has dated a lot, too, but I don't think
she's ever dated someone like an Olympic medalist." I skated
ahead of him, turned around, and skated backward so that I
kept going in the same direction but facing him. "She tried to
remarry once, but it didn't last."

"Did you have any contact with your father growing up?"
James asked, skating past me and falling back as he let himself glide. His coat was open and it flapped as he sped up
again and then fell back.

"Not after he left, no. There was no custody battle, none of
that. My mother wouldn't talk about it, and I was too young
to know about things like child support. By the time I was
old enough to ask, that was about the last thing I could imagine bringing up to my mother. She let it slip to my aunt—who
told my sister, who then told me—that he left behind a large
pile of money when he went away. Not large enough for us
to live off for the rest of our lives, though. From the way
things went around our family, my guess was the money
lasted about five years, by which point she had gotten fed up
trying to get a second husband and got a job instead."

He took my mittened hands and swung me into a turn,
then pulled me along behind him with powerful strokes of his
skates. "It's funny. The more I find out about you, the more
we have in common."

"I could say the same thing!" I sped up and went past him, daring a skippy little jump I remembered how to do. He chased after me and we raced around the rink, slaloming around other couples until he caught up to me and we slowed, his arms around me from behind. I tightened around the glass inside me, which I'd forgotten until then, until I could feel the hardness of him through his trousers, pressing against me. "The real thing," I murmured.

"Soon," he assured me.

Although it had been a pretty warm spring day, at night it had cooled off a lot, and of course we were on ice, so sharing a pot of hot chocolate and fondue afterward was heavenly.

So was the way he tugged on the glass inside me as we rode back downtown. He kept to his rules, though, and did not let me come, though it would have taken very little effort to push me over the edge by the time we reached my apartment.

"Is this really going to make me ready for you?" I asked with a frustrated whine as he pulled the glass free and wrapped it up. "Or is it just a kinky game?"

"Now, now, sweetness," he said, pulling me close and nuzzling me. "What did I say about either/or? So often it's both. And this time, it's definitely both."

Tuesday he was in the car when I hopped in. He kissed me deeply as soon as he pulled me close, as if he hadn't seen me in a long time, though it had been less than a day. "I can't stay," he murmured in my ear. "But I have time for this."

He slid his hand into my panties and jiggled his hand at my mound until when he slid one finger between my lips it met copious cream. "Lie back and take your pants off," he whispered in my ear.

I did, spreading my legs as I had done so many times before.

"Spread your lips, too, sweetness. Let me look at what's mine to claim."

"Mmm, James!" My cheeks flushed at his bold words.

His eyes lit up, and he answered, "Karina..." He used two fingers, working deep inside me, in and out, until my hips were rocking into each stroke. Then he switched to the phallic-looking dildo, running it up and down my clit and teasing me with it, swirling it at my opening but not putting it in.

"Ah, fuck! Please, James, please!"

"Just because I put it in doesn't mean you can come," he reminded me.

"I...I won't, I promise!" I didn't think I could come from that by itself, though he'd made me very aroused with the teasing and the smooth strokes and circles on my clit.

"All right." He pushed an inch of it in, then pulled it out, making me wail. Then he was fucking me with just the tip.

"Think about how good it'll feel when it's my cock doing this," he said. "Is one inch going to be enough for you?"

"No!"

"Two inches?" He pushed more of it into me and pulled it out.

"No!"

"Three inches?" More of it went in, this time the bulbous head rubbing my G-spot and making me see stars.

"More, more, please!"

He slid the entire thing inside me then, until it bumped my cervix, which made me jump but didn't actually hurt. He fucked me with long, slow strokes of the dildo, in and out in a steady rhythm until I lost track of time passing.

The alarm on his phone pulled me back into real time.

"I'm so sorry I have to run," he said. "But I'll see you to-morrow for the next one. All right?"

I could only whimper while I got dressed again.

"Do you feel all right? No pain?"

"Only the pain of deprivation," I moaned. "Is it the end of the week yet?"

"Not yet, sweetness. Soon." He kissed me again, leaving me breathless and swollen-lipped on the curb outside my apartment.

Wednesday we met in the morning, on the steps of the New York Public Library. He snuck me into the men's room at the back of the microfilm department and had me bend over in the wheelchair-equipped stall, holding the railing. The next toy was more phallic in shape than the previous, with a bulbous head and ridges along one edge. As he fingered me and teased me, he stroked himself and lay his hard length against one of my buttocks. While I held the toy, he teased at my holes with the head of his cock, smearing my juices around with it and thrusting across the openings without going in. Then he put the toy inside, easing the large head past the point of resistance in my vagina. I tensed for a moment, expecting it to hurt, but his other hand never stopped moving, one index finger circling my clit ceaselessly while he worked it in.

In the stall next to us, some guy was having a coughing fit.

I tried to keep quiet as he worked the glass all the way out and then all the way in again several times. He had found the spot that would make me groan and squeal, and it was diffi-cult to keep quiet. He bade me put my back against the wall and lift up one leg onto the rail. I touched myself while he pushed and pulled at the toy sticking out of me.

I couldn't keep quiet though as I got closer and closer and finally had to pull my own hands away with a wail or I'd go over the edge. I had spasms deep in my pussy then, but nothing that spilled out into full-blown orgasm.

"Good girl. That's enough," he whispered, and kissed me on the hair. "I'll see you late tomorrow night. Now, do you want to take the piece home or shall I hold on to it for you for now?"

"Oh, could I take it? Please?" I asked.

He chuckled and caressed my cheek. "Can you tell me why you want to when you're not allowed to come?"

I had to think for a moment. My reaction had been entirely emotional. I just *wanted* to. I tried to articulate a reason. "Um, because I miss you when we're apart and it'll make me feel like I have a piece of you with me?"

He nodded and kissed me, sweetly and deeply. "All right."

He pulled a strappy thing from his trench coat pocket and handed it to me.

"Wear this tomorrow," he said. "It'll hold the glass in place inside you. I'll meet you at your library, about twenty minutes before closing."

That meant that on Thursday I went to the library with the straps and the glass hidden in my backpack. Becky had given me the idea that we should write a paper together on feminist interpretations of the various versions of the King Cophetua paintings, and I was curious to find what previous scholars had written on the subject. Some of it was so horribly wrongheaded, but I supposed that was true of any scholarly pursuit. Two hours before closing time, I went into the women's room and put the glass in, then fastened the straps on to hold it inside me, just like he'd said. Under my jeans you couldn't see a thing.

At twenty till eleven, he waltzed in, showed a guest pass to the guard at the door, and came to plant an almost chaste kiss on my cheek where I was waiting at the reading room. He led me immediately into the stacks and then from behind, put one hand over my mouth and the other into my underwear. He aroused me relentlessly for the next ten minutes, muffling my helpless cries, then letting me go.

"They'll be looking for us soon," I said, panting and breathless. "They're closing up and know how many came in and went out."

"Then we'd better be quick. Bend over, pants down."

He loosened the straps and then cut right through my panties with a knife and slid the glass free. The next thing I felt was the head of his cock against my opening. I tensed, wondering if all we'd done so far that week had been enough, wondering what put him in such a hurry. Maybe he was succumbing to all the need built up through the teasing. I wondered if he had been denying himself orgasm as well.

"Just the tip, sweetness," he said.

He pushed in then, and I stifled a moan. He felt so good! I was eager for more, especially when he fucked me like that, pulling out and pushing in, that small amount of him, at the sensitive edge of my opening.

He moved quickly, pulling back and replacing himself with something hard and rigid. Another of the glass pieces, I assumed. He slid it in and I gasped in intense lust.

"Buckle up," he whispered.

I adjusted the straps and zipped up my jeans as quickly as I could while he sauntered to the end of the shelves.

"Ah, yes, found everything we needed," I heard him saying. "Thank you."

I hurried to join him but the guard had already moved on to look for someone else. We slipped out with one minute to spare before closing time.

Stefan was waiting at the curb, standing beside the door, ready to open it.

I moved toward the car, but James spun me back to look at him. "Alas, my sweet, I have something to take care of. Will you be all right walking the few blocks to your home?"

"Yes," I said, trying to hide my disappointment.

"I do have some instructions for you."

"Yes?"

"How do you feel about sleeping with this one inside you tonight? Call me when you wake up in the morning and I'll come and remove it."

I felt my insides twist pleasantly at the idea. I'm not even sure why that made me gush with lust. "I would love to. What time?"

"Whenever you wake."

"What about my roommate?" I had a sudden panic that he was going to push things too far, that she was going to freak out and so was I.

"You'll come down to the car, dearest," he said, caressing my hair the way he knew I liked. "No need to bother your roommate."

"Oh. Thank you."

He laughed. "Don't thank me for keeping our best interests in mind."

"Oh, like almost getting us caught by security was in our best interests?"

He grinned. "Almost caught was part of the plan. We each have the things that thrill us."

"No kidding." I put my arms around his neck to kiss him good-bye. "I'll call you in the morning."

Of course that morning was Friday. I woke up, brushed my teeth, and ate half a muffin, then brushed my teeth again because of the blueberries. Still in my pajamas and bathrobe, I called him.

"I'm outside," he said, sounding already quite amused. "You have sixty seconds to get down here."

Thank goodness I'd brushed my teeth! I ran down and into the car, which was not quite in front of the building but parked at a hydrant with lights flashing. Stefan shut the door behind me and then went around to the driver's seat to get the car moving.

James was fully dressed in a business suit and tie. Although his first order of business was for me to strip down to nothing but the straps, he seemed to want to talk, not touch me sexually, at first.

"You were telling me you had a job interview a while back, didn't you?" he said.

"Yes." I sighed. "But the guy I interviewed with . . . he was there with my advisor that night you and I met in the bar. I'm pretty sure he threw my résumé out after that."

"What sort of a job was it?"

"Graphic design. I took some computer design courses when I first started grad school. It pays better than making lattes and cappuccinos."

"And ostensibly it would be some kind of art?" he asked, though he was giving me the skeptical eyebrow again.

"I guess. Renault introduced me to him, so it seemed like it would be an easy job to get."

He pursed his lips unhappily. "If he'd offered you a job, you would have taken it?"

"Well, I suppose. At least until I figure out what I want to do with my life."

"Like when you went into grad school five years ago, thinking you'd figure out what you wanted to do while you were there?"

"Basically." I felt a little defensive. "You know, I have a parent who is already critical of my life. I don't need you acting like one, too."

"I'm sorry. I wasn't trying to be critical. Is your mother very judgmental? I'm curious what she's said."

"Well, to hear my mother tell it, grad school is a waste of time, and the only way I'm ever going to have the love of any man is if I pretty myself up and pretend I'm stupid."

"You don't honestly believe that, do you?"

"Of course not."

"It can be difficult to ignore the things we hear over and over all our lives," he said.

"True. My mother found a formula that worked for her. You'd think I'd get off a little easier since my older sister's a lesbian. But no, that just made her all the more desperate to turn me into a girly girl." Something clicked for me then. I knew my mother measured her worth by what the men in her life thought of her. It hadn't been quite clear to me until now that she measured *my* worth by what the men in my life thought of me. And she measured those men's worth by what they thought of her. Brad had bowed and scraped for her and, at least when we were with her, had treated me like a princess. Yet he was no Prince Charming. My mother thought he was solid gold, and when I was with him, she treated me like I was, too. I was back to being spun dross now that he was gone.

Warm hands enfolded mine as he moved close to me. "Karina. I know I've always insisted on honesty, but that goes tenfold for what I am about to ask. The ball gown. Did you choose it because you wanted it or because you thought I'd want to see you in it?"

Okay. That was not the deep, soul-searching question I was expecting after his intro. "Both, of course," I said. "Hey, aren't you the one trying to teach me life isn't *either/or* but *and*?"

"Indeed, I am." His voice was soft and he kept my hands in his. "And I will without any doubt enjoy seeing you in it. I just feel the need to say this: I don't value you more when you pretty yourself up. I definitely don't value you more for conformity of any kind."

Which prompted me to ask, because my mouth was moving faster than my brain, "Then when do you value me most?"

He pulled me close and I snuggled against him. "If this statement were merely a prelude to sex, I would say I value you most when you are completely naked and vulnerable to me. However, it is closer to the truth to say I value you most when you're being honest with me, and with yourself."

"Perhaps it's because when I'm naked and in your bed, it's easiest to be honest," I added.

"You may be right." He nuzzled my hair. "Few people ever escape all the trappings, costumes and roles that society requires of us to be that naked, to be that honest with ourselves."

I tipped my head back and kissed him under the chin. "Which is one of the reasons being with you is special."

"Is it?"

"It isn't just about the sex," I explained. "You're protective of me without smothering me. You make me feel precious without making me feel like a china doll or a trophy. You make me feel like it's okay to be beautiful in my own way. It's hard to explain."

"No need to explain," he murmured. "I understand."

"I've been so disconnected from everyone else. I was never really connected with my boyfriends except by a kind of optimism that we would connect eventually, if we loved each other enough. But you know what? I couldn't fall in love with someone I didn't feel a connection with. I could have a romance, a courtship, always hoping for it to happen, but it didn't with them..."

I trailed off, realizing I had basically told him I had fallen for him. Saying "I love you" to someone who isn't ready to hear it is always game-over. Isn't it?

Stefan rapped on the window. We were slowing to a stop at the curb on a midtown avenue surrounded by skyscrapers.

He hugged me, hard. "Bad timing. This is the wrong moment to end this conversation," he said. "Wait a second."

He took out his phone and texted someone. "There. Now they think I'm in traffic, but it only buys us a few more minutes. Karina."

"Yes?"

He shifted so that we were facing each other. He licked his lips as if struggling to find the words he wanted to say. What came out was, "Don't ever change, sweetness." He kissed my hands, my fingers, my eyelids, then almost chastely my lips. "And remember I prize your honesty above all things."

I think that was his way of saying I hadn't made a mistake saying what I did. Or almost saying it.

"Now lie back. I should take the glass out."

"Must you?"

"Your body needs a break," he insisted, "even if your heart wants to keep me here forever." On the word *here*, he brushed his hand down my abdomen.

I lay back on the seat and he moved the straps aside and slid the dildo free. Then he crawled up my body to kiss me.

"The next thing that goes inside you is my cock," he breathed.

"Could you try it now?" I whispered back. "Just for a few seconds?"

He growled a little. "That will, I'm sure, leave you unfulfilled."

I laughed. "Isn't that the point of this whole week?"

"Perhaps. I will be, too, though."

"Aren't you already?" I teased. "The more you tease me, the more you tease yourself."

His hands hurriedly undid his trousers and the next thing I felt was the length of him rutting against my inner thigh.

Then he stopped, his hips jerking up. "This isn't the time for this."

"But—"

"Hush. I don't want to rush this with you, Karina." He spread kisses across my cheekbones. "I treasure you too much to do that."

I groaned. "All right. For fuck's sake. Go to your meeting or whatever it is."

He kissed me hard and then was out of the car before I could say anything more. Through the tinted windows I could see him buckling up quickly as he walked across the plaza toward a building's entrance.

I pulled my robe back on as Stefan lowered the window.

"Back home?" he asked.

"Yes." I leaned tiredly against the back of the seat. Phew. "Do you know anything about this ball he's taking me to? I think he meant to tell me more about it but I, um, distracted him."

"Ah, yes, that." Stefan was silent for a few moments as he navigated through the heavy flow of traffic on what I could now see was Sixth Avenue. We weren't far from Radio City. "It's tomorrow night. We'll be picking you up at seven o'clock."

"That's it? That's all you know?"

"I'm sure he'll text you more details if necessary," Stefan said.

"Come on, Stefan. This is a big deal! I need to know at least what kind of shoes to wear. Will there be actual ball-room dancing?"

"I've never been permitted inside to see," Stefan said. "But there is a ballroom—that much I do know."

"Is this like a regular thing? Who's throwing it? He said it would be a bunch of rich, overprivileged people."

Stefan snorted at that. "He should be one to talk. But yes. It's in a very rich person's private home."

"A private home with a ballroom?"

"Yes. That level of rich."

"I'm not even sure I can imagine that kind of money."

"I'll tell you one more thing about the person hosting the party. They're rich enough to have paid for my college education without blinking."

"Really? Where did you go?"

"Yale."

"Yale!"

Stefan nodded. "And then to bodyguard school after that, which was nearly as expensive, especially when you consider I wrecked a car in the process of learning evasive and tactical driving."

"What!"

He smiled at me in the mirror, with a cat-who-licked-the-cream sort of smile, and I knew he wasn't going to say more. All right, fine, so the party would be at the house of a person so rich they basically lived on a separate planet from me. I suddenly wondered if a secondhand dress was going to be good enough.

"Man, now I'm really nervous about this."

"Clearly I shouldn't have told you anything," Stefan said.

"Well, I better go do my shoe shopping this afternoon. Not that anyone can see my feet under that voluminous dress. Shoot. I wonder what I can afford."

"Does it matter, if no one will see your feet?"

"Well, you know, if there's a grand staircase, at some point you have to walk down it, and when you're holding your skirts out of your way so you don't trip and fall and break your neck, everyone gets to see your feet then."

"Having never worn a ball gown, I can't say I knew that, but I do now," Stefan said. "Thank you."

"I've never worn one either," I admitted. "That's something I read in a book somewhere."

He chuckled. "I can see why he likes you. You're real."

"And most people aren't?"

"No, they really aren't. They're exceedingly fake. Although New York is not as bad as Los Angeles. I think many of the people you meet there are actually androids. There's no other explanation for it."

"Have you traveled a lot?"

"A fair bit. His business takes us all over the world, and yet he's a recluse at the same time. Otherwise I think we would go more places. Los Angeles, London, Seattle, Milan, Paris, Miami. It's mostly just New York and London."

"What's London like?"

"A complete nightmare to navigate. They drive on the wrong side of the road there."

Stefan regaled me with tales of vehicular jeopardy all the way back down to my building.

Thirteen

Leather, Leather Everywhere

James finally let me out of suspense late Friday night when we talked on the phone. "Look," I said. "I need to know what shoes to buy, or if this is actually the kind of party where I won't be wearing them long."

His laugh sounded low and rich, even through the phone. "Well?"

"What did Stefan tell you?" he asked.

"He didn't tell me anything, which only increased my suspicion that this party is going to be full of shenanigans."

"Oh, is that what they're calling it these days?" he joked. "All right. I'll clue you in a bit. This is a society of mostly well-heeled people who have some unorthodox ideas about sexual recreation."

"There's that word again! Recreation."

"Well, it's an interesting word, because many of them do seem to approach it like a hobby or a sport. Others are committed to the alternative lifestyle. Oh, what am I saying? Many of the same people are both highly committed to an alternative lifestyle and also, well, you'll see. Besides, it makes perfect sense to get the exhibitionists and the voyeurs together for their mutual benefit."

"I suppose it does. You still didn't answer the question about the shoes. Will there be actual ballroom dancing?"

"Yes. We have some appearances to maintain, after all."

"We do?"

"Oh, I don't mean you and me. I mean this secret society overall. Think of it as an extended form of group foreplay. There's a veneer of aristocracy atop the whole thing. Which perhaps makes it all the more fun when the veneer cracks." He paused. "I'll bring you shoes."

"Wait, did you just say you'll bring me shoes? You don't even know my size."

"Of course I do, sweetness. Did you forget I rented our ice skates?" He quoted my own words back to me. "You're an 'eight, sometimes seven and a half in styles that run big.'"

"All right. And I guess that means my secondhand ball gown is all right?"

"I assure you it's fine. And don't forget the tiara."

"Hey, I thought a little more about what we said in the car today."

"Which thing we said?"

"The bit about how it isn't necessary for me to pretty myself up for you. Or my own self-esteem, for that matter. Wearing a pretty dress when you're a single girl, it doesn't work."

"Doesn't work?"

"Think about it. If a girl dresses really cute, is she really going to impress that boy she thinks is cute? Or is she only going to attract a lot of unwanted attention from men? I've never been big on all the unwanted attention. I mean, seriously, it's gross most of the time. I'm not interested in those guys, young or old, so getting compliments or appraising looks can be downright creepy. And then there are the actual creepers who do shit like hover around trying to see your tits. Ugh. Why why why would I want to do anything to encourage that?"

He made a murmur of agreement.

"I don't put on makeup. I don't style my hair. I don't wear cute shoes. I don't wear frills or skirts or anything the color pink. Because it only leads to trouble. And I wouldn't want to date any guy who only noticed me because of how cute my hair was." The guys I had dated weren't much better, I thought. "Here's what's different, though. I want to be pretty for you. I wish I was prettier, in fact."

"Karina, you are far prettier than you give yourself credit for."

"That's not the point. The point is that for you, I pretty myself up because we both enjoy it. We have fun with it. I don't mind exposing my femininity, literally or figuratively, when I'm with you. Heck, I don't even mind other men watching me and appreciating what they see, as long as I'm with you."

"A large number of voyeurs will be present in the crowd tomorrow," he said.

"They can look all they want, because they'll know I'm yours," I said. "Isn't that right?"

"That's exactly right," he said with some vehemence, which made me feel warm and tingly inside. "Now, about tomorrow, would you like to go back and see Mandinka? She does beauty above the waist as well."

"Oh, that's a thought."

"Would you like to bring your roommate? She could get a facial or a pedicure herself, too."

"Well—"

"Don't insult me by offering to pay for it," he said. "I'll set up appointments for you both. You might want to bring the dress and change there."

"This'll be fun!" Once again, he'd thought of everything. Instead of me stressing over whether my hair and makeup were right, I'd have Mandinka work her magic. Everything was going to be just perfect.

* * *

I broke the news to Becky that we weren't going shoe shopping after all. She was in the kitchen fighting with our toaster, which was fussy about actually toasting both sides of the bread sometimes. "He's buying me shoes," I told her.

"Great! How much do you think we can spend?" She pulled the toast out with a fork and put it back in facing the other way.

"No, no. I don't mean he'll pay for it. I mean he's getting the shoes for me."

"But I got you a bag!" she protested. "What if your shoes don't match?"

"No one will see my shoes under the dress," I pointed out. "What bag?"

"Look at this. I thought you'd need a place to put your cell phone and stuff." She went to the shelf by the door to dig in her own purse, which was larger than most tote bags I had ever seen, and pulled out a plastic shopping bag wrapped around something. "Tada."

I discarded the plastic bag and was left holding a very cute blue satin purse, square, on a long string. It fit my cell phone and a few other things perfectly. "It's awesome!"

"Can you text him a picture of it and tell him to get something that will match?" she asked.

"I'm sure if what he gets me matches the dress, and this matches the dress, then it'll all match," I assured her.

"But I was looking forward to going shopping with you." She sighed and sat on the futon. "All we've done is work work work all week."

I didn't mention that I'd done some other things, too, but I did say, "It's okay, Becks. We're going to spend some time together after all. He booked us spa appointments."

She sat up straight. "Spa appointments?"

"A pedicure and facial for you and pedicure, hair, and makeup for me," I said. "At the place he sent me once before. They're really nice there."

"Ooh! I'm liking him more and more. Will he be there? What am I supposed to call him?"

I realized I wasn't so sure. "I don't think he'll be there," I said. "And I'm not sure what you should call him. I call him 'James,' but even his staff doesn't use that name. It's . . . only for me."

"Oooh. Special." Becky's eyes widened. "Well, obviously I can't call him that. If I'm going to thank him, I want to be able to say, 'Thank you, Mister So-and-So.' Or whatever would be appropriate. Wait, are you telling me you still don't know his last name?"

"I know who he *is*. He's J. B. Lester, the glass artist, but no one's supposed to know that's him. I haven't asked what alias I'm supposed to give people who aren't in the know!"

Becky blinked. "Huh. Isn't J. B. Lester a pseudonym? I can't say 'Mr. Lester' if that's supposed to be a secret, too. Especially if it would get you in trouble for telling me!"

"I don't think he'll be there," I repeated. I was sure that he'd told me the truth, that his name was James and that he was the glass artist J. B. Lester, but he still hadn't told me the whole story.

"So, what happens in a facial?" Becky asked.

"I haven't the slightest idea, but it's supposed to be fantas—"

"Do you smell something burning? Oh no! The toast!" She ran into the kitchen and unplugged the toaster, just as wisps of black smoke were starting to curl up from it. Her toast was fine, but the toaster itself was done for. "Well, I guess I can spend the money I was going to spend on shoes on a new one of these."

We arrived at the spa at five, right before closing. This time Mandinka and another woman were there for the two of us. The big surprise was that Becky knew the other woman.

"Mistress Mischief!" she exclaimed when she caught sight of her. "Oh my gosh, I had no idea this was where you worked. Karina, this is one of my friends from the LL fan club."

The woman had jet-black hair but very pale skin. "You can call me Jesse here, Becks," she said as she led us to the changing stalls.

When I gave a questioning look, Becky said quickly, "Oh, see, lots of folks have fan names. They're usually two words with the same letter, like Lord Lightning. So, um, yeah." She was blushing a little.

Jesse let the cat out of the bag. "Becky's fan name is Baroness Babelicious."

"We were drinking at the time," Becky said weakly as she shut the curtain, but we were all giggling about it by then, even her.

Becky had a facial while I got shaved, and then we both got pedicures, which made Becky shriek and giggle because of how ticklish her feet are. After that, all three of them hovered around me to do my hair and makeup. Okay, Becks mostly kibbitzed and made play-by-play commentary like, "Oh, that shade makes your whole face glow" and "Oh my God, so glam!"

They put the tiara on to sculpt my hair around it and ended up adding little jewels to my face and eyes. They also did something I'd never seen before. I mean, my idea of makeup was you brushed some red powder on your cheeks. They used a kind of bluish shadow not just on my eyes but also on various places on my face and down my neck and cleavage.

With the dress on, I have to admit it looked stunning. *I* looked stunning. The makeup made it seem like the dress and I fit together somehow, instead of it being something I put on. All the glittery crystals helped with that, too.

He hadn't said one way or the other what to wear under the dress of course, so I wore nothing. No bra was necessary since so much support was built into it. And I figured if I was going to need underwear, he would bring it along with the shoes.

Which meant that when it was time to go, I suddenly realized, "Oh, should I put my sneakers back on to walk to the car?"

Becky shook her head sadly. "I still think it was a mistake to let a man pick out shoes."

"Well, if his own clothes are anything to go by, he's got

very good taste," I assured her, and Mandinka and Jesse backed me up.

While we were debating what I should do, someone knocked on the glass door.

My breath caught before I had a full look at him. He wore a midnight-blue jacket that went almost down to his knees. Unlike a regular tuxedo, this one had no lapels and a short collar, almost military-like. Instead of a regular necktie, he had a silvery-looking cloth knotted and pierced with a silver and diamond pin, and in one ear he had not one but two studs, one diamond and one sapphire. Stunning.

Mandinka unlocked the door and let him in. He kissed her hand, then came over to where Jesse, Becky, and I were standing by the counter.

He only had eyes for me. He dropped to one knee, kissed the back of my hand, and then rose, still holding my fingers lightly in his. "Shall we, madam?"

"Um, shoes?" I asked.

"If someone could get the door please?" he asked, and Jesse hurried to hold it open.

I squealed as he literally swept me off my feet. I held his neck tightly as he carried me to the door. I waved good-bye to Becky and then closed my eyes as we headed down the steps of the stoop and across the curb to the waiting car.

I had to let go to step into the limo, and it took some help from both him and Stefan to get the whole dress inside, but soon we were under way.

And of course he had found the perfect shoes, silver ballet flats. Why hadn't I thought of those? They were silver leather with just a few rhinestones dotting the toe.

He had something else for me, too. He held out a flat

velvet-covered box large enough to hold a small dinner plate.

"What's this?" I asked, expecting to open it and find a rhinestone-studded dildo inside.

"Open it," he said.

I lifted the lid. It took me a moment to register what I was seeing. Not a sex toy at all, but a fine silver necklace, worked to look like vines and tiny leaves, with bits of glass clinging to it like dewdrops, some clear, some blue. Then it hit me that they might not be glass, even given his penchant for it. "Are they real?" I breathed.

"Yes, they are. Sapphires and diamonds. Allow me?"

He took the box and lifted the necklace free, then undid the clasp. I turned so he could loop it around my neck.

"Gorgeous," he said when I turned back around. "You are beyond a fairy princess right now."

"No dildo tonight?"

He gave me one of his hawklike looks, his eyes alight with desire and excitement. "I was serious when I said the next thing you'll have inside you is my cock."

I swallowed, feeling the anticipation run straight through me. "Good. I suppose that means I don't have to worry about you lending me to a gang bang."

"Well, at least not first thing," he teased.

At least I think he was teasing.

Stefan took us onto the highway and James took me into his arms and held me. The whoosh of the road noise was soothing and a little hypnotizing. I could feel where one of his hands was against the ribbing of the dress, warm and solid.

When I was a little girl, I once fell asleep in the car on the way home from a party. I think it was my sister's christening day and we had a big party at my aunt Tera's house. We stayed late. My sister got to sit in the front seat with my mom, because she got car sick easily and my parents believed she didn't get as sick if she sat in the front. So in the back were me and my dad. Troy hadn't been born yet.

My father was not an emotive man, but I remember his hand on my hair, petting me like a cat, and I sat thinking that was the most extraordinary feeling before I fell asleep.

I felt a little like that in the back of the car with him. There was so much affection in the way he held me.

Wasn't he everything my mother told me a man should be? Caring, totally into me, and wealthy to boot?

I tried to imagine bringing this man, holding me while I dozed, home to meet her. "Yes, Mom, I'm totally head over heels for him, and he's filthy rich!" Not that I'd say it that way, but that's what she'd hear, and at least I knew that would go over well. The bit where he was a mysterious glass artist who did kinky performance art installations? Not so much. I wondered how he'd respond to her interrogation.

Surely he'd have the perfect answers to her questions, like he did for everything. I had never looked forward to bringing a man home before. It had always felt like a necessary step in a relationship, a kind of obligation to fulfill. But I wanted him to come home with me, not because I thought my mother would like him but because, for once, I didn't care if she did.

Not that I was likely to bring him home anytime soon. We still had a lot to learn about each other, but I couldn't help thinking about it.

"Tell me what this party will be like," I said, a little sleepily. "Is it really a secret society?"

"*Secret* is a relative term. Many of them are very rich, meaning they are well placed in society. But they're also quite kinky, which means identities need to be protected. Some keep their sex lives secret from their families, others from their business associates. You'll hear people called by many names and titles tonight. Most of them are not real."

"Like Baroness Babelicious?" I asked with a snort.

"What?" he asked, as if he hadn't heard me. "Who?"

"Oh, nothing. Turns out my roommate has an LL fan club name. Always two words, both starting with the same letter, to match with Lord Lightning. Somehow during a drinking binge a couple of weeks ago she got tagged with *Baroness Babelicious.*"

He chuckled, almost nervously. "And I take it this is a somewhat inappropriate name for her? She seemed pretty enough."

"Oh, it's so funny because she was this total nerdy mouse who never left the house for anything but class and studying at the library. She's got a whole closet full of punk and goth clothes, but she never wore them anywhere. So, you remember the night we met? She's this huge Lord Lightning fan and she finally got up the courage to go out and meet some other fans. She's totally come out of her shell!"

"That's fascinating," he said.

A short while later we exited the highway and soon were pulling into the circular driveway of what looked more like a castle than a house. We joined the line leading up to the main walkway.

"What will Stefan do while we're enjoying ourselves inside?" I asked.

"I think Stefan reads a lot of e-books these days," he said seriously. "Also, the drivers get together and play cards and eat cake."

"Cake?"

"The catering staff brings it to them through the kitchens. Cake and coffee so they can stay awake, of course. Here we are now, be careful of your dress."

Someone opened his door for him and he leapt out, while Stefan got out and opened my door. James was there to offer his hand to me and I carefully put one silver-slippered foot out the door, then the other, before I stood.

The night had turned chilly, and we walked up to the main doors together, one of his arms around my shoulders, which had only the lace jacket over them.

The doorman seemed to know him, addressing him as Mr. Jasper, and when he asked who I was, he gave my alias as Ashley.

"I have her to thank for all this," I said as we made our way through a grand entrance hall.

"Who?"

"Ashley," I said. "She was the one who called in sick at the last minute, so I took her name tag and her shift at the bar the night we met. Do I look like an Ashley to you?"

"Not particularly," he said. "But it works for our needs, plus the name bears the same meaning as a favorite character of yours."

"Character?"

"Cinder-ella," he said.

"Wow, so it is." That hadn't occurred to me before. "And I'm to call you Mr. Jasper tonight?"

"Just Jasper, if you need to use a name when we are with

others, though you might hear me called by other nicknames as well."

"Even more?"

"I used to do a lot of role-playing in the past, as you might have guessed."

I was about to ask him what else I might hear when a woman stopped us in our tracks. She was neck to ankle in a sleeveless sheath of perfect silvery satin, slit up to the thigh, with elbow-length gloves to match and a pillbox hat with netting over her eyes. She was already a tall woman, and with her feet in strappy, towering heels plus the hat, she was taller than he was.

"Lucinda," he said with a slight nod.

She returned the nod without addressing him, all her attention focused on me. After a few awkward moments, her perfect lips split into a smile. "So this is what the cat dragged in," she said.

Was she talking about me? This had to be the Lucinda his assistant had been warning him about at the doctor's office.

"If you're going to be unpleasant—" he began.

"Oh, but it's unpleasantness that has made my presence necessary, isn't it? Point the man out to me and I will be sure to take care of the matter."

I wondered what she could possibly be talking about. James's world of secrets suddenly seemed to loom dark and large.

"Thank you." He cleared his throat. "I shall."

She stepped aside, and he swept me past her without attempting introductions. By the time we reached the entrance to the actual ballroom, she had gone into a side parlor and I could no longer see her when I looked back.

I was the one to give him the inquisitive eyebrow for once. "A bitter ex," he said, as if no other explanation was necessary. And it wasn't, except for the bit about taking care of unpleasantness. Maybe I could grill Stefan later about it. Before I could mull it over further, we were in the ballroom, and my eyes were captivated by the sight of about a dozen couples, all in formal wear of various kinds, waltzing. It was like a time-travelers ball almost, with couples in elaborate tailcoats and gowns—Victorian, Renaissance—and one couple in formal kimonos.

He led me on a circuit of the room, waving off the waiter carrying the tray of champagne flutes. We paused to exchange meaningless pleasantries with a few other couples, who seemed to recognize him without having anything of substance to say. Well, what could they say if they didn't really know who he was? You couldn't inquire about anyone's family or business. We had exactly two conversations that went beyond "how are you," and one was about an art exhibit that we and another couple had seen.

The other was about the party itself, in which we joined two men in discussion.

"Jules, Jules," one of them said, snagging my partner by the sleeve. "Did you see that terrible film? Arnold, I tell you, you never should have brought Kubrick here."

"He'd already been to a party in London." Arnold shook his head. "The whole film was supposed to be set in London in the 1960s, you know. That's why it makes no sense. Don't you agree, Jules?"

"I never saw the film, I'm afraid," James said.

"I do agree the premise was ridiculous, though, certainly," Arnold continued. "There are kinky nightclubs downtown that openly advertise in the newspaper. One needn't join a secret society to get one's ass spanked."

"Arnold. Language," the first man said with a nod toward me.

Arnold's eyes crinkled with laughter suddenly. "I find it likely the word *ass* is less offensive to the young lady than seeing yours will be," he said.

"Bah." They moved off together, the first one still trying to argue and the second one waving good-bye to us with a merry twinkle in his eye.

"Jules?" I asked.

"Another nickname," he said.

"For Julian?"

"For what I wore." He ran his finger along the twining vine of my necklace and then leaned over to kiss me softly on the temple.

"Oh. *Jewels.*" I tried to imagine him wearing something other than a distinguished suit and couldn't. "Diamonds and sapphires?"

"Diamonds," he said with a smile. "And jasper and blood-stone. Are you ready for some dancing?"

"With you? Anytime."

A very small orchestra was playing the music live. They were finishing a piece when he led me toward the middle of the floor. The ballroom was not as huge as I imagined it would be, but there was room easily for twenty couples to dance. The ceiling was high enough that there were balconies that opened from brightly lit second-floor rooms.

"Done this before?"

"My mother forced me to take six weeks of ballroom dance before my cousin's wedding when I was sixteen," I said.

"That counts," he said with a little smile as he took my hand. "Did you dance at the wedding?"

"With my not-so-little brother, who had gotten out of the dance lessons by virtue of being a boy, I think. So you can imagine what a disaster that was. He couldn't lead, stepped on my feet, ugh. Although, better him than my grabby cousin."

While I spoke, he led me easily into a turn, and we were dancing. It was another waltz, which we fell into easily, as he was a good leader. We didn't talk for a while, just moved to the swaying tune. Dancing requires you to be in the moment in a way that talking or doing a lot of other things doesn't. You see and feel your partner, the other people in the room, the music, your own feet, your own breathing. His eyes looked like greenish agates in this light. Or maybe jaspers.

Eventually we fell into conversation. "Those men were saying there's a society like this in England, too?"

"It won't surprise you to know that rich people have always come up with ways to indulge their eccentricities," he said.

"Even their perverted ones?"

"Especially their perverted ones," he said with a low laugh. "But yes, this group is something of an offshoot of a group there. The group's been there since the 1820s. This one, since about 1980 or so, I believe."

"How does one become a member?"

"You have to be recruited by another member."

"How did it start?"

"A handful of people from here had either been as guests or were members of the UK group. You must attend two parties as a guest before you can submit your name for membership."

"And it's made up of all wealthy people?"

"That's not the main criterion, but it does somewhat work out that way. In England it's a matter of class and influence more than net worth. Here, it's a bit more complicated. It's a matter of who's found worthy of membership."

"Influential, you mean like politicians?"

"We don't get many politicians, actually. They are too afraid of being exposed or blackmailed. We used to wear masks, but they really didn't actually hide most people's identities. It was more of a tradition and no better than a false sense of security and anonymity. It's a curious dance we do here, of course, because although the membership committee needs to vet each applicant, and therefore needs to know their real names, many prefer to interact anonymously when they're here. But anonymity never lasts. People get close, they form affinities... eventually that becomes business alliances and other real-life connections. That's human nature. People join a group to connect, after all, and that desire to connect drives them."

"If it's not politicians, then, is it mostly Wall Street types?"

"In this room are more than a few captains of industry, some high-ranking scholars. Some actors and other entertainers and artists."

"Artists? Visual artists?"

"All kinds. Painters, musicians, sculptors, playwrights. Artists are always considered interesting by the nonartists, always looking at the world in different ways from the rest of society. Artists are always outsiders."

"How do you get outsiders to join a group, then?"

His laugh was private, just for me, as he murmured in my ear, "They like the sex."

I was expecting that at some point a bell would ring and everyone would start stripping their clothes off and having a massive orgy, like something from a Hieronymus Bosch painting. But it wasn't like that at all.

Gradually people began to drift out of the ballroom, and then a woman's squeal from up above made my head turn. On the balcony, a woman was bent over the railing and completely naked except for her improbably tall shoes and her jewelry. Her hair was in an updo, but her partner, a woman in a gray tuxedo, pulled the pins free and her hair cascaded over the balcony.

The woman in the tuxedo held something up that looked like the pull rod to a set of Venetian blinds—long, slender, and plastic. Then she pulled it back like a tennis racquet and swatted her partner on the rear with a forehand. The woman bent over the railing squealed with what sounded much more like glee than pain. The one who had hit her grinned crookedly, an unlit cigar in the corner of her mouth, and did it again.

My partner slid his arms around me. When had he shifted behind me? We were at the edge of the dance floor now, looking up at the women.

"They look like they're having fun," I said.

"I'm certain they are," he answered. "One of them is a fashion designer. The other is an editor at a fashion magazine."

"Sounds like a perfect match."

"Oh, it's quite funny. They ran into each other here some years ago and were quite antagonistic toward each other. Until they finally had it out. They've been together ever since."

"Had it out?"

"I think it involved some form of naked oil wrestling. The winner got to lead the loser around by a leash the rest of the night."

"Which one of them won?"

"I don't know. I wasn't here that night. They appear to take turns on top."

"Really?"

"Is that such a surprising concept?"

"Well, all the BDSM sites online make it sound like people are either dominant or submissive, no in-between and no switching."

"You know you can't believe everything you read on the Internet," he said with a chuckle. "Come on, let's see what's going on around the house."

He led me back into the hallway, and we could hear the sounds of sex and spankings coming through the parlor doorways. At the foot of the stairs a woman in a gorgeous red ball gown was being attended by a man who knelt and kissed her ring. She then very slowly lifted the edge of her voluminous skirt, showing the pointed toe of her daintily slippered foot. He lowered himself on all fours to kiss it as well, and then she moved to put her foot on his neck. He reminded me of a puppy, lying down before an alpha dog.

We moved on toward the gardens. "In the summer, much happens out there on the patio and in the courtyard," he said. "Not much to see there on a chilly spring night like tonight, though."

"That man called her *Your Highness*," I said.

"He may have. The society has many members who inherited both their wealth and their influence. The idle rich need their hobbies. But it's much more likely they're play-acting than that she's royalty."

"Is he really submissive?"

"What do you mean by *really*?"

"Is he a timid guy who likes to be bossed around in real life?"

"Actually, I think he's the CEO of a well-known tech company, if I'm not mistaken. Many people in positions of high responsibility enjoy giving up the decision-making to someone else when it comes to bedroom games."

"And he becomes her plaything."

"Perhaps. He certainly looks deep in role."

"He plays the part well." It was hard to imagine the CEO of a big corporation groveling. "And she can do whatever she wants to him?"

"It depends on what they negotiated. Every couple is different, but there are always rules."

"Like our rules."

"Exactly. It's more likely there are certain limits she has to respect, but within those limits she can be creative. Otherwise he won't feel like she's in charge."

"He looks so vulnerable like that, with her foot on his neck."

"She wouldn't injure him, I'm sure. But some men find it difficult to experience vulnerability in real life. It's not safe. And yet so many men can't experience their full emotions unless they're made vulnerable. I'm sure he craves the emotional experience as much as the physical one."

"Maybe that's another and-not-or situation, though," I said. "The physical and the emotional can't be separated. Not when someone's stepping on your neck, anyway."

He led me past a room where a woman was sprawled across a chaise lounge, her bosom spilling loose from the bodice of her gown while a completely naked man suckled one of her nipples and another did something under her skirts. Only the lower half of his body was visible. In the next room, a man and a woman were in their underwear, their hands against the grand marble mantelpiece above the fireplace, while a man and a woman, still in their formal wear, took turns lashing them with short whips. The woman cracked her whip in the air and I jumped: it sounded like a gunshot.

The two naked people had jumped, too, and the woman started laughing. The man wiggled his butt enticingly and received a lash for it. A crowd had gathered around them, a dozen or so people, to watch.

I suddenly clutched at my partner's arm and turned my face away. "That's . . . that's . . ."

He shielded me from the sight of those inside the room with his body and murmured in my ear, "Your Professor Renault. I know."

"You know!" My throat went tight with outrage.

"Yes. It's his third visit as a guest. His name has been submitted for membership."

My stomach turned and I pulled away, but he didn't let me go far before he steered me to a parlor where we were alone and could sit. "I'm totally disgusted."

"As well you should be."

"These people, it's . . . that's . . ." I couldn't even put it into words. "That's disgusting."

"Back up, Karina. What's disgusting?"

"This group of perverts! God!" I shook myself like a dog, as if I could shake that feeling of the willies away. "Ugh!"

He gave me a moment, then tried again. "So, you see one idiot predator in our midst and have decided everyone's like him?"

I didn't answer right away and received the skeptical eyebrow from him.

"Well, you're not," I admitted.

"Look around," he said. "Have you seen anyone who looked like they were being victimized so far?"

"No." Everyone looked like they were having a grand time, especially the ones on the receiving end. "You can't possibly let him join."

"Lucinda is here to keep an eye on him tonight. We take every issue of consent very seriously."

"What if he doesn't do anything wrong?"

"If he had even a single report of sexual harassment on his record, I doubt he would have made it this far."

"I get it! Okay! I should have reported it. But I didn't. And now it's too late."

"It's never too late."

"And that girl never called me! Oh man. I wonder what happened to her." My shoulders slumped. Maybe she hadn't even gone to his office after the scene I made about it. Or . . . "Maybe I'm the only one he did it to."

"You're very special, sweetness, but I highly doubt you're the only one." He held my hand. "You could guarantee his rejection by making a report."

I swallowed. "I'll think about it," I said. "Is that what you brought me here for? To convince me to do the right thing?"

He pulled my hand to his lips and kissed my knuckles gently. "Don't be silly. I brought you here to fulfill your Cinderella fantasy, and to fuck you in front of some of the most influential people in the world."

Oh. Right. My heart was suddenly beating much harder and the dress seemed almost too tight to breathe in. "Even him?"

"Even him. Sweetness, there is no chance he's recognized you even if he has caught a glimpse of you. You are a completely transformed creature from your usual. However, I do have something that will undoubtedly keep him from recognizing you."

"You do?"

"Yes. I will trade your dress for it."

"What is it?"

"A blindfold, my sweet." He got to his feet and pulled a satin blindfold with elastic straps from the inner pocket of his jacket. It was midnight blue to match my dress and had a rhinestone stud.

I couldn't help but laugh a little. "You really plan ahead, don't you?"

His grin matched mine. "Always." He gave me a serious look then. "If you're not comfortable with him here—"

"I'm not afraid of him," I insisted, standing up, too. "Besides, wasn't he at the gallery last week? He's already seen my ass."

"Let's go upstairs first before I put this on you. I think there's a room there that'll suit our needs." He slipped the blindfold into his pocket, took my hand again, and led me toward the grand staircase.

Fourteen

Love Just Kissed You Hello

Upstairs there was a long hallway with rooms upon rooms. Some had their doors closed, but many were open. He told me that an open door was an invitation to watch, but not necessarily to join in. No one was going to touch me without permission. He didn't say it but I understood that meant not only my permission, but also his.

We went into a large room with a balcony overlooking the ballroom. The two main pieces of furniture were a large round bed, larger than a typical king size, and a sort of tubular frame.

He helped me to undress down to nothing but jewelry, draping my things over a chair, then asked me to help him do the same. I was a little surprised since with most of the couples I'd seen, the dominant partner was still clothed.

Helping him out of the jacket, I felt like I was peeling away layers of his armor. I slipped his shoes from his feet, one, then the other, and eased his briefs down over his hips.

His cock was already eagerly rising, but he pulled me against his leg and said, "Make me hard."

I slipped a hand down to it and stroked the loose skin up and down the thickening shaft until it tightened. I could feel his heartbeat in my hand as I stroked, and an answering throb seemed to beat between my legs.

He led me to the frame and then opened the top drawer of the dresser against the wall. I'd assumed it held someone's clothes, but no. It was full of rope.

He selected a few coils from several he dug out and laid them atop the dresser for later, bringing one over to me.

"So," he said, brushing his hands over my hair and down my back, over my buttocks and up my stomach, fingers pausing to tease my nipples, "you're not my slave, not my servant, not my minion. You don't have a collar, you don't have a title, and you don't have a job other than pleasing me. Stand on one foot. Bring the other one up as high as you can. Hold on to the frame if you need help balancing."

I put a hand on the frame and bent one knee, picking it up as high as I could, pointing my toe like a ballerina, though I was no longer wearing the ballet flats. Doing so parted my lower lips, and the scent of my desire wafted up like waves of heat. He slid a finger down to spread them farther, barely brushing at my clit and running his fingertips up and down the newly shaven skin.

Then he wrapped the rope around my thigh and shin so that my leg would stay bent at that angle, and then he tied the whole thing to one pole of the frame, raising my foot so it was in the crook of my other knee, like a ballerina caught in the middle of a spin. A couple came in. Our first spectators.

He retrieved the blindfold then and settled it over my eyes, stealing a quick kiss from my lips and stealing my breath away at the same time.

I felt him drape a rope over my shoulder, his fingers always caressing my skin as he prepared to do whatever he was going to.

He wrapped the ropes around my upper body much like he had that time in the hotel suite, tightening around my breasts and making my nipples extra sensitive. Then he pulled on one arm, gently lifting it from my side. It was the opposite arm from the leg that was bound, and he made me stretch to the side and back some, the rope that coiled around that arm pulling taut to another part of the frame. The other arm he bound upward. Now I must truly have looked like a dancer caught in mid-movement.

"Do you remember that first time in the car," he murmured close in my ear, "when I spanked your cunt for the first time?"

"Yes."

"I wonder if it will feel different now," he said, as if sure that it would.

I could feel that his hand was cupped at first as he tapped on my mound, standing close enough to press his lips against my hair while his hand did its wicked work. *Tap tap tap.* Only soon it was less of a tap and more of a clap, as he relaxed his hand and slowed the rhythm. My arousal shot up and continued to climb as he slowed even more, each blow now a full slap, right on my exposed cunt, catching both the fleshy lips and my clit.

At first, the sounds I made were soft moans, but as his hits rose in intensity, so did my pitch. By the time he was smacking me full-on, each cry was a wail.

It dropped to a groan as he paused and circled my clit

with one fingertip. I could hear the murmurs of people watching.

"You're so engorged," he whispered. "This is what happens after a whole week of teasing without release."

I shook on my one standing leg, bouncing up and down with impatience. "I want it now!"

"Patience. Should I let you come before I'm inside of you?"

"Please?" I tried bargaining. "I could always come again after you're inside me."

He clucked his tongue and I could hear the smile in his voice. "Nice try, sweetness. But I would rather torture you some more."

His torture consisted of more slow circles of his finger, through the wetness gathering below and then over my clit. He was right: I don't think it had ever been so swollen. If he would just flick his fingers back and forth across it a few times, that would probably be enough to send me over the edge.

He clucked his tongue again and withdrew his hand, moving his attention to my buttocks. "I'll let your front side cool down a little," he said as he let the first spank land.

I yelped, but once he got going in a steady rhythm, it didn't matter what sounds I made. His slaps on my ass started light, but they soon grew heavy and each blow made me scream. The harder he spanked, the longer he waited between hits, as if waiting for the sound of my scream to fade between each one. In the silences between, I could hear my own breathing and the rhythmic whimpers of another woman nearby having sex or at least being masturbated.

I could feel him move under my outstretched arm, and a warm hand slid down my cunt so that one finger was curled just enough to penetrate me while the palm pressed against my clit. His other hand rubbed my buttock.

Then that hand struck, and my body jerked against the palm on my clit. I gasped. "Oh God, that'll make me come."

"You're forbidden from coming," he said. "I expect you to warn me if you get too close." With that, he began spanking me steadily, making me cry out.

I was so desperate to come by that time that I seriously considered cheating. What would he do, punish me? Wasn't that what we were doing anyway? My brain was foggy from lust and hormones and endorphins.

He wouldn't be happy if I did that, though, and I wanted him to be happy.

I wanted to be happy. "Stop! Stop-stop-stop! Oh God..."

He stopped and let go, so that the only thing touching me was ropes, and I spasmed on them almost like having an orgasm, except it was a false one. I hadn't gotten there, and that left me even more in need. I was making a whining sound like a neglected puppy.

Then I felt his cock rubbing against my leg. His mouth was at my ear. "You don't know how hard it is not to shove myself inside you right now. I'm completely on fire."

I could only whine in answer.

I could hear him groaning, almost growling, as he teased me with the tip of his cock, running it up and down the slick seam of me, between my legs and between the widespread lips. Then he took a deep breath and stepped back so that I couldn't feel him anymore. I could make out a murmur of voices from the edge of the room as I listened, trying to guess what he was doing.

I heard something rip before he stepped up to me again,

and the tip of him felt cold and squishy. That jolted me a little.

"You put on a condom?" I asked.

"House rules," he said. He teased more, then pulled back again. "I think I had best cut you down and move you somewhere more comfy for this."

He snapped his fingers and someone else must have helped let the ties loose. I felt the ropes around my rib cage loosen and my breasts come free. I still had the rope tied around my leg, but I was no longer attached to the frame or held in position. He carried me to the bed and helped me to scoot back until my head was on the pillows.

He kissed me, deeply, and the pillow felt downy and luxurious under my head. His cock slid between my legs, teasing us both. My one leg was still bent from the ropes, but my knee was pointed up at the ceiling and I moved so that the other knee crooked also. He lay in the valley between my legs and then lifted up on his arms, positioning himself. The head of his cock swirled against my opening, which was gushingly wet and aching to be penetrated.

I gripped him with my knees. "Stop."

He held still and I couldn't hear anyone. "What's wrong?" he asked, his voice hoarse with desire.

I knew what I had to do. I knew what I wanted. But it took me a few more tries before I could get it out. "Who's here now?"

Our voices were so soft that even if spectators were standing over us, they wouldn't be able to make out anything we were saying, but I wanted to know. "Hardly anyone," he answered in his most soothing voice. He chuckled a little. "Plain old sex is boring to them, after all. There are two couples making out against the wall and two people out on the balcony."

"Good."

He tried to move but my knees still held him in place. I felt the tip of him rubbing at the opening. He made an involuntary noise, very much like the puppy whine I'd made. "Karina—"

"Not until you tell me your real name," I whispered.

"It really is James."

"I know it is. I mean the rest of it. Your full name."

He went still and rigid above me, then shook as if he had swallowed a cough. "You can't be serious."

"Serious as a heart attack. You want in, you tell me who you are."

"I won't take you without your consent," he said, as if that were the issue.

"The price of my consent is your name," I said.

"You don't know what you're asking."

"Don't I?" I whispered vehemently. "You're the one who goes on and on about the value of honesty, of loyalty! Where's the honesty now, mister?"

"I . . . There are reasons I haven't told you."

"Bullshit. I think you're so used to hiding it, you don't know how to stop."

"I promise I'll tell you in the future."

"I don't believe you. And if I can't believe you, this whole thing is . . . is nothing."

I could feel him trembling now as he held himself above me, but perhaps also as my words had an effect.

"You're right," he whispered. "I don't want it to be nothing."

"I know," I murmured back. "I feel like if I don't demand your name now, you'll never give it to me. I'll never truly know you. And if you don't trust me enough to tell me now, you'll never trust me."

"I do trust you, Karina."

"Prove it," I hissed.

He pressed his forehead against mine, as if thinking, as if resting a moment. Then I felt his mouth move to my ear, his breath warm and making me melt, but not enough to give in, until he whispered, "James. Byron. LeStrange."

I relaxed my grip and he plunged in. I'm sure if I had not made the demand I had, he would have worked his way in gradually, but having held him back and having asked a price, the price I paid in return was the whole length of him splitting me open in one searing thrust. I couldn't even scream as everything in my body clenched tightly around the intrusion.

One of his hands brushed over my nipples made hyper-sensitive from the squeezing of the ropes. The touch seemed to make something in the center of me blossom, and to my surprise he thrust even deeper, creating a burst of pleasure in me. His mouth was at my neck then, triggering the spot that always made me wild, his thumb on one nipple, tweaking and circling, and his cock withdrew several inches before plunging back in.

On the thrust I saw stars, my skin tingling everywhere he was touching me, and my hips rocked to meet him on the next thrust. And the next, and the next. If it had hurt in that initial moment of penetration, all trace of it was gone, as this felt like the best of the heavy, smooth glass inside me, but also the heat and friction of a real body and the tension of his desire.

It was everything I had ever dreamed sex could be. Each

thrust was a treat, an explosion of pleasure in its own right that made me want another and another and another. And he had finally told me! I felt the last barrier between us crumble. I clung to him with all my limbs as I neared orgasm and made myself come as I banged my hips against him, smacking my clit between our bodies until I screamed. And still he did not stop. He flattened me into the bed with his thrusts, sometimes fast for a while, so fast I could barely catch a breath, other times slow and relentless with a snap at the end of each long plunge that made me gasp.

He urged me to turn over and I got on all fours. He flattened me against the bed again while his cock hunted for my opening. From this angle he felt different and I moaned, thrusting my ass up.

His hand reached around me and made me come again with harsh, fast rubbing on my clit. I screamed into the pillow as he wrung an orgasm from me and then plowed right on to a third, fourth, and fifth, by which time I was screaming at him, "I can't, I can't, I can't!"

"Yes, you can," he hissed as I came again on the vicious rubbing of his fist. "Change positions."

This time he lay on his back and pulled me to lie on top of him, also faceup so that I was wide open for him. The blindfold kept me from seeing the ceiling above us, but I didn't need to see to feel every inch of him. He didn't penetrate as deep this way, but there was still plenty of him inside me, and he used slow strokes now, rocking his pelvis under me.

James Byron LeStrange. It suddenly hit me that J. B. Lester was a bastardized version of that, and I had been right about James being his real first name. He had wanted to tell me. I know he did. But he had to be pushed to go all the way.

I wondered what had happened to him in the past to make him trust so slowly. Who had hurt him so much that I had to pry this hard to get him to let go of his name? Lucinda? Or had it been someone else?

"Turn over again," he said, his voice harsh with need.

I rolled onto my back and reached for him. I heard a snap, and the next thing I felt was the warm condom in my hand.

"I thought there were rules?"

"I'm breaking them. It's time you understood, Karina, that you truly, truly make me naked before you." He plunged into me again and began to fuck me.

It was like he had said at the beginning. He wasn't my master; he wasn't my boss; he wasn't my owner. He was just...James.

Those were the words that came out of my mouth when he suddenly slowed, whimpering from how close he was, thrusting deep and holding a moment, then thrusting again when that wasn't enough, five, six times like that. "Mine," I whispered, feeling the twitch and throb that was probably him ejaculating inside me. "My lover. My partner. *My James.*"

He thrust twice more and then lay limp atop me, panting hard, as if he couldn't catch his breath.

And then, as I felt the hot juices running out of me, as he slipped free of me, I realized he was sobbing.

"Are you all right?" I reached up to stroke his back.

He pulled free of me suddenly.

"It's okay, love," I said. Plenty of people cried during incredible, emotional sex. At least in the books my mother liked to read.

I felt the bed shift. All right. Give him a moment. Maybe he was overwhelmed. It had taken him so long to let me even see his cock; this must've been as intense for him as it had been for me. I wondered if he was going to get a cloth and wash me like he usually did. Such a small thing, but it had made me feel so cherished. I let a flood of images of the previous hour rush through my mind. Mmmm. A night to remember.

Then I realized he hadn't returned. Was the bathroom far?

I sat up and lifted the corner of the blindfold. I was alone in the room. The door was closed.

I pulled the blindfold off and looked around.

There on the chair was my dress and all my things. Everything of his was gone. I blinked in disbelief. Did he want to be fully dressed to . . . to what? And why wouldn't he have gotten dressed in here?

I tried to get off the bed and found I couldn't stand up with the rope still around my leg. It took me some tugging and cursing until I loosened it enough to slip free. I ran to the room's balcony and looked down. There were various couples and groups milling around. The staff had changed over the hors d'oeuvres displays. A whole roast pig was being carved at one serving table. A bit farther down was the largest roast beef I had ever seen being sliced. The crowd was partly in their formal wear now, partly in various stages of nudity and silk robes, and some even still wore their artful ropes.

There was no sign of him.

I tore open the door and looked in the hallway, panic starting to climb up my throat. Where was he?

I ran back into the room, wondering if I could find something to put on besides my dress, but every drawer of the dresser was full of rope. Damn it. I pulled the dress up hurriedly and held it up since I didn't want to take the time to try to get it zipped up by myself, jammed my feet into the slippers, and grabbed the lace jacket and my purse and ran out into the hallway.

The first people I ran into were the queenly woman and her groveling guy. She was in a different dress now, one much less formal, and he was in nothing but a collar. She held the leash. Damn, I realized, I couldn't ask for him by name. Wait, they knew him as Jules. "Have you seen Jules?" I asked her. "The man I came in with?"

"Sorry, dear, I only just emerged from a private room," she said.

I ran down the stairs and looked wildly around the ballroom again, but didn't see him.

Then I thought, *Oh, you're stupid. Use the phone. There's probably an explanation.*

I took my phone out of the little purse and hit the speed-dial entry that went straight to him.

A male voice answered, but it wasn't him. "Karina—"

"Stefan?"

"I'm waiting for you outside."

I hung up and ran to the front door. Maybe he was sick or hurt and had turned to Stefan.

When I arrived, Stefan was standing, very stiff, beside the back passenger door. He opened it and bowed formally. I could see no one else was inside.

I ran up to him. "Where is he?"

Stefan shook his head. He looked very serious. "I am directed to take you home."

"Home!"

Stefan wouldn't meet my eyes. He gestured to the interior of the car, with a half bow and a scoop of his hand.

The doorman was standing at the front door, watching impassively. I wondered if he was under orders not to let me back in.

I was half tempted to scream at Stefan that he shouldn't bother taking me home but should take me to the nearest bridge so I could jump off. I've never really been a drama queen, though, so I didn't think I could pull it off. Besides, my worth wasn't what some man thought of me. Wasn't that what I'd said?

I climbed glumly into the back of the car, and Stefan shut the door behind me with a solid *thunk*.

The party went on, but for me it was over. It was all over.

Fifteen

Love Dares You to Change

I went through every kind of mood swing you can imagine sitting in the back of that dark limousine on the highway. I was upset, confused, scared, angry, confused again, righteous, hurt. There was still so much I didn't know and didn't understand. I played the scene over and over in my mind.

Finally I banged on the glass until Stefan relented and lowered it. I put on my toughest "New York City Do Not Fuck With Me" voice. "Okay, what the fuck is this all about?"

"I don't know. All I know is I'm to take you home." His accent was extra-thick.

"And you're not supposed to speak to me."

"No."

"But you are."

"Karina . . . I don't know how to say it, but—"

"I told you so? Is that it? You told me once he fucked me he'd leave me, didn't you? But then you told me that was a lie to try to scare me off. Which is it, Stefan?"

He shook his head.

"Are you going back for him later?"

"No. I am to go straight home."

"Quit it with the Boris Karloff routine, Stefan. It's not going to work. I know your English is perfectly fine, you Yale rat."

"Ah, fuck, Karina, what am I supposed to do? He told me to take you home. That's all I know." He gripped the steering wheel tightly.

"Okay, then speculate about what happened."

"I would love to know what the hell happened," he said, hunching his shoulders a little. "I definitely didn't predict this. You're right, the whole love-'em-and-leave-'em thing was just to scare you. Why don't *you* tell *me* what happened in there?"

I wasn't quite ready to go into the details, but my mind was running a mile a minute. "Okay, first of all, does the name Lucinda mean anything to you?"

He sat up straight suddenly. "It's just a name," he said carefully.

"The name of a woman he used to know," I said. "A bitter ex, he called her."

"She was there?"

"Yes."

Stefan shook his head. "There is no way he left you for Lucinda, so put that out of your mind."

"Oh my God, I hadn't even thought of that as a possibility!"

"Then why did you bring her up?"

"Because I thought hearing about her might jog your memory or something." I clung to the edge of the window to the front seat. "Can I come up there?"

"Don't try to climb through," he warned, as if he were afraid I might actually do it. "Look, there's a rest area. Let's pull over where nothing bad can happen to you."

"All right. Might as well visit the restroom while I'm at it."

I had to gather my skirts to make it up the wheelchair ramp into the rest area. Stefan put gas in the car while I went to the ladies' room.

When I saw myself in the mirror, I felt like crying. My makeup was a wreck, the dress was askew and still not zipped properly, and the tiara was digging into my forehead and making a red mark.

A woman came in after me. "Are you in line?" she asked, clutching her woven straw handbag and pointing to the two stalls past the mirror.

"Oh no, please go ahead," I said, edging aside so she could get past without having to step on the dress. She went into the smaller of the two stalls.

Right. I should do that. I went into the wheelchair-equipped stall, which had the high seat and room for my skirts.

When I came out, the woman was washing her hands.

"Um, if it's not too much trouble," I asked her, "could you zip me up?"

"Oh, darling, of course," she said. She had frizzy, graying hair and put her glasses on so she could see the zipper. "I don't want to make assumptions, but it looks as if you've had a bit of a rough night."

"Oh, I'm all right now," I assured her. "A, um, limo driver is taking me home."

"Well, that's good. Dumped the boy who messed you up, did you? Good riddance. He can find his own way home." She patted the back of the zipper and then reached into her handbag. "Here. If you ever need it, and if you don't, you might have a friend who does. Okay?"

It was the business card of a rape crisis hotline. "Oh." I must have looked a little shocked.

"You might not think it's such a big deal, or worth the trouble, but sometimes it helps to talk to someone," she said.

"Um, thank you. Really." I put the card into the purse with my phone.

The woman was shaking her head as she went out. "Tsk. Ruining a girl's prom night like that," I heard her say.

Stefan was waiting beside the car. He opened the door for me—the front passenger door this time.

"Here." He handed me a little grocery sack after I sat down and then went around to his side of the car. In addition to a Gatorade, the bag was full of chocolate bars.

"Stefan?"

"You look dehydrated. And, you know, all those TV commercials make it look like chocolate makes women feel better. I didn't know which kind you like, so I bought one of each."

I teared up looking into the bag. "You are the sweetest thing."

"Consider it a bribe, or a thank you, or whatever, for telling me about Lucinda," he said. "So we're even."

I drank some of the Gatorade and then capped the bottle and stuck it in the cup holder. Halfway through the first chocolate bar, I started to feel a little more human. "Okay, so to pick up where I left off. First, we ran into Lucinda. Then he tells me she's there tailing this creeptastic professor of mine."

"A professor?"

"A guy who tried to solicit me for sexual favors in order to allow me to graduate."

"Ah, creeptastic. I get it now. And he was there?"

"Yes. James told me he—" I broke off as Stefan turned to look at me so fast he nearly swerved the car.

"He told you his name!"

I nodded and pointed ahead.

Stefan put his eyes back on the road, but they were very wide. Fortunately there was barely anyone on the road at that point. We were on what seemed a fairly rural highway, two lanes on either side of a picturesque, tree-lined divider. We passed under an arched stone overpass.

"He told me his name was James Byron Lestrange."

"Wow." Stefan shook his head in confusion. "I wonder what made him leave."

"I've been asking myself the same question. Why would he confide in me and then leave me?"

"Hang on, hang on." Stefan drummed his fingers on the wheel. "So he told you and then left right away?"

"Yes." I decided not to mention the mind-blowing-sex part.

"And it didn't occur to you that he left because he told you his name?"

"What, you mean because I burst the bubble of anonymity the magic was lost?"

"No. I mean, he's a very secretive person, Karina. You know. He ... exposed a big secret to you there."

"Oh, come on, was he any more exposed than I was?" I argued, but then I remembered something. "Oh."

The last thing he said when we were in bed: *"It's time you understood that you truly, truly make me naked before you."*

He'd made other little comments about his own vulnerability in the past weeks, but I'd brushed them off. I thought about how Stefan and the beautiful assistant whose name I hadn't learned had both considered *me* the one who was dangerous to *him*, not the other way around.

"I forced him to say it," I confessed weakly.

"You what?"

"Forced him to. Or coerced him. It didn't feel like I was violating him at the time." Oh God, I felt like sinking right into the seat and disappearing.

Except, wait. "Didn't I have a right to know it? He's known my name for weeks! Aren't two people in love supposed to share everything? He was the one who went on and on about honesty!" Now I was getting pissed off again. "He made a rule that I had to be honest all the time, even to other people. I finally ask him for the truth and he flips out and dumps me?"

"The rules aren't always the same for everybody . . . ," Stefan hedged.

"That's bullshit, Stefan! What's so special about his name, anyway? What's the big deal? I'm not about to go telling the whole world that the mysterious glass artist J. B. Lester is actually that guy in the back who acts like an art dealer."

Stefan nearly banged his head against the steering wheel. "Are you really in love with him?"

"Yes. And I know he's in love with me even if he's afraid to say it. I didn't want to tell him directly because . . . because that always wrecks things, you know?"

"And forcing him to give up his most closely held secret wouldn't?"

"Stefan, come on! He had to start acting like a normal human being sometime!"

Stefan looked at me sideways. "Conformity is not his strong suit."

I put my face in my hands. "Did I actually just say that?

You're right. That was completely stupid. Of course I don't expect him to suddenly become someone he's not." Hadn't I told James how miserable my mother's attempts to make me conform had made me? "I meant the game had to end so a real relationship could begin."

It looked like we were going through a more thickly settled area. Yonkers. "Are you sure?"

"Okay, you're right. No either/or. We could have the game and still begin a real relationship. I was so sure we had something special. I'm sure he's in love with me."

"Or was."

"Shit." I started to get teary again, and Stefan opened the glove box and apologetically handed me a pristine, white handkerchief. "Well, I'm completely sure I'm in love with him. It makes no sense, to be in love with someone whose real name I didn't even know."

"I'm not under the impression that love always quote makes sense unquote," Stefan hazarded.

"Oh fuck you for being right." I wiped my eyes with the handkerchief and it came away a little smeared. "What am I going to do, Stefan? Does he hate me now?"

"I don't know, Karina." He swallowed and took a deep breath. "That's the first time he's ever summoned me up to the house half dressed, standing in the front drive. He looked . . . crazy. Like pulling-his-hair-out crazy. The doorman put his own overcoat around him, out of embarrassment I think, or taking pity on the insane. When I pulled up, he threw the phone at me and said if you called to tell you I was taking you home. When I asked if I would be returning for him, he said no. And then he stalked back into the house."

"Did he seem angry?"

"Yes! And hurt and out of his mind. I haven't seen him like that since, well, since Lucinda."

"How long ago was that?"

"Five or six years." He shrugged. "Right at the beginning of . . ." He trailed off then and shook his head.

"What aren't you telling me?"

He blew out a long breath. "Listen, Karina, his name is a very big deal. I worked for him two years before I learned it."

"Did Lucinda know it?"

"I doubt it, and she got under his skin in the worst ways." He pressed his lips together as if he were trying to stop himself from saying more. "Just telling you his first name was a huge step for him."

"He told me his name was James a long time ago."

"He was very captivated by you, Karina. Right from the beginning. Right from that first night."

Hearing him say that gave me a flicker of hope. "Do you think he'll come around?"

"If he really loves you? Maybe. I don't know, Karina. He's very stubborn."

I sighed and broke into another of the chocolate bars. This one had caramel in it. I chewed for a moment in dejected silence. "It occurs to me if he really loved me, he would have told me his name without me having to insist."

"I don't know about that," he said. "I told you, that was a big deal. He lives life differently from other people."

"And that makes him happy?"

"That keeps him safe," Stefan said.

We were mostly quiet the rest of the way, passing the George Washington Bridge, majestically lit in the night sky, and then down the West Side Highway.

Eventually we were turning onto the block where my apartment building was. Stefan pulled the car to a stop at the fire hydrant. I sat there a moment.

"Thanks for everything, Stefan," I said. "I...I hope I see you again."

"I hope so, too, Karina. But if not, take good care of yourself, all right?"

"All right." I climbed tiredly from the car, clutching the grocery sack, the handkerchief, my small purse, and the lace jacket to my chest.

"Wait," Stefan called. "This is yours, too." He fetched the velvet-lined case. He gestured to the door and carried it over with me. Once I got the vestibule door open, he handed the case to me without a word.

Upstairs, Becky was waiting, watching a movie on the Internet.

She took one look at me and I burst into tears in her arms.

* * *

That night, I told her the whole story, every detail, every little thing he'd ever said to me, teaching me to read minds, teaching me not to lie, telling me to report Renault, the glass art, the performance art, everything. I felt like I had to tell the entire story, like leaving anything out was going to prove it was all a dream, completely fake, while telling it all I could prove it had really happened. No, no, it really happened! The only thing I left out was his name. Because, well, that name had been trouble enough, and she understood.

Becks was rapt. She didn't interrupt except to ask a question here or there or to exclaim "Oh my goodness!" She teared up when I did, and she hugged me when I finally got to the end.

Then she said, "I just have one question, Rina."

"What's that?"

"Where did you get one of Lord Lightning's handkerchiefs?"

I stared at the white cloth in my hand. Embroidered white on white in one corner was the letter *L* and a lightning bolt. "You're sure this isn't yours?" I asked, in case we had gotten mixed up.

She shook her head. "Mine's framed on my bedroom wall."

"Stefan gave it to me. Tonight. It's brand-new."

It all started to make sense. Stefan playing the music and then quickly turning it off when he realized it was still on. All the comments James had made about performers and masks. The money. The secretive ways. Him being in the bar that night, alone, a few blocks from the Garden. No wonder they thought I was dangerous. I remembered how scared he seemed that night, when Stefan turned the car toward the crowds blocking the streets.

Becks had clearly come to the same conclusion. She was crying a little. "You had unbelievable epic hot sex with the most wanted man in the world . . . and you scared him off," she said. "What are you going to do now?"

"I don't know," I admitted. "I do know that first thing Monday morning, I'm going to report Renault for being a pervert."

Beyond that, the whole future was murky, like clouds in a crystal ball. Of handblown glass.

The sexual journey of Karina and James continues...

Please turn this page
for a preview of

Slow Seduction.

One

I stepped off the plane in London, already tired and sleep-deprived. By the time I got through customs, it was even worse. Martindale said I should tell them I was there on vacation and not to mention work, but the customs agent seemed so friendly, inquiring about my visit, it hadn't occurred to me it was anything more than idle chitchat. I mentioned looking forward to the show at the Tate. His questions got more and more pointed until I finally had to say I was there for a job interview—just an interview!—and that if I got a job, the Tate would be handling the paperwork. I guess there was a terrible glut of art historians looking for work in the UK if they were out to protect their jobs so fiercely.

Either way, it was a lie. Reginald Martindale, the museum curator James had introduced me to, wanted me as a tour guide for special groups through the pre-Raphaelite exhibit they were opening in a week. Only a temporary job, but it was still a job of sorts, and a good excuse to leave New York.

I still didn't have my degree. After I'd reported my thesis advisor for sexual harassment, all hell had broken loose. I told the truth: He'd said he'd approve my dissertation if I granted him sexual favors. He lied and said that I was the one who came on to him, trying to get him to pass me in exchange for favors instead of rewriting my thesis. The full inquest period was sixty days, which made me miss graduation anyway. At this point, my thesis draft was in the hands of the department for evaluation and Renault was being forced to take academic leave until the inquest was over. I wasn't hopeful about the thesis. It was a first draft—I'd expected to work on it after he read it—and I knew I had cut corners in it. On top of that, he had friends and allies in the department and the dean's office who defended him and didn't believe me. Some had called for a misconduct investigation of me. Others had called me a slut.

Right now, I had done all I could do and had taken all I could take. It was a good time to get away from school for a while.

As soon as I got through customs, I bought a refillable phone from an airport vending machine and studied the "top up" instructions for a long time before I figured out how to use it. You'd think it wasn't English, but maybe that further proved how tired I was. I went into the small newsstand and paid the cashier, who gave me a receipt with a code on it. I texted the code to the number and magically, the phone worked.

I sat down on a bench with my suitcase and texted a number I'd memorized: *I told a lie today, but it was sort of a necessary one. You know I try not to tell them at all, but it was a customs officer at Heathrow giving me the what for. I was afraid he'd send me right back to New York City. I'm in London.*

When I sent the text, it made a pleasant whooshing sound, as if it were flying through the ether directly to James's ear.

James Byron LeStrange. I had no idea if I would ever see him again. I clung to a few ragged hopes that I would. For one, the phone he had given me never died. Someone was still paying for it. Maybe he hadn't noticed, in his vast riches, that the account was still being paid? But maybe not. I had hurt him badly the last time we saw each other. I knew that now. But in the months that had passed since that fateful night, I had not stopped loving him.

I sent him a text every time I told a lie. Sticking to the rules. Being a good girl. Even if Stefan, his driver, was the only person who saw the texts, I hoped he'd relay the messages since he was the last person with the phone. The texts never bounced, anyway. And Stefan knew all about me and how James had abandoned me, so I didn't mind him seeing the messages, if he still had the phone in his possession.

I hoped they weren't breaking Stefan's heart. He was a nice guy and a friend when I needed one.

I figured out how to get a transit card and then caught the Underground to King's Cross, where I had booked two nights in a cheap hotel. The place was barely a step above a hostel, with shared bathrooms, but at least I would have a private sleeping room.

It was nearing the end of August. I hadn't seen James since the beginning of April.

At the hotel, the clerk was a young Indian man, unfailingly polite, his shirt buttoned all the way up the collar but with no tie. He explained what time breakfast was, apologized that the water pressure in the shower was not very good, and handed me a card with the Wi-Fi password on it. When I got up to my room, I found it was so small I literally could not get in without crawling onto the bed.

The window was open and I could see the towers of the St. Pancras train station at the end of the block.

I decided to try out the old phone and see if it worked internationally. I turned it on and found the hotel's Wi-Fi signal. I decided not to chance running up a huge roaming charge and connected that way.

I texted: *I got called a slut and a whore for reporting sexual harassment at the hands of my thesis advisor. Yet when I rode naked in the back of a limousine and screamed from orgasm as we drove through the streets, I was cherished and praised finally. I know which world I'd rather live in.*

The next morning, I made my way to Martindale's office. Here's where I confess I told another lie. I had told Martindale I was coming for the job. I had jumped at the chance to see this major exhibit, 150 paintings, and to get out of New York, but I had one more ulterior motive. I was there to pump him for information about James. Rumors were swirling through the Lord Lightning fan community that he was in England somewhere and that he might not be retired after all. If he was here, maybe I had a chance. And if Martindale knew anything, maybe that furthered my chances.

I had to find out.

I was in my best clothes, rumpled from being crammed in my bag on a transatlantic flight. Martindale was also unfailingly polite and didn't mention the wrinkles. He sat behind a desk strewn with *objets d'art* and I recognized a paperweight as James's work. I waited until we had gone through all the formalities, and I'd given him the briefest sketch of how strife in the art history department had led me to leave the university without my degree in hand.

"You think you'll have it eventually?" he asked.

"It's mostly a matter of paperwork," I said. "I may have to go back to defend, if they'll let me. It's very political."

"Well, I certainly understand how political both the art world and the university system can be. For what it's worth, I thought your doctoral dissertation to be top-notch. You wouldn't be here if I didn't."

"Thank you." I blushed a little from the praise. "I have a favor to ask, though, if I could?"

"Of course, my dear, what is it?"

"Our mutual friend, the man who introduced us. I've...fallen out of touch with him. I would love to at least know how he's doing? If that's not too much to ask?"

Martindale folded his hands on his stomach. "Yes, the enigmatic J. B. Lester. Well, you know, he can be a bit of a recluse."

"I know."

"He's been impossible to reach lately. And he owes me a piece."

"Oh," I said, since I didn't know what else to say.

He stared at his hands for a long moment. "It's funny you should ask about him today, as I did get a small package in this morning's post. It contained no letter, no explanation, just some photographs."

"Photographs? You mean, like actually printed on photo paper?"

He barked with laughter. "Yes, dear, actual photos. Take a look and tell me if you think they look like his work."

He handed me the envelope and I shook out a small stack of four or five pictures. My breath caught the moment I saw them. I had no doubt they were from him.

The pictures were of a shoe. A slipper. A glass slipper.

-To Be Continued-